Kat felt terrible. "I've ruined yo sorry, Easton."

He reached for her hand and squeezed it. "You could never ruin anything for me. I'm here because I want to be. I always want to be here for you, Kat. Why can't you understand that? I can't seem to prove that to you, even after all this time, after all we've been through together. Why can't you believe that?"

"Because I don't deserve you." There, she'd finally said the words. "Why would anyone give up his dream and spend years helping someone recover? What's in it for you? Nothing I can see, except a sense of duty fulfilled. I don't want to be your duty. I want to be your—"

The truck swerved off the road and he put it in park.

"My what, Kat? Look at me."

She sighed and turned her head.

"What do I need to do to convince you my love for you is unconditional? My proposal last year was not a scheme to trap you here. It was an honest request for you to spend the rest of your life with me. The last five-and-a-half months have been miserable without you. We're connected by our hearts, whether you want to acknowledge it or not."

Dear Reader,

When I wrote Love on the Edge, I had no idea it would become a series. As friends and family read my first draft, one after the other wanted more of Crane's Cove, specifically to know what happened to Molly and Jack, why Kat was back suddenly and why there was so much tension between her and Easton, why Caroline was so dramatic, etc., - and the more I thought about the answers to those questions, the more those secondary characters became more active in my head. They all want their stories told. I chose to tell Kat's story next because I couldn't get her out of my mind. Her backstory began to meld to form a character that pulled elements from several people I knew, and she became real to me.

A few of my family members have sustained traumatic brain injuries (TBI's). One was crushed by a horse, another was involved in a car accident that took the life of his son. Living so far from them, our family lived for the updates and prayed fervently. It's heart-breaking for those who love them, and so painful for them to rehabilitate. My grandmother's case was a little different; she had a sinus infection that leaked into her brain and threatened her life. After a major surgery that required removing part of her frontal lobe, I was able to be with her for extended amounts of time over the several years it took her to recover. Kat's symptoms and tricks for remembering things are inspired by what I witnessed during my grandmother's recovery, interviews with several mothers who are caring for children with TBI's, and friends who sustained TBI's in sport-related accidents.

Writing this story wrecked me at times, as I recalled that night at St. Luke's Hospital when the doctors told us Gram might not make it. I thought about the terrible accidents and the grief of not knowing what would happen next. Caring for someone with a traumatic brain injury takes a strength many do not know they possess. It's easy to get frustrated from the blank stares after you've given instructions or waiting for them to realize they just made a match playing a memory card game. It's heart-wrenching when they realize they can't add simple numbers and don't understand why.

But the brain is a beautiful thing. It can be re-trained. It responds to commands from your own voice more than anyone else's. Self-talk and speaking things into existence can become reality. We can teach the brain to believe and do just about anything. With a loving support system, prayers, and coping techniques similar to those Kat uses throughout this story, many people suffering from TBI's can live a fulfilling life.

If you or a loved one have suffered a TBI, I am praying for you. Have faith.

Kerry Evelyn

Love on the Rocks

KERRY EVELYN

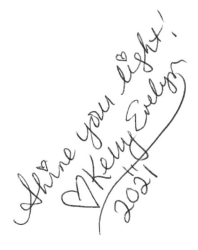

Swan Press

Love on the Rocks
Kerry Evelyn
www.kerryevelyn.com
Kerry@kerryevelyn.com

Published 2018 by Swan Press

Edited by Racquel Henry of The Writer's Atelier, and Nicole
Ayers, Ayers Edits
Cover photo by Robert Hare Photography
Cover models Sarah Masry and John Kelley
Cover design and formatting by Valerie Willis, Battle Goddess
Productions
Proofing by Laura Perez, Palmas Publishing

Printed in the United States of America
First Printing: September 2018
Swan Press

Paperback ISBN: **978-0-9995861-2-9**
EBook ISBN: **978-0-9995861-3-6**

Dedicated to

For my Gram, Evelyn Marshall,
whom I miss dearly,
and all victims and families affected by traumatic brain injuries.

For I know the plans I have for you," declares the Lord,
"plans to prosper you and not to harm you,
plans to give you hope and a future."

Jeremiah 29:11

Love is patient, love is kind. It does not envy, it does not boast,
it is not proud. It does not dishonor others, it is not self-seeking, it
is not easily angered, it keeps no record of wrongs. Love does not
delight in evil but rejoices with the truth. It always protects,
always trusts, always hopes, always perseveres. Love never fails.
And now these three remain: faith, hope and love.
But the greatest of these is love.

1 Corinthians 4-8, 13

Chapter 1

Kat Daniels leaned back in the oak barstool and crossed one booted leg over the other. She frowned into the tumbler of amber liquid and ice in her right hand, considering again how she had ruined everything. *God, what am I doing here?* She had let go of the love of her life, and coming back to town to work at his family's resort was not working out as she had hoped and the solution was certainly not to be found in a shot of whiskey.

The seaside pub in Crane's Cove was surprisingly empty for a Sunday night in June. She was hoping she wouldn't run into anyone she knew, but she expected a crowd of tourists at least. People she could talk to and then never see again, people to help distract her from her own regrets and the events of the last few weeks.

You know that's not what you need, her inner voice scolded. She pushed the thought away and brought the whiskey to her lips. She took a sip and waited for her throat to recover from the burn. Picking up an extra shift at the resort hadn't distracted her, so she'd skipped dinner and Uber'd to the pub with a plan to drink herself numb.

"Hey, Kat."

"Hey, Kev," she said to her old friend. He'd been working for his father's construction business since high school, and it was evident by the way his shirt hugged his chest he was still very hands-on. Kat tossed back the whiskey and placed the glass on the bar.

He nodded to it. "Can I buy you another one?"

Kat sighed. If she'd wanted to be social, she would've hung out at the bar in the resort dining room. Saturday night's events always drew a crowd on Sunday nights, and this week's beachside potluck hadn't disappointed. The guests were an especially lively bunch. Too bad most of them had departed earlier that morning to avoid the storm.

She shrugged. "If you want. On the rocks, please." Kat absently twirled a long chestnut lock of hair as Kevin settled in the stool next to her.

He ordered another round and gestured to the half a dozen or so patrons in the pub. "Pretty slow tonight. Guess people are prepping for the storm. Good to see you here."

"Same." Kat averted her gaze and watched the bartender place two new tumblers on the bar. "Thanks, Paddy."

Paddy leaned toward her. "Don't drink that one too fast now, Kat." The owner of the pub had been a friend of her parents. She hadn't known he still worked the bar or she'd have gone somewhere else. His kids had taken over when he'd retired a few years ago. Seemed like even they had better things to do on a Sunday night.

Paddy shot Kevin a warning look and headed for the other end of the bar, where a trio wearing University of Maine ball caps had just settled in.

His back now turned to her, she chugged the whiskey in one swig as an act of defiance.

Kevin raised a brow. "Well, then."

She shrugged. "Tough weekend."

"Yeah, I'll bet." He sipped at his drink. "So how long have you been back in town?"

Kat sighed. She uncrossed her legs, shifted in her worn jeans, and rested her forearms on the edge of the bar. Kevin mimicked her actions and waited for her answer. She spoke straight ahead. "A month or so."

He nodded. "Well, welcome home. You want another one?"

"Why not?"

He finished the drink he was holding and waved Paddy over. The disapproving bartender set down another round and glared at him.

"I don't think he likes me," Kevin joked.

Kat swallowed the drink in one gulp. "He's just grumpy tonight." The whiskey was achieving the desired effect. The muscles in her thighs began to feel tender and tingly, relaxing her and at the same time making her more restless. "Paddy!"

He returned to their end of the bar, crossed his arms,

and narrowed his eyes sternly.

She giggled. "You look so mad."

"You're drinking too fast, Kat. Wouldn't want to see you find any trouble," he said, looking directly at the man occupying the bar stool next to her.

"Oh, he's fine." Kat waved her hand absently. "Me and Kev go waaaaaay back."

"Huh," Paddy grunted.

She laughed. "Another round, please. This one's on me." She grinned at Kevin. "This night may not be a total bust after all."

Paddy brought the next round. Kat picked up a drink and handed the other to Kevin. "To lonely Sunday nights," she toasted.

They clinked glasses, downed the whiskey, and set the glasses on the counter. Kat felt the now-familiar cloudy sensation in her head take over. Over the past several months, she'd learned to find moments of solace from more than a few ounces of strong whiskey. She pulled on a different strand of her long hair and wrapped it around her finger. She twirled it as she studied Kevin's face. She tried to focus on what he was saying.

"So what brings you back to town? Last I heard you were on the barrel-racing circuit. How'd that go?"

She darted a glance to her empty glass. "I got tired of it."

"Really? All those wins get you down?"

Kat looked up at him. "Stupid people got me down." *And their persistent text messages.*

He smirked. "On the tour, or here in town?"

Kat noticed him looking at her left hand, currently half-wrapped with hair. She quickly put her hand in her lap and covered it with the right one, sitting up and squaring her shoulders. "Both."

He leaned toward her. "I see."

"What do you see?" She blinked, straining to keep him in focus. *Concentrate, Kat.*

He tilted his head. "You don't have a ring on your finger anymore. How long has it been gone?"

"Christmas."

"Ouch."

Kat was starting to feel agitated. "I don't want to talk about it." She slid off her seat. "I'm gonna go play a song."

She felt his eyes on her as she walked over to the jukebox. She fed the vintage machine two quarters and selected a song from the eclectic variety. *Good. Someone appreciates my attention.* Too bad it was the wrong guy. She liked Kevin, but she'd never date him again. They were meant to be friends, that's all. Her heart had long ago taken up residence elsewhere, and wouldn't be moved.

She jumped as Kevin appeared at her side. "Hey!" She smiled. "Didn't see you coming."

"Sorry to startle you. Wanna dance?" he asked as the beginning verse of "Home Alone Tonight" began to play.

Kat tilted an ear toward the speakers and frowned.

That wasn't the song she selected.

"I don't know how to dance to this song. It's more of a my-life-sucks kind of sing-along song."

He snorted. "That's funny." He held out his hand. "Try?"

"I'll try anything once." She offered her hand.

Kevin raised a brow. "Really?" He took her right hand in his left and placed his right hand on her slim waist.

Kat rested her left hand on his shoulder and they shuffled to the music. A thought came to her as she listened to the lyrics. "Hey, we should take a selfie!"

Kevin smiled. "Whatever you want."

Kat pulled her phone out of her pocket and held it out to snap a picture. "Smile!" She grinned stupidly as Kevin squinted his eyes and held up his fingers in a sideways peace sign. She punched in a brief message, hit send, and replaced the phone in her pocket. "Ready for another shot?"

"I'm game if you are."

"Great! It's nice not to drink alone," she added softly.

"Yeah," he agreed. Kat tugged him back over to the bar. "Two more, please, Paddy."

The older gentlemen looked her over. "How you getting home, Kat?"

She shrugged. "Uber?"

"I can bring her home," Kevin offered. "You still live in that big house on the cliff?"

"Yep, big empty creepy house on the cliff." She

shuddered.

"You're all by yourself?"

The bartender shot daggers at Kevin. "She's got her uncle over there looking after her," he said firmly to Kevin. "I'm sure Old Man Wetherby wouldn't mind coming to get you, Kat."

"Nah. He's prolly fast asleep. Kev's an old friend. He can bring me home. Where's my next round?"

Paddy placed the drinks and a bowl of the bar's version of Chex Mix on the counter without a word. Kat giggled after he disappeared through the swinging doors that led to the kitchen.

"I don't think he likes you."

Kevin shrugged. "Never has. Another dance?"

"Sure. Gonna bring my drink, though. Think I should sip this one. Liiiiittle tipsy!" She grinned up at him. "Your eyes are very blue, Kevin. And kind. I like that. Better than green eyes that are mean." She knew she was talking nonsense. She didn't care. The man with the green eyes certainly didn't seem to care anymore.

He led her to the dance floor. Someone from the UMAINE group had added several songs to the queue. Kat sipped at her drink and swayed with Kevin to the Y2K playlist. She'd have to talk to Paddy about the music selection.

Easton Crane checked the latches on the horses' stalls

one last time and headed for the fridge in the break area at the back of the barn. He pulled out a local craft beer and popped the top, ignoring the vibration in his pocket from an incoming text message. He dropped heavily onto a nearby bale of hay and scanned the two lines of stalls that faced each other. All seemed well, another weekend of trail rides and riding lessons in the books. He took a long, slow sip from the bottle before he reached into his pocket.

Looky who found me at the pub! A long-forgotten, familiar anger burned in his belly at Kat's silly grin and his old rival's snarky pose. Easton put the phone back in his pocket without replying. He couldn't figure out what Kat's game was. He'd been ready to spend his life with her and then she took off barrel racing. At Christmas, he'd given her an ultimatum. The tour or him. She'd called his bluff and given back his ring. She'd left again and reappeared about a month ago. His parents had rehired her to help around the resort, of all things. Talk about salt in his wounds.

His phone rang. He groaned and pulled it out again. *Paddy's Pub and Grill.* Nope, he wasn't doing this. He stared at the phone as it rang and went to voicemail. His caller ID app was worth every penny as far as he was concerned.

It rang again. *Paddy O'Hara cell.* He sighed and swiped to receive the call.

"Easton Crane. Cliff Walk Stables," he recited.

"Hey there now, Easton. Paddy O'Hara here. Thought you might want to know Kat is in here tearin'

it up. Lookin' like she's plannin' to leave with that
Kevin Conroy fella you played ball with. I don't know
that that's a good idea since she's barely standin' up,
and he's had a few, too. Thought you might come get
her."

Easton sighed. He pulled off his ball cap and used it
to wipe his brow. "Yeah, I don't think she'd appreciate
that, Paddy." Since she'd returned, he'd been struggling
to figure out why she was back and what she wanted
from him. Some days, she acted as if she wanted to pick
up where they'd left off. Other days, she was colder
than a frozen harbor, snapping at him for no apparent
reason or brushing him off when he tried to help her.

A few weeks ago, they'd been caught off guard
outside the dining room during an event at the resort.
When their song started playing, a magnetic force had
drawn them to each other. They'd danced, suspended in
time, hearts beating as one. A flood of emotion passed
between them as they clung to each other. When the
song ended, she'd bolted. Kat was hot or cold; there
was no in between. All last week, she'd barely said a
word to him at the barn.

"Welp, I called Old Man Wetherby and he didn't
pick up. She told me not to call Shelby; she's
babysitting her nephew tonight. Couldn't reach your
sister, Molly, either. Kat's got no one else. I guess I
could call up to the police station and see if one of the
guys can bring her home. But you know, they've been
understaffed since the Donovan kid decided to go to

Virginia and join the FBI like his ma."

"Won't she take an Uber?"

"Suggested that. She shot it down after Kevin offered. She's a stubborn one."

"Don't I know it." Easton inhaled deeply through his nose and let out a long breath. He looked longingly at his half-full beer. "All right. I'll head out there. Don't let her leave with him."

"No way in hell. I'll deck him myself if I have to."

"Thanks, Paddy."

Kat sang as Kevin twirled her around the dance floor. "Whoa!" She stumbled as he attempted to dip her. He twisted to avoid landing on her and she fell onto him in a fit of giggles. "Whoops!" She rolled off him, still laughing.

A shadow loomed above them. Arms crossed and frowning, Easton Crane, her former fiancé, stood before them, his emerald eyes cold. Her face fell and she swallowed hard. Kevin stood up and offered his hand. She took it and stumbled to her feet.

"Time to go home, Kat," Easton said, glowering at her.

She put her fists on her hips in defiance. "No, it's not."

"I got her, Crane."

Easton shifted his fiery gaze to Kevin. "Not tonight."

"What do you care?" Kat muttered. "You just want to ruin my fun."

Easton tensed.

Kevin set his shoulders back. "She doesn't want to go with you. She's made that clear."

"She doesn't know what she wants," Easton growled.

The men glared at each other. Kat didn't dare look at him. She could sense he was tired and weary under his anger. Paddy approached the trio.

"Everything all right, fellas?"

"I'm here to bring Kat home," Easton said, still focused on Kevin.

"And I'm telling you that I'm going to bring her home," Kevin challenged. He stepped forward.

Easton held his ground.

"Oh, please don't fight." Kat sighed. She looked at Easton, her eyes searching his for a sign of warmth. He continued to glare at her. She took another step back, overcome with the maelstrom of emotions she saw in their depths. She shouldn't have looked into his eyes. Another step back. Right into a barstool.

"Whoa!" Easton reached out to steady her. He was quick. It was like he knew she was falling before she actually fell. He used to be able to anticipate her every move. He'd always caught her before she fell when she was in therapy. *Push that thought away, Kat. That was a different time and a different Easton.*

"Easy there, Kat," Paddy soothed. He turned to

Easton. "You take her home. This guy"—he gestured to Kevin—"is gonna sit at the bar and have some coffee and snacks till I decide he's not a danger to himself or anyone else."

Kevin grumbled, but conceded. "I'll call you tomorrow, Kat." He followed Paddy to the bar.

Kat flicked her gaze back to Easton. "Why did you come?"

"Paddy called me."

"Oh." She'd hoped he'd gotten her text and felt something. Jealously, anger, anything really. Guess that ship really wasn't coming back to port.

Kat followed him out the door and into the cool summer night. She hugged herself as she trudged across the gravel to his truck. He opened the passenger door for her and she climbed in.

Easton drove in silence down Main Street. Kat leaned her head on the door frame and stared out the window. Her buzz had worn off.

"You know you shouldn't be drinking whiskey with your meds, Kat." Easton watched her out of the corner of his eye as he drove. She turned her body in the seat so that her back was facing him. His heart was still moved at the sight of her, even when she was a mess. He recalled the words he'd spoken that had prompted their breakup and wished he could take them back.

"What do you care?" she mumbled a second time

that night.

He tensed, squeezing the steering wheel. She was becoming more and more reckless, leaving a string of bad choices in her wake. Picking up the pieces was getting old.

"You know I care. Don't undo all your progress with bad decisions. You're so close to complete recovery. Why do you continue to take risks?" Easton slowed for a red light and relaxed back into his seat. He turned his eyes to her curled-up body facing out the window and softened his voice. She didn't need a lecture. She needed grace. "I was with you every day, Kat. Every day after your riding accident, through your therapy. I took college classes from the barn so I wouldn't have to leave you." His voice broke. "I *never* stopped caring." He fought to control the wave of emotions that descended and missed her stiffening at his words.

"Then why won't you forgive me?" she pleaded, her anguished whisper barely audible.

The light turned green and Easton pressed his lips together as he released the brake. Up and down Main Street, several businesses had already boarded up. It'd still be a day or so before they knew if the storm would hit with hurricane-force winds, but some weren't taking any chances. The boards reminded him of how much work he still had to do at the stables to prep for the storm. He didn't have time for Kat's drama or impulsivity.

Ignoring her question, he made the turn onto Crane's Cove Road and wondered if Old Man Wetherby would be able to prep her historic Queen Anne-style home sufficiently. He should take a look around after he saw her inside.

Crane's Cove Road wound itself over a granite cliff that declined in elevation as it passed the town's premier resort, the Cliff Walk. Owned by Easton's father's family for generations, the expansive acreage accounted for half of the town, from the high Acadian peak above the resort to the beach in the cove below. Beyond the family land, a scattering of town buildings and mom-and-pop businesses lined the road before it turned, hugging the peninsula that jutted out a half mile into the cove, ending at the Point, and then back again to the town landing and marina. Large residential homes dotted this section of town, most built by those who had profited from the whaling, fishing, and shipping industries over a century ago.

Kat's house was one of these homes. It was left to her by her great-aunt Katherine, affectionately known as Auntie Katie, upon her death last summer. The house was expansive, its rose-painted shingles towering three stories above the rocky base, visible from all points in the cove. A windowed turret extended upward and peaked beside a widow's walk. An attached walkway led to a gazebo overlooking the cliff.

Below the house by the road, the original carriage house had been restored and converted into a groundskeeper's cottage by her great-uncle Charley, who had returned to his childhood home two decades ago to live with his sister after the tragic boating accident that had claimed Kat's parents and maternal grandparents. Devastated by the loss of his youngest sister, his niece, and their husbands, he'd surprised everyone in town when he'd shown up after swearing he'd never come back. Charles Wetherby was the older half-brother of Katherine and Charlotte, Kat's grandmother. He'd never gotten along with his stepfather and had joined the marines on his eighteenth birthday. He'd come back, compelled to help his sister raise their grandniece, and had been devoted to Kat ever since. In his eighties now, he was slowing down, but the inner Marine inside still pushed his physical limits.

Refusing to live in his stepfather's house, the retired sailor had gutted the smaller building, added a loft apartment, and used the space below to store his Boston Whaler and a pool table. Before her accident, Easton, Kat, and their friends had spent many a night in their teens shooting pool with the old man and listening to his stories. He was getting older now, moving slower, sleeping more. Easton knew it was only a matter of time until Kat was truly on her own.

He turned off the road and onto the long driveway that led to the house. The cottage was dark, but the old man's ancient Ford Ranger was parked in front of one of the large garage doors. Easton pulled in next to it and hopped out before Kat could ask any questions.

He jogged to the door and knocked. The blinds were

drawn. Probably the old guy just went to bed early. He knocked again.

"Easton, what are you doing?" Kat hissed through the open truck window. "Let the man rest."

"Just checking on him. Paddy said he didn't pick up when he called." He frowned at the lack of response.

"He goes to bed at seven now so he can be up at dawn," she huffed. "I'm sure he's fine." "Thanks for the ride. See ya." She opened the door and stepped out.

"Wha—" He watched her, arms crossed, purse hanging from the crook in her elbow, march up the hill toward the main house. "Kat, wait—" He glanced at the cottage door, shrugged, and hurried to catch up with her.

"You don't need to follow me home."

"I just want to—" He paused as he reached her side. What did he want? They reached the steps that led to the wraparound porch. She dug her key out and jammed it into the lock.

"Please," she pleaded. Her eyes welled with tears. He reached up to wipe them, as he had done so many times. She left the key in the slot and swatted his hand away. "Don't."

Easton stepped back, emotionally struck with a pain that was far greater than the swat of her hand. He knew what he wanted. He wanted the old Kat back, regardless of her traumatic brain injury. He didn't care if she couldn't find the right word to say, or sometimes forget words or what she was doing. He wanted the Kat that fought hard every day to walk again, talk again. The

Kat that loved helping him in the barn, caring for the horses and teaching little kids all about them and how to ride them. The Kat that sparkled with a love of life and found fun in everything, despite sustaining more loss than most people could handle. Where was she hiding inside this risk-taking, angry, impulsive woman who stood in front of him? And had she run away to cope with mourning Auntie Katie, or was there more to it? Was it because of him?

She went in and slammed the door. He stared at it for a moment before shuffling to the corner of the porch that offered the view of the sea. Straight out and down below, Crane's Light, the floating lighthouse his family had purchased from the Coast Guard back in the '60s, signaled to him. When Kat had left him at Christmas, he'd emptied his savings into the lighthouse with the goal of fixing it up into an exclusive guest suite for the resort. He went out there every chance he could, and he was set to have it ready as a honeymoon suite for Matt Saunders and Lanie Owens when they tied the knot in July. The Coast Guard still operated and maintained the light, so it had been in decent shape to begin with. After the storm, he'd finish painting the trim work and bring in the smaller appliances and pieces of furniture. With Kat now teaching the children's riding lessons on the weekends, he'd have plenty of time to spend at the lighthouse—as long as the hurricane didn't destroy it.

Easton trudged back down the hill to his truck. He opened the door and sat for a few moments, staring up at the lit windows on the second floor he used to climb into a decade ago. So they hadn't boarded up. He hoped they'd follow the evacuation orders. A shadow appeared in the bumped-out base of the turret. The outline of the broken woman he had loved for so long sat in her window seat, head on her knees.

Before he could entertain the idea of scaling her porch as he'd done countless times in his youth, he started the truck and drove back to the resort.

Chapter 2

Early Monday morning, after scarfing down the pancakes her uncle had left warming in the oven, Kat headed out to the resort to make sure Mocha was all set for the impending storm. The Cliff Walk offered limited boarding space and services to the town residents in exchange for use of the horses for guest trail rides, but Kat preferred to take care of her horse herself.

Before Mocha, she'd ridden Callie, who had been Easton's grandmother's favorite horse. The older Mrs. Crane, known around the barn as Ms. Vivi, had gifted Mocha to Kat as a foal after Kat's accident as an incentive to motivate her recovery.

What had started with a trail ride for Kat's tenth birthday had sparked a love of riding. Auntie Katie had told Kat how Ms. Vivi had remarked to her how much Kat reminded her of herself at that age. Not long after her birthday trail ride, Kat was offered lessons in exchange for helping around the stables after school. In a short time she had developed her natural talent in the saddle and was competing and winning jumping events all over the East Coast. Summers in New England, spring and fall shows in the Mid-Atlantic states, and winters in Florida. Auntie Katie was Ms. Vivi's best friend and would spend most of her afternoons watching Kat learn and perfect her show-jumping skills. She'd been thrilled to spend her deceased husband's fortune on Kat's passion.

Kat had become fast friends with Ms. Vivi's grandsons, Easton and JC, who worked in the stables. The boys traveled with Kat and Ms. Vivi to the events that weren't local. A tear fell as she remembered the trip that had changed everything. It had been over six years ago, but it seemed like yesterday when she remembered the excitement of the event. She'd saddled up Callie, executed a perfect warm-up, and was ready. One minute she was clearing jumps and the next she was opening her eyes to the back of a white cotton bandage in a hospital. She had no memory of the fall itself. Perhaps her brain protecting itself was best.

Kat ignored the buzzing of her phone and parked her cherry red Jeep Grand Cherokee in the small lot beside the barn. It was brand new two years ago, a gift from Auntie Katie to celebrate getting her license back. She'd been seizure-free for over two years.

The gift included a brand-new, top-of-the-line saddle with ostrich leather accents and a lightweight horse trailer for Mocha. The SUV was an unusual choice for towing, but it suited her just fine. The rodeo could be a judgy crew, so she'd learned to let the comments and snickers roll off her in regards to her vehicle. Neither she nor Auntie Katie had envisioned her barrel racing and traveling when she'd purchased it.

She walked around the barn to the open doors that faced the paddock. A rustling around the corner made her look up. Easton stood perched about sixteen feet up on a ladder in the maple tree that cast its wide canopy over Mocha's side of the barn.

"Look out below!" he called. Girlish giggling carried over the salty breeze. Kat frowned and pulled the sides of her jacket together. The winds had already begun to pick up. The storm was still several hundred miles offshore, and they had several hours to go before the rain would begin. She shivered as she peeked around the corner.

Below Easton, Maddie, Meggie, and Mellie,—or the Triple M, as the friends liked to be called collectively— gathered fallen branches, which they tied and stacked against the barn.

"Incoming!"

More giggles as Maddie called out, "I got this one!" The branch thudded onto the ground. She ran to it and dragged it to where the other girls stood.

Easton climbed down, wiping his brow. He took a few steps back from the ladder and surveyed the canopy of the tree. Kat sucked in a breath. The curve of his bicep peeked out from under his rolled-up sleeves. His jeans hugged every muscle of his lower half. As if he could sense her, he turned. His classically handsome face lost the grin he'd awarded to the girls and his eyes darkened. Kat pulled her head back and pressed her whole body to the wall. She took a deep breath to steady her racing heartbeat and squeezed her eyes shut, praying he'd ignore her.

"Hey, girls," he called. *Good.* He seemed to be continuing what he'd been doing before she arrived. "I think I heard a vehicle pull up while I was up in the tree. Wanna go see who's here?" *Darn.*

Kat straightened herself and rushed into the barn and to the first stall on the right. "Hey, sweet girl."

Mocha greeted her with a whinny and a happy grunt. Kat reached up to stroke her between her eyes. She unlatched the stall door and was pleased to see that it was already mucked out and stocked with fresh water and hay.

"Those girls are taking good care of you, aren't they?" She peered into the empty grain bucket. "Looks like you enjoyed your breakfast." She scooped up a handful of baby carrots and a couple of sugar cubes from the bag in her jacket pocket. Mocha gobbled them up and gave her an appreciative snort. "Wanna go for a ride? There's a storm coming, so I don't know when you'll get out again." Mocha awarded Kat with a nuzzle and blew air out her nostrils. Kat laughed. "I'll be right back."

She opened the stall door as the girls entered the barn. She smiled. The three girls had started much like she had. It was Maddie's sixth birthday that started their love of everything horses. Eight years later, when they turned fourteen, they began working at the resort and had been dependable barn hands for the last two summers. They had no trouble taking over Kat's duties last year when she decided to leave the stables and barrel race full time.

The only difference now was the absence of Easton's grandmother. After Kat's accident, Ms. Vivi sold off the jumps and limited the barn to trail rides and children's lessons only. When Kat had recovered enough to ride again and assist Easton at the barn, Ms. Vivi had literally hung up her saddle and moved into an apartment complex for retired seniors on the other side of town.

"Hey there, Kat!" Mellie greeted her. "Can we help you with anything?"

"Sure. I'd love some help saddling up Mocha. She seems a bit edgy. Likely she senses the storm coming."

"Happy to!" Maddie answered.

"Great!" Meggie chimed in. "We'll grab her stuff."

The girls headed for the tack room and Kat turned back to Mocha. "You ready, sweet girl? I thought we'd head up to the meadow and then work on the barrel pattern. Does that work for you?"

Mocha neighed and snorted her response. Kat grinned.

The girls returned with Mocha's gear. Mellie handed the aqua saddle pad to Kat. She positioned herself on Mocha's left side and tossed it over her back.

"I love that color on her," Mellie commented as she

handed Kat the half pad. "It just pops on her gorgeous chocolate-colored coat, you know?"

"Totally," Maddie agreed. "Someday when I'm a famous rider, I'll dress my horse just as flashy as Kat dresses Mocha."

Kat smiled. "I have no doubt you girls will have the best-dressed horses in southern Maine." She took the saddle from Maddie. "I can picture the headlines now: 'Triple M Saddle Club Wins First Downeast Equine Fashion Show.'"

The girls beamed. "Do you really think we can do that, Kat?" Meggie asked. The most serious of the three, she was often the one to bring her friends back to reality when their imaginations ignited.

"I think, no, *I know*, you girls can do anything you set your minds to. Focus on the goal. Break it down into small parts and small goals and crush one after the other." She adjusted the saddle, positioning it above the withers and tugging on the saddle pad to line it all up so Mocha wouldn't get pinched. Maddie moved over to Mocha's right side and reached under to hand the girth to Kat, who grabbed it and tightened the cinch.

Maddie turned to Meggie, who handed her the bridle. "I agree with Kat. We just need to learn everything we can about horses and fashion—and I suppose leather making and sewing, too." She frowned. "So not glamorous."

"Well," Kat said as she slid the bridle over Mocha's head, "you already know that most things related to horses are the opposite of glamorous. Take mucking, for instance."

The girls giggled.

Kat adjusted the browband and stroked Mocha's muzzle. She took the reins. "Ready, girl?"

Maddie, Meggie, and Mellie stepped aside as Kat led Mocha out of the stall. Kat stepped up, slid her left boot into the stirrup, and swung her right leg over the saddle. She landed with a slight thump. Mocha grunted.

"Sorry, girl. I'm a little off today," she whispered. Turning to the girls, she gave a little wave. "Thanks for your help. Will I see you when I get back?"

"Oh yes, we're here all day to help Easton prep for the storm," Maddie said.

Kat felt a twinge of guilt. She was off Mondays and Tuesdays, but hadn't offered to help.

"Great. I'll leave her in your capable hands when we return then. I've got some prep to do myself still." She gave Mocha a little kick and steered her around the paddock toward the trailheads.

"Have a great ride, Kat!" Maddie called.

"Thanks!"

Kat guided Mocha toward Mountain Walk Trail and leaned forward in her saddle. Within the pines, the upward climb into the Acadian woods was tranquil on any day. Today was extraordinarily quiet. It seemed even the wildlife was hiding in preparation for the storm. All was still except for the occasional wind gust rustling leaves and needles on branches.

And her cell phone. She ignored the vibrations in

her jeans pocket. She'd check it later.

They emerged from the trees into a small dirt clearing at the overlook. She stared out into the cove. Straight out, waves crashed against the Crane's Cove lighthouse. She wondered if Easton had secured it yet. She hoped so. It couldn't be safe to head out there at this point. Off in the distance to the left, her rose-colored home peeked out from the pines along the short peninsula. At high tide, the waves were already crashing higher than she'd expected along the rocky dike. On the right side, the land rose into a higher cliff than the one her house sat on across the cove. She recalled the conversation she had had that morning with her uncle. He refused to evacuate.

Kat slid off Mocha and led her to the low hand-created stone wall that lined the outer perimeter of the overlook. Below the haphazard structure, a chain-link fence ran the perimeter a few yards out. Beneath her, the resort jutted out like a stepping stone. Glimpses of the main lodge, stables, and cabins dotted the greenery with shingled roofs and chimneys. Beyond the road, graying teak stairs led down to the beach. Someone had removed the colorful buoys that hung from the beach shack, and the kayak rack sat empty. The beach chairs and umbrellas had been locked inside. They were all taking this one seriously. All it took was a little shift of the wind to devastate.

She climbed back up onto Mocha and followed the trail to the meadow. Nudging the mare into a trot, then a lope, they rode the perimeter a few times before heading back down Pine Walk Trail to the stable area. Her cell buzzed again, and she ignored it. She didn't want to talk to anyone. As soon as it stopped buzzing, it started ringing. She stopped Mocha just short of the trailhead and pulled out her phone. *Kevin.* She swiped the red dot. It could go to voicemail.

Her cheeks flamed as she recalled her behavior the night before. Her life had truly fallen apart. A text message from her former boss had sent her over the edge and straight to the pub.

Kat, when are you coming back? It's been weeks. Don't make me come find you.

She shuddered and kicked Mocha gently with her heel, steering her toward the barn. She didn't feel like working on the barrel pattern after all. Maddie saw her approach and hurried over.

Kat handed her the reins and dismounted. "Thanks, Maddie. We took a loop up to the overlook and ran a bit in the meadow. She's not too hot, but I'm sure she'd love a good rubdown and a treat or two." She stroked the mare's cheek with her right hand and pulled some more baby carrots out of her left pocket. Mocha nibbled them greedily. "Here," she said to Maddie. "Take the rest and give them to her when you're done. If she's good, you can give her a few sugar cubes, too."

"Will do," Maddie said.

Kat turned back to Mocha and planted a kiss above her nostrils. The horse returned the sentiment and nuzzled her face. "You be a sweet girl for Maddie."

Maddie led Mocha into the barn and Kat scanned the grounds. Easton was on the roof of the barn, banging a hammer. She walked around to where he could see her and called out, "You need any help before I go?"

"Nope. Go home and force Old Man Wetherby to come to the lodge."

"You know he won't. He rode out Hurricane Bill and Superstorm Sandy and who knows how many typhoons in the Pacific. This storm doesn't scare him."

Easton set the hammer down and glanced out to Kat. "It should. One bobble and we're toast." He sought her eyes with a sincerity that took her breath away. "Are you staying with him or coming back here?"

Kat inhaled deeply. She hadn't expected that look he gave her. She could feel the warmth in it all the way from the roof to where she stood. He had to still care. The eyes couldn't lie, could they? A little bit was enough to keep her hope alive. "I haven't decided. Molly offered to let me bunk with her at the lodge, but I'm worried about him being alone out there if the storm surge is bad." She sucked in her bottom lip. "And then there's Mocha—you know how she spooks in thunderstorms."

Easton shook his head. "Stay with Molly, please. He knows the risks. It's not his first storm. And your horse will be fine."

"True, but he and Mocha are all I've got left. He shouldn't be alone. It's been five years since Sandy, and Auntie Katie isn't here this time to stop him from doing something stupid. He's so old, Easton. I couldn't live with myself if something happened and I wasn't there to help him." Her phone rang again and she let it go to voicemail.

"Aren't you going to answer that?"

"Nope."

Easton grunted and picked up his hammer. "Do what you want. Mocha will be fine if that's what you're worried about. I'll bunk in the office for the duration."

"Really?" Her eyes misted. "That's—"

They turned toward the parking area as a Ford F-350 roared up and parked next to Kat's SUV. Kevin stepped out and nodded up to Easton before turning to Kat. "You lose your phone?"

Kat sighed. "Nope, just been busy." She glanced up at Easton. She stifled a laugh at the murderous expression on his face. He must have some major beef with Kevin.

They'd always been rivals, competitive in academics and on the field. The three of them had shared many classes throughout their school years, especially in high school. Thanks to the teachers' unoriginal seating arrangements, Conway, Crane, and Daniels were never too far from each other.

"I can see that." He shielded his eyes with his hand and assessed the roof. "Need some help up there?"

"I'm all set."

Kevin shrugged and looked back at Kat. "Tried calling you. Wanted to know if you needed any help prepping for the storm? I've got all my tools and some boards in the truck."

She shook her head. "We should be all set, but thank you. I hired a service to board up the house."

Kevin raised his eyebrows and scrunched his face into a pained expression. "Not those tarp-and-board guys in Bar Harbor?"

"Yep."

Kevin groaned. "Why didn't you call me? Those hacks hire college kids with zero experience who want to make a quick buck. It's temp work. Likely they're just bangin' nails however to get those boards to stay." He crossed his arms. "Want me to take a look at least? Make sure they're secure and won't blow off?"

"Couldn't hurt, I guess." She called up to Easton. "If you don't need me, I'm heading home."

"All set here," Easton replied through gritted teeth.

Why was he always so mad? God, please warm his heart to me.

"Let's go. I'll follow you." Kevin hopped in his truck and roared the engine. "See ya, Crane."

Kat stole one more glance at Easton. He resumed banging at the same board. She sighed and got into her car. Time to go try to convince the old man to evacuate again. She'd have to worry about Easton later.

Easton's fingers squeezed the hammer. The red SUV disappeared from sight followed by the man he detested most. Kevin had no integrity, no backbone. He ran from anything that got too hard and moved on to the next easy thing that appealed to him. He'd been that way his whole life, but it hadn't mattered to Easton until he'd abandoned Kat after she'd fallen off her horse and sustained a traumatic brain injury.

After a year of his persisting, Kevin had worn Kat down and finally wooed her by asking her to the homecoming dance on Acadia High's morning news their senior year. They'd been dating for three months when Kat, Easton, JC, and Grandma Vivi journeyed to Florida for the Winter Circuit. Kat was expected to place, and at seventeen, she was hopeful that consistency would advance her to the Indoor Circuit that fall. It was her biggest show to date, and Kevin had opted to stay home, insisting she'd do great and that the basketball team needed him more than she did. That was a fact, but if Easton had been her boyfriend, he'd have dropped everything to watch her. She was magnificent, beautiful, and commanding.

Though Easton had called Kevin from Wellington as soon as he knew which hospital Kat would be airlifted to, Kevin remained in Maine. When it was evident it would be a long recovery, he'd broken up with her to "give her time to heal and focus on herself." It was Easton who'd missed the senior prom to binge watch movies with her, and it was Easton that wheeled her up to the stage to get her high school diploma.

He was always too shy. For years he and his brother

traveled all over with Kat and their grandmother in her old RV, towing Callie, Grandma's dark bay, and all the gear. He was too afraid to tell Kat how he felt, afraid of how things might change if she didn't feel the same. He could handle pining. He knew he couldn't handle rejection. Not from her. It would wreck him. *And it did.*

Grandma Vivi had lived for those trips. She shared with them once that she'd never really been cut out for running a resort. She much preferred her horses to people. Their Grandpa John, on the other hand, had lived for hospitality. It was in his blood. When he passed away unexpectedly, Easton's parents had taken over the operations, allowing Grandma Vivi to work the stables full time. She was thrilled when she discovered her best friend's grandniece had a natural aptitude and talent for riding. Her own children and grandchildren loved horses, but not in the way she did. With Kat, it was as if she were a young girl again. Those were the best years. He'd give anything to have them back.

It hadn't been fair. Easton often wondered why God hadn't prevented Kat's accident. Pastor Porter had reminded him that God had saved her life, and that Easton should focus on praying for her recovery. No miracle was too big or too small for God. He recalled the verse the pastor had shared from the book of Romans, that in all things God works for the good of those who love him, who have been called according to his purpose.

Easton clung to that verse then, and recalled it still, when life's events didn't make sense to him or when they made him question his faith. Sometimes, he grew discouraged looking for the good that the verse promised. When he thought about it objectively, Kat lost her horse, her future career, her ability to process, friendships, and academic aptitude. She'd lost her aunt. She could no longer devour books or compute higher level math. Kat had lost so much, and why? What was God's purpose? After her aunt died, Kat pushed him away, desperate to find meaning for herself. If God had a hand in it all, she needed to know why so much suffering was necessary.

Easton climbed down from the roof and put his tools away. He pulled on the hoodie he kept in the office. The pressure and temperature continued to drop steadily. The horses could feel it, too.

Over the last few days, he and Matt Saunders, a guest he'd become friends with over the last month, had assisted him and Terrance, the resort's landscaper, with hurricane prep. They'd trimmed branches, secured equipment, and brought in anything that could turn into a projectile. Only a few more things remained on his to-do list. He needed to bring in Kat's barrels and check that the hay and feed were stocked. After that, he'd secure the sheds at the back of the paddocks to make sure the old-fashioned open-aired landau carriage, the sleigh, and all the large equipment was set.

Easton opened one of the sheds and sucked in a breath as he stared at the landau. He'd last taken it out to drive Matt and Lanie to the formal. The night played in his head. Kat had found him holding up the wall outside the dining room. He'd heard the words of their song faintly through the walls and had reached out to her before he could think any better. For a few moments, they were back in time, swaying to their song. It was just them, holding each other up, their hearts beating in sync.

Easton slammed the door on the landau and the memory. He snapped the padlock shut and began walking toward the main lodge.

He texted the girls that he was taking a lunch break and set off. He reminded them not to forget to eat their lunch, as they often did, and to text if they needed anything. They were good barn hands, and their friendship reminded him a lot of him, Kat, and JC at that age.

As if his ears had been ringing, Easton's phone lit up with JC's picture. He hadn't talked to his brother in a few days. He swiped green. "Hey, man."

"Yo, bro. Looks like that storm's gonna hit ya, huh? Category one. Not so bad, right? You gonna watch it from the overlook? I bet the surge will be awesome!"

Easton couldn't help smiling. JC had a positive spin on everything.

"Nah. Gonna ride it out equine-style."

JC laughed. "Dude, the barn is the last place I'd be. All that noise. Where are Kat and the old man gonna hang?"

"Not sure. You know Molly's moving into the lodge? Mom and Dad insisted on everyone evacuating the cabins and she asked Kat to bunk with her in one of the empty rooms. Mom offered Old Man Wetherby a room, but I'm pretty sure he'll decide to stay at his house. Kat doesn't want to leave him, though."

"Yeah, I see her point. He's all she's got left." For the second time that day, that comment riled Easton. It wasn't true. Kat had *him.* He corrected himself. *Could* have had him. She'd made it clear—at Christmas of all times—that she didn't want him.

"Not my problem anymore." Easton swallowed a lump and narrowed his eyes. He would not allow his feelings to get the best of him. The new, tough Easton did not show emotion, did not give his heart away, did not allow anyone to penetrate the walls he'd put up. He would not play the fool again.

Chapter 3

Kat parked at the top of the driveway. Kevin pulled in behind her and was out of his truck and at her door before she turned off the ignition. *When did he get chivalrous?* She opened it before his hand could reach the outer handle. He stepped back as she exited her SUV.

Kevin turned his eyes from Kat and squinted at the younger twenty-somethings on the roof of the covered porch. It was clear they were struggling to place the heavy board and drill in the screws at the same time. "How much did you pay them, Kat?"

"Likely too much, from the looks of it. I probably should have called you." She bit her lip and looked at him. "It's just that it's been awhile, you know?"

"Yeah." He pulled his eyes from the motley crew on the roof. "No worries." He opened his mouth and closed it, as if he wanted to say more and thought twice. "Mind if I climb up and offer some help?"

"Not at all. I'm going to head inside and pack up some stuff. Come find me when you're done." She pulled her jacket close and looked up at the darkening sky. "Hopefully the rain will hold up until you guys finish."

"Will do." He jogged over to the ladder propped against the front of the porch and readjusted it before climbing up.

Kat returned to her SUV and grabbed her purse before heading inside. On the kitchen counter, a sandwich wrapped in wax paper sat next to a plastic container of sliced apples and a stainless steel bottle labeled "iced tea" on a strip of masking tape. Her eyes welled with tears. The old man seemed really happy to have her back home. She hadn't thought he would have missed her so much when she left, but she was learning that his gruff exterior belied his inner feelings.

She'd left him alone last summer, after his sister died, and had only thought of herself. Though he'd doted on her since she was a little girl, he'd never been overly affectionate. She hadn't considered once how he might feel about her leaving. She understood now how much he cared. He had aged over the last year, more than she could have thought possible.

She swiped at her eyes, frustrated at the easy tears, a side-effect left over from the brain injury. The anti-anxiety meds helped to a point, but didn't keep her from getting emotional over the smallest things, especially at the most inopportune times.

She unwrapped the sandwich, tossing the wrapper in the trash and biting into it while she headed upstairs. As she chewed, she surveyed her room from the doorway. Auntie Katie had given her the tower room when she'd come to live here. Situated over the old-fashioned formal sitting room off the foyer, the tower section stretched two stories above the porch roof. At some point, one of her ancestors had cut open the second-floor ceiling and installed a spiral staircase leading to the attic loft above. Window seats on both the second and third floors provided occupants with a cozy niche. Kat had positioned her bed so that the headboard faced away from the trio of windows with the seat, creating a separate nook for curling up with books and staring out at the ocean.

Above, in the attic space, the walls were lined with books going back over a hundred years. Kat's personal collection lived in a small bookcase that backed up to her headboard. The books mocked her, reminding her daily that she'd never be able to read like she had before she'd fallen off her horse. It was a painful process, reading, and frustrating to have to stop to take breaks. She rarely remembered what she'd just finished reading, and resigned herself to watching movies instead. Never before her accident would she even consider watching a movie before she'd read the book.

Five years ago, she was still at the rehab facility, and her aunt had packed up what she thought was important in preparation for Superstorm Sandy. The house had come through relatively unscathed, as it had in every storm for the last hundred years or so. Auntie Katie had done some upgrades afterward, installing hurricane windows and a new roof as a future precaution. Kat wasn't too worried, but she knew the slightest bobble of the storm could be the difference between tree debris in the yard and total devastation. *Or getting back to the marina safely or overturning a sailboat and drowning.* She pushed the thought away.

She plopped on her bed. *If I had to leave and never come back, what would I take?* Her eyes immediately found the old picture frames with Auntie Katie and Captain Huttleston before he died, Uncle Charley, and her parents and grandparents.

This time, she didn't stop the tears as they flowed. It wasn't fair. She'd lost so much. She'd only been four when the Whitby cruiser hit a swell and overturned, taking her parents and her maternal grandparents with it. She never knew her paternal grandparents—they passed away before she was born. Neither of her parents had siblings, so no aunts, no uncles, no cousins. Only her great-uncle, Charley, was left, and he'd be gone soon, too.

A picture of her standing by Callie after her first show. Herself, Easton, and JC as young teens with Ms. Vivi in front of the RV when they started traveling. Easton's lanky arm was slung around Kat's shoulders. His smile was proud, genuine. When was the last time she'd seen him smile like that?

Why me, God? Why did I have to lose so much? What's next for me?

Kat reached for the throw pillow she'd quilted in

middle school for Auntie Katie and buried her face in it. It still smelled like her, the faint scent of Chanel No. 5 mixed with fresh laundry. She fought with all she had to control her body-wracking sobs. She'd talk to her doctor about upping the dose of her meds. She loathed her weepiness.

Her heart jumped at the unexpected knock on her open door. Kat dragged her face up from the pillow.

"You okay? One of the guys thought he heard crying so . . ." Kevin averted his eyes and nodded toward the large window to the left of the tower windows, directly across from the doorway he stood in. She appreciated that, although she wondered if it was for her benefit or because he couldn't stand the sight of her crying. He shifted his weight from one foot to the other, hands in his pockets, as he waited for her reply. It was obvious she made him uncomfortable.

"I'm fine. I just get super emotional sometimes." She rubbed her eyes.

"Okay, then." He put his hands in his pockets and continued to stare at her.

"What? Do I have snot on my face?"

The side of his mouth turned up slightly. Was he trying not to laugh?

"No." His brows knitted and he tilted his head.

Why didn't he just leave?

"Kevin, if you have something to say, please, just say it."

He leaned into the doorframe. "I want to be your friend again, Kat. I'd actually like to be more than your friend, if you'd consider it. We never really got a chance back then, did we?"

She stiffened. Was he serious? Did he not remember choosing his team over her after her accident? "No, Kevin, *you* never really gave *me* a chance. You wanted me on your arm at the homecoming dance, and to show me off to all your cocky friends at games and parties. You were never affectionate unless your boys were around, egging you on. It was like I had the plague. We surface-dated, Kevin. You didn't want to get to know me. And as soon as things got hard—" Her voice cracked and her vision blurred as fresh tears filled her eyes.

"You gotta understand. Easton was always there, one step behind us, everywhere we went. And when he wasn't, JC was glaring at me from across the room. They were like your family, and I was afraid"—he looked at the ceiling—"never mind."

They were like your family. Family. Kat sucked in a breath. A lump started to form in her throat. "Never mind what? Kevin, if they intimidated you, then you're weaker than I thought."

He tensed. "I was a chump. I admit that. And I ran from anything that got hard, you called that right. But time changes things, changes people. I'm not the same punk kid I was, I promise you that."

She let out a breath. "I'm sorry, Kev. We can be friends. But that's it. I need to make things right with Easton. I don't know if he still loves me but I'm not giving up that he does." She swallowed the lump and met his eyes.

"It's fine." He crossed his arms and shrugged his shoulder, as if her rejection didn't matter. The room darkened slightly as the wooden panel over the large window was drilled into place. "But if it doesn't work out—"

"Then I will need a friend I can trust to lean on," she said firmly, her eyes meeting his to reinforce her point.

"Count on it."

Kat nodded and stood up. She gestured to her bureau. "I've really got to pack . . ."

"I'll go make sure those bozos finish it up right."

"Thanks, Kev."

She crossed the lush carpet to her closet and pulled out her biggest suitcase. Plopping it on the bed, she unzipped it and assessed the compartments. *Head to toe, accessories, hair. Makeup, purse, and outerwear.* The rhyme was a brain cue trick Auntie Katie had made up for her when she was relearning how to dress herself. In her head, in her room, in this big house, even in the barn, Auntie Katie was everywhere. Try as she might, she couldn't figure out a way to mend the hole her passing had left in her heart.

Back and forth to the bureau and closet, she put together several outfits in case her stay at the lodge extended past a day or two. Pajamas, underthings, a bathing suit, sandals, shorts, pants, tanks, shirts, a sundress, a sweater. What else? She went into her bathroom for her toiletry bag and makeup. She stuffed the clothes into the deep compartment and moved about the room gathering the pictures in frames. She placed them between her clothes so they wouldn't break during transport. She tossed in the pillow she'd cried into and scanned the room one more time. As an afterthought, she opened her nightstand drawer and grabbed a handful of Jack Daniels nips for her purse. Best not to be underprepared.

Outside, the trio continued to cover her windows. When only one window remained, Kat sank into the window seat to take in one last view of the sea. Out past the Point, Crane's Light appeared to bob on the waves. The lighthouse stood like a sentry, guarding the harbor and the little town from the unpredictable ocean beyond. The wind had picked up again, pushing the whitecaps that pounded at the rocks in the dike below, protecting her house and the rest of the peninsula.

Kevin climbed up on the roof and reached down to receive the board from one of the hired men below. He waved to her after he leaned it next to the window she was sitting in. She waved back and stood up. Time to go.

Easton had intended to grab his bag lunch from the resort's kitchen and eat it on his way back to the barn. Instead, Meemaw, Matt's grandmother, beckoned him over to the stove. It fascinated him how this tiny, bossy woman with a cloud of white hair and a personality bigger than the sky had seamlessly inserted herself into the resort's operations.

"Mmm, doesn't that smell just fine?" she drawled. Her eyes closed as she breathed in the aroma streaming up from the industrial-sized pot. She turned her head and commanded his eyes meet hers. "You ever had Brunswick stew?"

"Can't say I have."

She peered down at the lunch bag in his hand. Her lip twitched, noting her disapproval. "Why don't you give it a try before you head on out again? It'll really stick with you."

Easton looked down into the pot to get a better glimpse. How could all that smell so appetizing? The shredded meat and vegetables didn't appeal to him. "Maybe later."

"Suit yourself," she chuckled. "This here stew is a staple at our place back home on a stormy night. I know you folks probably prefer chowder or chili. There's just nothin' like a thick, hearty soup to fill your belly when the sea winds howl."

Meemaw had been visiting from Savannah for the past two weeks. She'd come up for the Memorial Day holiday to spend time with her grandson, Matt, after his fiancée's stalker had been apprehended. Matt and Lanie had left yesterday, but Meemaw had wanted to stay since she'd been enjoying her vacation so much. She'd insisted she wasn't afraid of the hurricane, and since she was retired, she was her own boss.

Easton's mother, a recipient of leftovers from several of the dishes Meemaw had prepared at Matt and Lanie's cabin, had given her full rein of the kitchen when she asked. Meemaw even offered to give the staff lessons in southern cooking. "You know, Matt and Lanie's wedding food has got to be just right. Let me help ensure that." Easton had overheard the conversation and smiled at the recollection.

Matt and Lanie's wedding was set for the Fourth of July. He frowned. Today was June fifth. There was a lot to do between now and then, especially if the storm left significant damage in its wake.

The kitchen door swung open. Easton and Meemaw looked up from the pot and grinned simultaneously.

"Well! It's always nice to be greeted with a smile!" Carol Crane, Easton's mother, strode toward the stove to give her son a hug. "Oh, Brunswick stew! Easton, have you tried this yet?"

"Later, Mom. Gotta head back out to the barn." He raised his lunch bag. "I'll eat my sandwich on the way."

Carol shook her head. "Still my picky eater. Someday you'll get bored with the same stuff over and over again and realize what you've been missing."

"Ma, you've been saying that my whole life. I'm not gonna change."

She reached up and cupped his chin. Her eyes grew serious. "Change is always necessary to move forward, sweetheart."

He narrowed his eyes. His mother was always

trying to make everyday occurrences into teachable moments. "Nah. I don't like change. I'm good."

Meemaw piped in. "Bless your heart, dear."

Easton's mouth twitched. Did Meemaw just insult him?

His mom laughed and patted his shoulder. "Someday, sweetheart. Someday."

He shook his head.

"How's the prep going? Barn all set?"

"It's just about done. The girls have been a big help. Timing of the storm worked out since they're done with school now and can help all day."

"That's wonderful. Just be sure not to overwork them. And the lighthouse? It's secure?"

"Yep. Matt and I went out there Friday and brought back everything that might get wrecked if the windows blow. Coast Guard will take care of the rest."

"Sounds like you're doing a fine job, then. I'll mention it to your father so he can cross all that off the list."

"Thanks." With a nod to his mother and Meemaw, he left the kitchen.

A few hours later, all prep work done, he returned to his cabin to get what he needed for a night in the barn. It was raining steadily now. He flipped the television on for the latest update. The five-o'clock track put the storm slightly more west. *Not good.* The storm was still moving slow, always a bad sign, and the outer bands were already arriving. He wondered if Kat had made it back to the resort yet. He pulled out his phone and called Molly.

"Hey, bro! Heard you were sleeping with the horses tonight. Are you nuts?"

"Hello to you too," he grunted. "Yeah, it's fine. Kat was worried about Mocha getting spooked, so I offered to stay there before she got it in her head to." He ran his fingers through his hair. "You need anything, Molly? I can come by after I grab a shower."

"Hmm . . . I'm already at the lodge. Setting up for the dinner crowd now. I'm glad most of the guests left yesterday. I managed to grab my stuff in between helping the cabin guests that did stay get set up here. Pretty sure I brought everything I need. Kat's in the room now setting up her stuff. She picked up a shift working dinner with me tonight. If I think of something, I'll call you."

"Okay." He could hear the disappointment in his own voice. *If you want to see Kat, suck it up and get some of the stew for dinner.* He shuddered. No way. *Get over it. Get over her.* "Did the old man come with her? Ma offered him a room."

"Nope, he wouldn't come. She's a little bent up about it, so I plan to wine her up good tonight so she won't think too much. We're gonna have ourselves a little hurricane party later."

Easton's grip tightened on the phone. "Molly, her meds—she shouldn't be drinking."

"Oh, chill, little brother. She can have a couple glasses of wine if she's not going anywhere. I'll be watching, I won't let her overdo it." Her voice hardened. "You know, you could fix this whole thing with just a few words to her."

"You make it sound like I can just wave a wand and go back to last summer. It's not that simple."

"Why can't it be?"

"It just can't."

"You need to let go of that pride or fear you're holding onto, and just give her another chance. You've known she was the girl for you since forever. Don't be stupid, Easton. People make mistakes. How 'bout some grace?"

"I gotta go. The shower's not gonna take itself."

"Hardy har, Mr. Subject Changer. Think about what I said, really hard. Don't sacrifice your future for your pride."

"Yes, Ma," he joked.

"Thanks for the compliment. Stay safe tonight."

Easton ended the call and plugged the phone into the charger on the kitchen counter. He pulled out a mug from the cupboard and turned on the Keurig. Likely to be a long night. A steady flow of caffeine would help. He turned the mug to read its message. "You read my mug. Social interaction quota met." *If only.*

He took the coffee upstairs. Two bedrooms and a bathroom, a perfect bachelor-pad space for him and JC. They'd moved in when his brother graduated high school, at the end of Easton's first year of community college. Their parents wanted to convert the family spaces on the third floor of the main lodge into penthouse-type guest suites, so the whole family had moved out. He and JC had chosen the cabin closest to the stables and their parents had a cabin built at the very end of Crane's Lane. Kat had been doing physical therapy at the time and would come often to visit and bond with Mocha. It was only a short push of her wheelchair to the cabin, and with JC away at UMAINE, they could be alone to watch movies and play cards, or memory games, or whatever the therapist was currently recommending. He'd pick her up at her house after her morning physical therapy and lunch, then bring her back at bedtime. Everything in this cabin reminded him of her.

Sharing the caregiver duties with Kat's aunt had given him purpose, and he fell in love with her more than he could ever have imagined was possible. He had almost forgotten about becoming a vet when he witnessed how Mocha helped her heal. Animals were powerful therapeutic tools, and he was given a new vision to build the barn back up to what it was in its old glory days. Maybe even start an equine-therapy program.

Easton had wanted a future with Kat more than anything. He regretted not being clear with her about his vision. He didn't want to rock the boat, so he stayed silent, believing they had their whole lives as a timeline. It was the perfect compromise. She'd lost her future career, and he'd given up on becoming a veterinarian. Together, they'd make a life together. But when Kat was well enough, she started barrel racing again. She'd become so reckless. He went with her to every event, mostly to make sure she was okay. If she got a concussion or missed taking her meds, she could experience powerful side effects.

He knew he couldn't travel with her when she went out on the tour. He couldn't leave work for more than a weekend, couldn't leave his parents hanging. So he came up with a plan he thought for sure would work: he proposed. She accepted, but grew distant while she was away. At Christmas—

No. He would *not* think about that right now. And he was done being her keeper. He couldn't watch her try to destroy herself anymore. To undo all their—*her*—progress. His heart wouldn't—*couldn't*—handle it. He'd already invested over half his life into her happiness. If she wanted to throw it away, then she was on her own.

He set his shoulders back and swigged the rest of the coffee. It was going to be a long night.

Chapter 4

Kat leaned back into the overstuffed pillows on the queen-sized bed. She watched Molly open a bottle of white zinfandel with expert precision.

"Ta-da!" Molly announced with a flourish as the cork popped off. "Wineglass, mug, or Solo cup?"

Kat laughed. "Whichever holds the most."

Molly opened the cupboard above the mini sink in the wet bar area. She tilted her head in thought as she stared into the recess. "Let's do mugs. There's a couple good ones in here." The Cliff Walk Resort had an extensive collection of mugs that the housekeeping staff rotated among the guest rooms and cabins. One never knew what might show up on a mug.

Kat reached for the mug of wine Molly brought to her. "I love Jesus but I drink a little," she read. "That's awesome."

Molly laughed and read from her mug, "I wish I was Felicia. She's always going somewhere."

Kat raised a brow and tried to hold a straight face. Both she and Molly burst out laughing, recalling the movie that inspired the words.

Molly snorted. "I can't even handle it! Bye—"

"Felicia!" they exclaimed together.

Kat put a hand on her waist. She was laughing so hard her side had cramped up.

Molly sat down on the corner of Kat's bed and sipped her wine. Her curly blonde hair was still pulled back into a ponytail, and she hadn't changed yet out of her serving clothes. Kat hadn't wasted a moment stripping off the white button-down shirt and black pants. She'd donned sleep shorts and a T-shirt as soon as she'd entered the room and pulled her hair up into a messy bun.

Kat sipped the wine. She'd have to pace herself with Molly watching. She nodded at the TV. "So, what are we watching?"

"Hmm . . ." Molly stretched past Kat to grab the remote from the nightstand. She flipped through the movie channels. "What do you feel like?"

"No chick flicks."

"Amen to that. *Hunger Games*?"

"Too depressing."

"*Gone with the Wind*?"

"Too old." Kat stared at the guide. "Something funny."

"*Guardians of the Galaxy*?"

Kat shrugged. "That works."

"Wow, that was enthusiastic." Molly continued to scroll. "Ah! *Charlie's Angels*!"

Kat squinted at the screen. "Looks intense."

"Oh, it is! I can't count how many times I watched this at sleepovers in high school. It's fun and empowering, and reminds you just how butt-kickin' you can be if you set your mind to something." She shot Kat a look.

Kat wrinkled her brow and grinned. "Sounds like I don't really have a choice after all."

"Nope. Pop the popcorn while I change?"

"Yes, ma'am."

Molly giggled. "Don't call me ma'am!"

Kat grinned. Molly was several years older than Kat, but no one would guess it by her playful persona and perfect skin. Easton's big sister had always seemed so glamorous to Kat while she was growing up, and though it had been a sad chain of events that had brought Molly home two years ago, Kat had been grateful for the time to get to know her on a deeper level. They'd become fast friends, and Molly had filled the void her best friend Shelby had left when she'd moved to Boston permanently after graduating from college in the city.

The microwave dinged and Kat emptied the popcorn into a large bowl. A loud thunderclap called her attention to the rain streaming down the window. Lightning lit up the sky. The outer bands had arrived earlier than expected, and with a threatening force.

She set the bowl on the bed and clicked the remote to The Weather Channel. Jim Cantore was reporting from Bar Harbor. Definitely not a good sign. This particular weather expert had a known reputation for appearing in the area that was expected to sustain the most impact from a storm.

"Molly—" Kat called.

As if on cue, Kat's phone buzzed. Her heart flipped at the chance it might be Easton. She swiped the screen to read the message. Her heart thudded when she realized it was from the boss she'd run from.

Hey, Hot Lips. Still haven't heard from ya. Saw you were getting a big storm. Take care of those horses. Call me.

DELETE. "Creep. Why doesn't he get the message?" Kat grumbled. A hot anger rose up inside her. Every time he texted her, the anger from the moment she left the tour resurfaced. Recognizing her overreaction, she inhaled and exhaled slowly to calm her accelerated heartbeat. *God, please help me. Deliver me from the sudden anger that boils up when I'm triggered.*

The bathroom door opened. Molly stuck her head out and glanced at the famous weatherman on the screen. "Well, crap."

"Do you think the horses will be okay?" Kat chewed on her lip. "Maybe Easton should let them into the paddock so they can move around?"

Molly shook her head and gave her a reproachful glance. "Kat, Mocha is going to be fine. My brother loves those horses more than his own family. He's even sleeping in the barn with them tonight."

"I know, but"—she shuddered—"there must be ." *If*

anything happened to Mocha . . .

"No buts!" Molly sat on the bed. "Except on the bed. Sit." She started the movie and relaxed into the pillows on her bed.

Kat sat. She was grateful for Molly's friendship. Oftentimes, breaking up with a significant other meant a breakup with their family, too. That hadn't been the case with the Cranes. They still treated her like family. *Family.* She sighed.

When she came back to town, Molly had called with her mother's offer of employment at the resort. Kat didn't need the money, but she needed to keep busy. She also couldn't help but think this was the Cranes' way of trying to get her and Easton back together. They had welcomed her back with open arms and seemed supportive, despite having left Easton. They'd all blessed her with unconditional grace. Except for Easton.

She forced herself to stop thinking of the past and pay attention to the three strong women on the TV screen. If only she could take care of the situation the way they did.

"What a fun job that must be," Molly said, sipping her wine. "I can totally picture myself as an undercover agent, kicking the booties of handsome criminals."

Kat cocked her head. "Really? You couldn't hurt a fly."

"I certainly could! And the first mystery I'd solve was why you left that tour with all those hot guys. I thought you loved barrel racing."

"I did." She lowered her lids to avoid Molly's eyes.

Molly lifted her brows. "And the hot guys?"

"Full of hot air." *And nerve.*

"Yeah. I figured you didn't break up with my brother for one of the guys on the tour. Although, seeing Troy 'Stetson' Boone every day"—she put her hand over her heart—"now *that* would make me swoon! Is he still single?"

Kat felt her expression harden. "Troy Boone is a sexist pig." She reached down the side of the bed for her purse. Her fingers clasped around a nip of whiskey. "And he's not the only one."

It was hard for her to read the expression on Molly's face. She excused herself to the bathroom so she wouldn't have to explain further. She locked the door behind her and swigged the whiskey. She studied her face in the mirror. She didn't like the girl staring back.

Easton gazed out into the darkness from behind the barn's half-door. Behind him, the snorts, whinnies, and grunts of the unsettled horses created a cacophony that almost harmonized with the howling wind and pounding rain in front of him.

He turned to his left. Mocha poked out her nose from the first stall. Kat's pride and joy. He could understand that. Across from her, his own horse grunted at him. Bolt had been Easton's horse for almost fifteen years. The chestnut quarter horse had been gifted to him from Grandma Vivi when he'd proved his devotion and commitment to the horses.

He closed the top section of the barn door and latched it. The wind whistled through the cracks. He glanced up at the clock above the door. 1:05 a.m. He should probably get some sleep before the worst of the winds arrived.

Easton returned to the twin air mattress he'd set up in the barn's office. He'd wedged it just inside the door and positioned it up against the side of his desk. He kicked the triangular wooden doorstop under the door to keep it open and lowered himself onto the quilts he'd rounded up. He relaxed back onto the pillow and shut his eyes as the exhaustion of the last couple of days caught up to him, dictating he stop and rest.

A few hours later, he woke to a barrage of thunderclaps, lightning strikes, and horse squeals. The storm was picking up. He reached for his phone, plugged into the wall behind him, and scrolled to find a real-time update. The eye had stayed far offshore, but they were still getting wind gusts upward of eighty miles per hour and were right on the edge of the red bands. The higher elevation protected the resort from flooding, but the wind was the bigger threat due to the sheer amount of trees.

The horses were going nuts. He jumped at an especially loud thunderclap. It was followed by a shrill screech and then a crackle of static. Easton jumped up.

That was close. He shivered.

A loud crack and then the sound of wood splintering propelled him to sprint to the other end of the barn. With a crash, the maple he'd trimmed up the day before barreled through the roof over Mocha's stall. *No!* Mocha skittered and danced to avoid the branches that strained through the ceiling at the back of her stall. The rain pouring in mixed with the dirt, mud, and hay beneath her, slicking the surface.

"Easy, girl! Easy!" The wind howled, and the rain stung his face. Easton reached to unlatch the stall door. He'd move her to the empty stall next to Buttons.

Mocha eyed him and reared back in panic as the tree limbs dropped even farther. Her legs flailing, she lost her balance on the slippery floor just as he opened the gate. Squealing, she went down hard on her side just as the back wall caved in on top of her. She squirmed under the weight, fighting to free herself.

"No!" All Easton could think about was Kat. She couldn't lose another horse.

He ran into the stall and pulled at the boards under the part of the tree that covered Mocha, desperate to free her. Her big brown eyes teared up from the intensity of the panic and pain.

She wouldn't budge. Soaking wet, he ran back to the office for his phone. "C'mon, Dad, pick up. I know you're not sleeping." The call connected. He didn't wait for a greeting. "Dad— tree through the roof. Mocha's pinned down. Grab who you can and get here fast! Use the door by the office!" He didn't think twice about barking orders to his father. They had to save Kat's horse.

Easton tuned out the symphony of the panicked equines as he scanned for anything he could use as a lever. Maybe the wheelbarrow? It leaned up against the tack-room wall near where the pitchforks hung. Worth a shot.

He rolled it down the barn. As he reached the end of the row, he realized he hadn't checked for damage in Dottie's stall. He set the wheelbarrow down and peered in. Fear gleamed in the eyes of the Appaloosa in the stall next to Mocha. She could sense the distress of her stablemate. The tree had fallen diagonally over Mocha and toward the barn doors. Dottie huddled by her gate, away from the rain and a few branches that poked in from the right back corner of her space. Though frightened, she was okay.

Easton fell to his knees beside Mocha. She faced the caved-in back wall and had stopped squirming under the weight of the tree and barn boards. That wasn't a good sign.

"Hey, girl." He felt sick to his stomach and fought down the lump that rose up in his throat. He swiped the water from his face, not stopping to think if it was rain or tears.

Kat's beloved horse raised her head and turned it to him. She squinted at him, unblinking. Her lower lip tensed in pain. She groaned at him, then turned her head back the way her body was facing.

"Shh . . ." he soothed. "We're going to get you up. Kat needs you, and I need her."

The wall had come down over the lower half of her midsection, pinning her to the floor. If he could lift it off her, maybe she could stand up. The wheelbarrow definitely wasn't high enough. He glared at the shovel resting inside it in disgust. What had he been thinking? He hadn't. Even if he could stand it up and use the handles to create space, it might roll out and she could be injured further.

"Steady, girl." He rose and walked around her head. Her front legs were free and tucked up into her ribcage. He bent down and put his hand on her shoulder. She lifted her head and nipped at him. "Easy." He ran his hand down over her ribs. She shook but retained control. "Ribs seem okay." He peered under the wood at her flank and back legs. In the darkness, he couldn't tell how badly she'd been hurt.

The rain continued to whip inside. *Blankets.* Easton ran back to the tack room and grabbed the first few he saw. He returned to Mocha and gently laid them on top of her to protect her from getting further soaked.

"Easton!" Joe Crane flung the back door open. The wind took it from him and slammed it against the back side of the barn. Soaking wet, Easton's father appeared at the entrance of the stall. His eyes darted from the horse to the ceiling to the main doors that had caved in.

"She's pinned." His voice cracked as he called to his father over the roar of the storm. Resolving to control his emotions, he swallowed and pushed his shoulders back, shouting over the wind, "We've got to get this off her."

"Let's try to lift it." Joe pushed a branch out of the way and moved to the spot Easton had tried earlier. Easton stood on the opposite side of Mocha and took hold of that section of the fallen wall. "On my count. One, two, three!"

The men strained with every bit of exertion they could muster, lifting the load up a couple of inches. Mocha's legs flailed, but she couldn't maneuver out from under the debris.

"C'mon, Mocha! Move!"

The horse ceased her flailing. She whinnied at Easton. He swore and nudged her gently with his boot. "Move!" he begged. Kat would never forgive him if they had to put Mocha down.

"She's stopped trying to get up," Joe said. "Lower it back down easy."

Distress raw in his gut, Easton complied. Mocha groaned as the weight was brought back down onto her. "Chainsaw?"

"I think so. I'll run and get it from the shed. You wait here for the others."

Easton shook out his arms and stretched them above his head. He knelt beside Mocha's head. "Don't worry." His voice cracked. "I will not let you die."

Chapter 5

Kat's head throbbed as she listened to Molly on the phone. The tune of Destiny's Child's "Independent Woman, Part 1" had jolted her from a dreamless sleep. Molly must have added the ringtone during the movie. It was way too upbeat for the middle of the night. What time was it? She didn't want to open her eyes. She pulled a pillow over her head and turned her body toward the window.

"Oh no," Molly whispered behind her. "Of course. We'll get there as soon as we can."

That didn't sound good.

"Okay. Bye."

Kat's heart began to beat faster. What was it? Who was it? She pulled the pillow tighter over her head to block out news she wouldn't want to hear. *Please, God, let everyone be okay.*

Her mattress depressed as Molly sat on it. "Kat." It was clear Molly tried to hold her voice steady with the gentle tone. "Kat." She put her hand on Kat's upper arm. "There's been an accident at the barn."

No, no, no. Her stomach clenched. She shook off Molly's arm and bolted upright, blood rushing to her already thrumming forehead. She shivered from the panic that raced down her spine. "What?" she whispered, taking a deep, shuddering breath. "Is it Mocha?" *No, please God, not her, too.*

Molly nodded, her tone calm and firm. "We need to go *now*." The urgency in Molly's voice clicked and Kat sprang from the bed to the floor. She flipped open her suitcase, pulled on yoga pants and socks, and stepped into her wellies. Two minutes later, she and Molly were out the door. Molly filled her in on their way downstairs.

Carol was waiting for them in the supply room. She handed them each a yellow rain slicker and a flashlight. "Be careful. It's still nasty out there. Use the back door by the office. Joe, Terrance, and Jordan have already left. I'll be along once I fill Frieda in and leave her instructions."

"Thanks, Mom!" Molly and Kat donned the raincoats and bolted out the door. Kat didn't need the light. She knew the way to the barn by heart. The rain pelted against her PVC-coated slicker and stung at her face.

"Careful!" Molly screeched over the wind.

Kat leapt over a downed tree branch just in time. The dirt path from the kitchen to the stables was a river of mud and tree debris. Easton's cabin, situated halfway between the main lodge and the barn, appeared out of the darkness to her right. Heat flushed at her cheeks. This was his fault.

Molly scooted ahead of her and opened the door. Kat thundered in and flung off her hood. They hurried to the sound of a chainsaw coming from the other end of the barn. Kat swallowed the bile that burned in the back of her throat. *Deep breath.*

Time stopped as she stood, frozen, taking in the scene before her. Easton and Jordan held a blue tarp over Mocha. Jordan avoided her eyes while Terrance held steady a large branch Joe was cutting with a chainsaw.

"Mocha!" Dread pooled in the pit of Kat's stomach. She crawled under the tarp and sank into the mud. She lifted the horse's head onto her lap and began whispering in her ear. "It's okay, it's okay, it's okay."

Mocha gave a strained whinny and closed her eyes.

Easton looked up at her, his eyes burning with a swirl of grief and fear. She glared at him. *Good. This was all his fault. It was his job to take care of Mocha. He* should *feel guilty.*

Kat felt Molly sink down beside her. She leaned into her and sobbed silently, stroking Mocha's face as she watched the men work. She hated herself for crying, for displaying her emotions. They were all here to help her, to help free her horse.

Air whistled through the barn as the back door again opened. Carol, in a matching rain slicker to Kat's and Molly's, set down a large soaking-wet rectangular tote bag. She peeled back its plastic cover. "I have coffee and snacks."

Kat appreciated the gesture, but how could she eat or drink anything when her horse was pinned?

It was near four a.m. when all of the tree pieces that had been pressing on the downed wall had been flung away. Joe called over at Kat and Molly. "You girls take the tarp. Easton and Jordan, help Terrance and me get what's left of this wall back up."

Molly and Kat stood and held the tarp over the horse. The four men each grabbed a section of the heavy wood and slowly raised it off Mocha. Much of the tree's canopy was still overhead, and they were able to lodge the wall within some of the branches to prop it up.

They were rewarded with a low guttural growl, followed by Mocha blowing air out of her nose. She leaned up on her front legs, her back legs moving but not in the way needed for her to stand. She sank back down and fixed her pleading eyes on Kat. The horse was in pain, but she wasn't giving up.

Terrance took the tarp from Kat and gestured for Jordan to take Molly's end. Easton approached Mocha and began to examine her lower half for injuries. They could all read the concern and fear on Kat's face.

She trusted Easton with Mocha. Kat recalled the summer he had spent volunteering for Doc Hill, the local vet. He especially loved treating the horses and for a while had planned to go to vet school and specialize in large animals. There was definitely a need for it in their area of Acadia since the nearest equine vet was over an hour away. Lucky for them, Doc Hill had grown up on a cattle ranch out west and had ministered there before meeting his wife, who was from Bar Harbor. Easton had soaked up everything the doctor had taught him. She always wondered why he'd stopped with a degree in veterinary technology and never went any further. Working in the barn with kids and tourists, plus training horses, had been her dream, not his.

The expression on Easton's face as he examined Mocha was enough for her to know the injuries to her horse were serious. Easton's lips pressed together and he squinted his eyes as his hands explored Mocha's abdomen. She snorted in pain. Kat followed his glance to her back legs, crossed and unmoving. He scooted the length of her to check them. Gently, he pulled her right leg from the mud. She raised her head as Easton checked for range of movement. She blew air out of her nose and grunted again, her front legs now circling in an effort to move.

The wind whistled above the canopy of the tree. Kat looked up into the raging sky. *Please, God. Please let it be fixable. Please save Mocha.*

Easton finished his assessment. "Probably some injuries to her abdomen and her left hind fetlock. Fetlock could be broken. Doc Hill will have to confirm." The grave silence deafened Kat's ears as Easton's words sunk in. A broken fetlock would be a death sentence. Colic was a threat with abdomen injuries. The horse's clock was ticking. She needed to stand.

Joe stepped forward. "Carol, will you call Doc Hill so he can get here as soon as it's safe?"

"On it." Easton's mom nodded and left the stall.

Kat felt she was an outsider, watching a movie. She couldn't move, couldn't think. This couldn't really be happening, could it? Joe turned to Easton and Terrance. "We need to move her. If my mother taught me anything about injured horses, it's that time is of the essence. Easton, get the ropes. We've got to get her up. Kat, put her halter on and help hold her steady. Molly, we're going to need more blankets. We've got to keep her dry."

Kat and Molly hustled to the tack room and returned with the supplies. Kat slipped on the halter and arranged the attached lead line, ready to help and support Mocha. "Have you ever done this before?" Kat asked.

"Nope!" Joe moved to the other side of Mocha's head. "C'mon girl."

Someone had removed the soaked blankets. Easton and Terrance positioned a long webbed mesh rope under the upper part of Mocha's legs. "Ready," Easton said. Slowly, they eased the rope under Mocha's legs. The horse protested noisily and began to flail her legs. When her body was at a forty-five-degree angle from the ground, they pulled. Their foreheads dripped from the exertion and rain. Mocha's grunts and groans increased in volume as she struggled and strained, and finally stood on three legs.

Kat held the leadrope steady and Mocha rose up, grunting and blowing air. She gave her horse a tender look. "Good girl."

"We'll help her to the empty stall next to Buttons. Everyone lean in." Slowly, steadily, they guided Mocha at a snail's pace down the barn to the empty stall. Kat removed Mocha's halter and pressed her tear-streaked cheek into Mocha's. She cradled the horse's head in her hand.

Molly distributed the blankets and those who weren't supporting Mocha began to wipe her down. Outside, the wind shrieked and the rain continued to pelt the structure.

Easton cleared his throat and shivered. Only then did Kat realize how soaked he was. "I think this is all we can do for now. Thanks for your help." His eyes searched the group, but the one pair he wanted to see wasn't looking back at him. "I'll stay with her until Doc Hill can get here."

"No, you won't." Kat's jaw was tight. Five heads swiveled to her. "She's my horse. I will stay."

Sensing the tension, Joe rounded up the others and left the barn. Kat shrugged out of her slicker and entered Mocha's new stall, ignoring Easton completely.

"Kat—"

"I don't have any words for you." She couldn't think clearly, and didn't know why she was so angry. She just needed to be with her horse.

Easton stomped into his office. He closed the door and stripped off his soaking-wet clothes. No words for him? Hadn't he just done everything he could for her horse? Was she implying this was *his* fault?

Figures. Once again, he came to her rescue and she took him for granted. It'd been the pattern for as long as he could remember. When would he learn? *God, grant me the serenity to accept the things I cannot change, courage to change the things I can, and wisdom to know the difference.* The prayer for serenity also hung on Kat's bedroom wall, the words painted on a colorful canvas with a rainbow to remind them that God was always with them.

Easton changed into dry clothes and sank into the air mattress to check his phone. It was a miracle they hadn't lost power or cell service. The radar showed the storm moving out to sea. It had picked up speed over the water, bobbled east, and now the back end of it was on its way out. He put the phone back up on the desk and shut his eyes. The duration had been short, but the damage significant.

Sometime later, the loud vibrations of his phone on the metal desk yanked him out of his slumber. He reached for it. TORNADO WARNING. TAKE COVER IMMEDIATELY flashed across the screen. *Are you kidding me, God?* He jumped up and ran to Mocha's new stall, cursing himself for thinking of Kat first. Again. It was instinctual to protect her; she was a habit he couldn't kick. An addiction he couldn't recover from.

Easton wrenched open the gate. If he'd had a minute to appreciate the sight he would have smiled. Inside, Kat snored softly, arms crossed, as she leaned against the front corner of the stall. "Kat!" He reached for her and pulled at her arm. "C'mon!" He glanced at the horse. Mocha's eyes caught his. She snorted at Easton.

"What the—" Kat jerked awake. She shook out of his grasp. Her head swiveled from Easton to Mocha, squinting awoke and tried to focus. "Shh, girl. It's all right."

"Kat!" She stumbled as Easton grabbed hold of her again and tugged her out of the stall. He slammed the gate back into place. "C'mon!"

He towed her into the office and lifted up the air mattress. She sank down beside him, eyes wide. Seconds later, the shrieks of the wind and frightened horses became deafening. Easton tucked her head into his chest. The lights flickered off. Dust and debris from the ceiling tiles trickled onto the mattress, but the roof held.

"Tornado!" he shouted above the din. It was too dark to see her expression, but he felt it in her body as she shook against him. Kat pressed her face against his heart. He pulled her tighter.

Easton needed to hold her, needed to protect her. It went beyond his sense of chivalry. As much as he fought the forces that drew him to her, he knew in his heart this was the way it was supposed to be. She had broken his heart, but he was kidding himself if he thought he couldn't forgive her.

He couldn't tell how much time had passed. His phone alerted him that the threat had elapsed, and he carefully moved Kat off him. She lifted her head and blinked her eyes at him.

"I think it's over. I'll be right back." He returned a few minutes later and handed her a bottle of water. "The barn held. Come with me to examine Mocha?"

"Okay."

They entered the stall. Easton squatted by Mocha's back legs and examined her injured fetlock. "It's swollen up quite a bit. I'm going to rub some liniment on it."

Kat nodded and leaned her head up against the side of the stall. She closed her eyes.

"Do you have a headache?"

"Yeah."

"Be right back." Easton left to get the liniment, a roll of cotton padding, duct tape, and the Tylenol he kept in his desk drawer. It hurt him to see Kat and her horse hurting, but it fueled him to know he could help them. It was what he did. What he'd always done. He was a fixer.

"Hey," he said softly a few minutes later. "Here." He opened the water bottle she had pressed against her forehead and popped open the Tylenol. She stuck out her palm and he dropped two gel caps into it.

"Thank you." She swallowed them.

"You're welcome."

"What's all that?"

"Just something I'm going to try."

"Okay. Can I help?"

"Nah. I got it.

"I'm not helpless, you know."

"I never said you were."

Kat crossed her arms. "You imply it."

Easton sighed. He didn't want to argue, so he didn't respond.

Kat closed her eyes again. He studied her for a moment as he picked up the liniment. He rubbed it up and down Mocha's leg, gently. The horse grumbled but didn't fight him or cry out in pain. "All right, Mocha, I'm going to bandage you. Steady, girl." Easton wrapped the roll of cotton around Mocha's fetlock. He pulled a roll of duct tape from his pocket and wrapped it around several times. Mocha sighed and nickered softly.

Outside, the rain poured and the wind continued to howl. Inside, the horses were quieting down. It wouldn't be long until the sun came up and the destruction of the night before would be revealed.

Chapter 6

Kat stared at the pine tree that had fallen through the roof of Molly's tiny cabin. It was likely going to be a total loss. Luckily for Molly, the tree had come down over the kitchen and bathroom, so most of her possessions weren't ruined.

It had been a night to remember for all the worst reasons. Kat had stayed in the barn with Mocha until the storm passed. She was still fighting a headache and the pain of possibilities. She couldn't lose her horse.

Her phone vibrated. She checked the text and blew an exasperated breath out of her nose. DELETE. *Deep breaths, Kat.*

She blinked into the blinding sunlight. The tornado had touched down in the wooded area behind the employee cabins, then taken a path to the resort's gazebo, which was now a scattered pile of splinters from the trees to the access road. Where it had gone after that, they hadn't yet explored. She prayed it hadn't taken any homes. She'd talked to Uncle Charley after the tornado passed. He reported no damage, and as far as he knew, the tornado hadn't gone over the Point.

Molly leaned her head onto Kat's shoulder and sighed. Easton, Joe, and Terrance were working to get the tree off the cabin so they could tarp what was left of the roof. "I suppose I'll be staying at the lodge for a while."

Easton looked over from where he was stabilizing a large tree branch. "You can stay in my cabin, Molly. I'll be bunking up in the barn for the foreseeable future."

Molly lifted her head from Kat's shoulder and walked over to her brother, who pulled on a piece of what was left of the roof. She crossed her arms and gestured with her chin. "Why's that?"

He shrugged. "I'm the horse guy. I need to be there if there's a problem."

Kat squared her shoulders. "You don't—"

He looked past Molly. "Of course I do."

Kat opened her mouth and closed it. She didn't know what to say. She nodded at him and called to Molly, "I'm going back to check on Mocha. Call me when it's clear to go inside?"

Molly flashed a tired smile. "Will do."

Kat gave her a hug and strode back to the barn. She walked around to the main entrance of the barn, crushed under the weight of the monstrous maple. She thought about how angry she'd been earlier. She shouldn't have blamed Easton. It wasn't his fault the tree fell on the barn or that Mocha got trapped underneath. She tried so hard to neutralize her irrational and impulsive words and actions. They were most hard to manage when she panicked or felt like she was being thrown into survival mode.

She needed to get back to her horse. She rounded the barn and went through the back entrance.

Kat wasn't surprised when Jordan appeared outside of Elvis's stall. Being the son of the landscaper and resort manager, Jordan helped when and where he was needed, but he excelled with the horses. "Hey, Kat." He nodded toward Mocha's new quarters. "I took care of her first. She wasn't eating but she drank from a bucket I held up to her." The teenager wiped his brow with a flannel shirtsleeve. "Easton said Doc Hill will be here as soon as the road's clear."

"Thanks, Jordan." She peered inside Mocha's stall. She was sleeping, but still on her feet. Kat turned back to Jordan. "You got any help today?"

"No, it's just me. Dad's helping outside. Mom's in the lodge. The girls aren't coming today. Maddie has no power, Meggie has a tree down on her street, and Mellie's helping her mom at the church." His face reddened as he spoke about Mellie.

Kat smiled. He reminded her a bit of Easton at that age. Quiet and shy, yet strong and commanding. Gifted with animals. She'd noticed him watching Mellie over the last few weeks, helping her when he could, and if she wasn't mistaken, Mellie returned his affections.

"Who's left? I can help."

"Just Bolt. I got it. Thanks, though." He gestured to Mocha's stall. "You planning to sit with her for a while?"

"Yes."

"Okay. I'll grab you a chair."

"Thanks." Kat opened the stall door and slipped in. "C'mon girl. Wake up." Her beautiful horse opened her eyes and looked up at her. She fought back a flashback of Callie. She'd never seen her again after she'd fallen. If Mocha's fetlock was broken, if this was the beginning of goodbye, then she was going to be here every minute until Mocha took her last breath.

Jordan arrived with a folding chair and set it up against the inside wall. She thanked him again and sank into it.

Kat's stomach growled. She pulled out her phone. It was almost noon. She needed to call home and check on Uncle Charley again. She dialed his cell.

He picked up on the fourth ring. "Yes, ma'am," he said. She couldn't help but let out a soft chuckle. It was the way he always greeted her. There was a breathless edge to his voice. She wondered if he had run to the phone.

"You still good over there?" she asked.

"Sure, sure, it wasn't bad, not bad at all. Just another storm." He coughed. "S'cuse me. No windows broken, a few trees down. How 'bout at the resort?"

"That's great." She bit her lip and took a deep breath. "Molly's cabin was crushed by a tree." She swallowed and took another breath before continuing. "I didn't tell you earlier. Didn't want to worry you. The old maple fell on the barn and the wall caved in and pinned Mocha." She choked, fighting back tears. "Doc Hill is on his way. Easton thinks her fetlock might be sprained or broken."

Old Man Wetherby let out a long, low whistle. "Terribly sorry, Kat. Anything I can do? Does Joe need help?" He coughed again, this one starting a chain of coughs that lasted half a minute.

"No. You sure you're okay? You don't sound well. Are you overdoing it?" She knew better than to ask. He *was* overdoing it.

"Fine, fine. Just my pesky COPD acting up again. You stay with Mocha. I'll get everything cleaned up and put back out. When are those guys coming to take the boards off?"

"I'm not sure. They said within seventy-two hours after the weather cleared." She thought for a minute. "Don't you go trying to get those boards off."

He sniffed and ignored her command. "You just take care of that horse. Everything's okay over here."

"Okay." Her phone buzzed. She wasn't sure whether to answer it or keep him on the line. His cough concerned her. "I'll let you go. I'm getting a text."

"Bye, love."

"Bye."

Kat swiped to end the call and checked her text screen. Kevin. She groaned. What was with his sudden interest? Why can't you just have drinks and dance with a guy without him thinking you want more than just a little fun? *Wait. He might be able to help.* She opened the message.

Hey, Kat. How did it go over there?

Barn collapsed onto Mocha.

Holy! Is she okay? Got a few more trees to clear, then I'll be over. The main roads are a mess. See what I can do.

You don't have to. But she wanted him to. She felt a little guilty, taking advantage of his offer, but she'd be stupid not to take him up on it. Likely the construction companies in the area would already be booked for the foreseeable future. She wondered if Joe had contacted anyone yet about the barn. Molly's cabin and the gazebo also needed repair ASAP.

Sure I do. We're friends, right? That's your horse's stall. I can help, so I will.

Well, thank you. Molly's cabin is totaled. Maybe they'll hire you? Talk to Joe.

Thanks. Will do. See you soon.

She put the phone back in her pocket. It buzzed again. She sighed and pulled it back out.

Easton. *You in the barn?*

Yes.

Did you eat?

No.

There's food in the fridge. Eat something. Doc Hill is twenty-five minutes out.

Thanks.

He knew her so well. She often forgot to eat, especially when she was stressed. She didn't feel like eating. And she had forgotten to take her meds this morning. She hadn't been back to her room.

As if on cue, her phone buzzed again. *Did you take your meds?*

Kat sighed. How did he know?

No. I will after Doc leaves.

He didn't respond.

Mocha stirred. She walked over and stroked the horse's cheek. "Sweet girl. Doc's on his way. We'll get you fixed up in no time." But the clock was ticking. In addition to her injury, Mocha had been down for too long. It was okay for horses to lie down only for short periods of time. If they didn't get up to adjust their position, they were susceptible to multiple gut issues. Their muscles and nerves weren't designed to handle one thousand pounds of weight. Dehydration could set in after only a couple of hours. At twenty-four hours, the horse was in dangerous territory.

Kat also worried about Mocha's other hind leg. Horses who stand on only one leg for a long time can develop life-threatening problems in their good leg. *Lord, please don't let her founder.*

The back door to the barn slammed open. A few moments later, Easton appeared at the gate, arms crossed. "Your meds and lunch are on the break table. You should eat before Doc gets here."

Her face tensed and her eyes narrowed. "You didn't have to do that." She'd taken care of herself when she was on the road. She didn't need him reassuming his role of caregiver. And she resented him telling her what to do.

"You need to take care of yourself, or you'll be no help to Mocha."

She studied his face. Underneath that gruff tone, she heard the concern in his voice, saw it in his shimmering eyes. He still felt something for her, she knew it. She relaxed her expression. "Thank you." She stood up. "How did you get into—"

"I helped Molly carry some things to her room after we finished tarping her roof."

"Oh. I told her I'd help—"

"Dad and Terrance are moving what's salvageable. You can help her organize it later."

She frowned. He had it all figured out. She should ask Molly to come stay with her. She had a handful of empty bedrooms she could choose from. It'd be nice to have some company.

He moved out of the way to let her pass to the break area. Her shoulder brushed his and she felt that old tingle of electricity. *For Pete's sake, Kat. Get ahold of yourself.* She shook it off and rushed out of the stall, heart beating double time.

Easton's eyes followed Kat to the break area. Once again, he'd thought of her and she showed no appreciation. Without her meds, she could have a seizure. Or worse. Why was she being so irresponsible?

A truck roared up next to the barn. He walked over

to the back door. Kevin hopped down from the cab and nodded at him. *Not this guy again.*

"Heard you had some damage." His eyes flickered inside the barn, looking for Kat, no doubt.

"We did." Easton leaned against the door jamb, barring Kevin's entry.

"Got anyone to fix it? I can take a look."

Easton sighed. "Don't you have customers or sites to check up on or something?"

Kevin drew himself up to his full height so that he was almost eye to eye with Easton. He crossed his arms. "Nope. My father and brothers are handling that. I've decided to branch out and get my own customers."

"How entrepreneurial of you," Easton muttered. He moved aside to let Kevin through. "Last stall on the left."

"That's the idea. Company expansion and specialization. I like the outside work. They prefer inside remodeling."

Easton didn't care about the Conroy family business. He just wanted his barn fixed. And Molly's cabin. And the gazebo. They needed to get that rebuilt before the Fourth.

Kevin paused at the break-area alcove. "Hey, Kat."

"Hey, Kev. I'm glad you're here."

Easton watched her lips curl into a grateful smile. His blood boiled. He moved quickly over to them.

"This way, Conroy." He passed them and turned around halfway down the stalls when Kevin failed to follow him. "You here to visit or work?" he barked.

Kevin quirked a brow. "Be right there, boss." He winked at Kat, then followed Easton.

Easton glared at his audacity and continued on to the damaged area. Earlier that morning, he, his father, and Terrance had brought in a tarp and some spare boards from one of the sheds out back to better secure the wall. The boards wouldn't hold up for the long-term, but for now they sufficed.

"Pretty significant," Kevin said from behind him.

"How soon till you can fix it?" Easton wanted to know.

"Depends on your insurance. I can get a couple of my guys here to help you tarp it better, and once we get the go-ahead, maybe a few days, a week at the most."

Easton didn't answer. He pulled out his phone to text his father. Kevin moved closer to the damage and wiggled some of the boards, continuing his inspection.

Joe texted back and Easton put his phone away.

"Adjuster will be out tomorrow. We've got three projects if you can handle them." God, he hated this guy, hated to give him business, especially to give him more opportunities to see Kat.

"I can handle them. Kat mentioned Molly's cabin. What's the third project?"

"The gazebo. We need one rebuilt by July Fourth for a wedding."

"Shouldn't be a problem." Kevin used his phone to take pictures of the damage. "I assume this is the priority?"

Easton nodded. "Then the gazebo. Molly's going to stay elsewhere until her cabin can be rebuilt. I'm assuming it will be a total loss. She'll likely want a say in its rebuilding."

When Molly had returned after her divorce, she was given the only vacant staff cabin. It was the oldest on the property and needed work. They'd fixed it up, but no one in the family had been heartbroken by its demise.

"I'll check it out, draw up the paperwork, and talk to your dad." He held out his hand.

Begrudgingly, Easton shook it.

"Thanks, man."

Kevin sounded sincere, which made Easton even more suspicious. He wouldn't under any circumstance let him get near Kat. If he wanted her, he shouldn't have messed up all those years ago.

"Which way to Molly's cabin?"

Easton waved toward the barn's back door. "Take a left at the fork onto Crane's Lane, instead of a right to head back the way you came. Molly's cabin is the second to last on the left. You can't miss it. You remember where the gazebo is?"

Kevin nodded. Easton had seen him at too many events there over the years. "Got it. See ya."

Easton watched him say goodbye to Kat on his way out. He strode to the back doorway, ignoring Kat as he walked by her. Kevin's truck headed toward Molly's cabin. From the other direction, Doc Hill's Cadillac appeared.

"Doc!" Kat rushed to him. "I'm so glad you're here."

Easton watched her swallow, picking up on a cue he had become so familiar with.

"Kat," he whispered. "You need some water?" It was an old code phrase from when she was recovering. She had been embarrassed about her inability to control her crying. It provided her with a reason to excuse herself and pull herself together.

She stared at him. Their eyes locked, emotion pulling them like magnets. He strained to pull away. With that one connection, he felt everything she was feeling. Fear, anguish, hope. He couldn't take it.

"Yes. Excuse me," she said weakly.

Doc Hill reached the doorway. "Where's our beautiful mare?"

Easton gestured. "Second stall to the right." He followed the vet and peeked into the office. Kat was dabbing her eyes. Her other hand held a bottle of water. He had to fix this.

Doc Hill checked Mocha's vitals and gave her a thorough exam. "Everything seems to be working properly on the inside," he reported. "Some minor cuts, scrapes and bruising." Mocha grunted as he ran his hand along her neck.

"That's great, right?" Kat asked, arriving just in time for the assessment. She clutched the water bottle, her knuckles white from squeezing too hard.

"So far, yes." He continued his exam, removing the

wrap from Mocha's ankle. "I can't tell for sure if there's a fracture without an X-ray. If it's fractured, it's minimal, but you know even a minimal fracture can be deadly. Good call with the liniment and wrap. I'll X-ray, give her an injection of Banamine for the inflammation, and get an IV started. I can tell she's already a bit dehydrated." He looked around the stall. "You also need to watch for colic. We don't want her intestines twisting. Fetlock is my main concern. Tendons are sensitive. If it's torn, she may be fated to be a permanent pasture ornament."

Easton nodded. That had been his assessment as well. He knew Kat would be disappointed if she couldn't ride Mocha again, but putting her down would be beyond devastating.

Doc continued. "If it's broken, there will be some tough decisions to make." He looked directly at Kat. "She may not recover."

Kat's shoulders slumped. Without thinking, Easton put his arm around her and pulled her into him. "We'll do whatever it takes to save her," he stated firmly.

Doc Hill glanced from one to the other. "I'll do what I can. The rest is up to her." He scratched his head. "We need to get that swelling down."

Easton let out a long breath to calm his racing heart. "The swelling hasn't gone down much that I can see since I applied the liniment."

The doctor nodded. "Let's give her a few more hours before we start panicking."

Easton slid Mocha's halter back on and held her head steady while Doc set up a catheter in her neck. His eyes never left Kat, who winced as if she felt the pain the same as Mocha.

Doc attached the IV and held the bag up. "I'm going to leave that catheter in. Easton, you know how to do this, so I'll leave a couple extra bags with you. I'll write out specific times and directions. I'll be back later today, unless you have an emergency. Call me if anything changes."

"Yes, sir." He helped the doctor finish up and detach the IV bag. They listened carefully to the instructions and walked him out to his car. After they watched him drive away, Easton turned to Kat. "You should get some sleep."

She stiffened. "You should stop telling me what to do," she said, her jaw tight. She bit her lip and looked away, as if she regretted her words as soon as they came out. Why did she keep responding to him with anger? It didn't make sense. Why was her brain so irrational? *Remember, Kat. Quick to listen, slow to speak, slow to anger.*

His expression softened. "Habit." He spoke in a low tone. "I need to clean up around here. I'll keep a close eye on her and text you if anything changes."

"Fine." Kat conceded. She let out a slow breath. "I feel like I'm dead on my feet anyway. "I'll grab a power nap and then come back to check on Mocha before I head home." Concern clouded her features and her expression changed as she mentioned heading home.

"What aren't you telling me?"

She frowned and looked up at him. "I was just thinking . . . something didn't sound right when I talked with Uncle Charley earlier, but I can't remember what . . ." She cursed her brain for the millionth time.

Easton checked his watch. It was after two. He could run out to the Point to check on Charley if the roads were clear. "I'll go check on him. You go sleep. You *need* to sleep, rest your brain." The bags under her eyes contrasted with her pale skin. "Jordan can stay with Mocha while I'm gone."

For once, she didn't object. "Okay." She glanced up. "Thank you."

He caught her gaze, and his arms moved of their own accord. He pulled her to him. She slumped into him and rested her head in the space under his chin. God, he missed holding her like this. "Everything is going to be fine."

She mumbled into his shirt. "You can't possibly know that."

"Your lack of faith is disturbing." He felt her try to stifle a laugh into his chest at his attempt to quote *Star Wars*.

She lifted her head. A slow smile formed on her lips. How he missed that smile. And those lips. It took every ounce of self-control to keep his face neutral and remain still.

"Don't worry. I won't let the Dark Side consume

me."

His mouth twitched. "Good. Go. And be mindful of your thoughts . . ."

" . . . Or they'll betray me," she finished.

"Exactly." His smile widened. She returned it weakly and headed for the back door.

Easton grabbed the keys to his truck from the office and took a water bottle out of the fridge. Thirty minutes later, he arrived at Old Man Wetherby's cottage. The roads had been easy to navigate for the most part. Though the crews were already cleaning up, he'd had to drive around a good amount of debris. It had been slow going but steady.

Kat's great-uncle had already built a substantial pile of tree limbs and wayward shingles by the side of the road. Easton hurried up the yard to help him with a large branch he'd been dragging.

"I've got this," Easton said, reaching for it.

The old man let go and gave him an appreciative nod. "Good man." He took in a few full breaths. Thanks." He followed Easton to the pile, rubbing his left arm with his right hand.

"Are you all right? Did you hurt your arm?" Easton asked as he positioned the branch into the pile.

The old man shook his head. "Just sore and tired I think. Can't do what I used to do these days. Old age is a frustrating curse."

"I can imagine." Easton peered at him a little more closely. His face looked a bit gray underneath the white scruff he hadn't shaved off in the last couple days.

"You don't look as well as you usually do. What can I do to help?"

"I'm fine." He sighed and pulled a little white bottle out of his pocket. He popped two little pink chewables. "Baby aspirin. Probably just overdid it." He flashed a grin. "I'll take it easier. Just can't seem to sit still when there's work to be done." He glanced at the debris pile. "Do you know when Kat will be back?"

"Not sure." Easton shoved his hands into his pocket. His left hand closed around the gray fabric-covered button that he carried with him everywhere he went. It made him feel connected to Kat when she wasn't close by. Every time he touched it, he remembered the night it had come loose from its source. It had become a security token of sorts. He wanted to go back to that time.

Old Man Wetherby nodded. "Hard to pin her down these days."

"Don't I know it," Easton replied. He glanced up at the boards covering the windows. "You want me to help you get those off?"

"Nah. That Conroy boy already stopped by and said he'd take care of it first thing Thursday if they weren't gone by tomorrow night." He snorted. "He's got to know he ain't got a chance in hell with Kat, but I appreciate his efforts."

Easton's jaw clenched. "Let's hope his work is as great as his ego. Dad's hiring him for the projects at the resort." The prospect of seeing Kevin and his buddies daily for the foreseeable future grated Easton's nerves.

"He does good work from what I've heard." The old man gestured toward Easton's truck. "You should head back now and make yourself useful over there. I'm good here. Let Kat know?"

"Will do."

Chapter 7

Kat's eyes widened as she opened the door to the room she was sharing with Molly. At least a dozen plastic totes, three suitcases, and a handful of boxes were stacked or laid out on every available patch of floor space. She stared in dismay at the bed she'd been looking forward to curling up on. She was grateful most of Molly's stuff hadn't been damaged, but she needed to sleep.

"Molly? Are you in here?" she asked, peering around a stack of totes.

"In the bathroom!"

Kat turned sideways to fit between the end of the bed and a suitcase. In the bathroom, Molly was hanging a shelf filled with shampoos, conditioners, shower gel, and other such things over the showerhead. The counter was stacked high with makeup bags and hair tools.

Molly stepped out of the tub to greet her. "You look terrible. How's Mocha?"

Kat gave a half smile. "I'm fine, just sleep deprived." She glanced back at the bed purposefully, hoping Molly would read her cue. She felt terrible for her friend's situation, but it paled in comparison to the possible loss of her horse.

"Here, let me move that stuff." Molly squeezed by her and began to transfer a pile of dresses on hangers to the closet. "How's Mocha?" she repeated.

"She's got an inflamed fetlock. Likely a sprain."

"Well, she's a feisty horse. I'm sure she'll be just fine." Molly finished clearing Kat's bed. "Have you checked your phone?"

Kat shook her head.

"Didn't think so. Jane texted me earlier. Shelby probably sent you a text. Ms. Tracy is over at the church organizing aid for those who lost power. Grandma Vivi's building is without power and they don't know when it will be back on, so we're going over there later. Mom's getting things together. Wanna come?"

"I guess." It would be good to see Ms. Vivi. And Shelby. "Don't you have a ton to do here?" Kat pulled out her phone to read Shelby's text. "Okay, Shelby says your mom and Frieda are gathering supplies to drop off. We need to pick those up and stop by the church for more, then the four of us can head out to The Roosevelt."

"Three of us. Jane's little guy is sick again."

"Oh, poor thing! I always hate to see kids sick."

"Yeah, and migraines at his age. Crazy." Molly shook her head and moved to the window to close the drapes. "All right, let's catch a catnap." She glanced at the clock. "I'll set my alarm. Sleep till four o'clock?"

"Sounds perfect." Kat curled up on top of the bed and wrapped the throw blanket around her. She closed her eyes.

Molly's phone alarm drew Kat out of a dream. She and Easton were slow dancing in the gazebo that overlooked the cliff edge. She sighed. She didn't want to wake up and face the multiple disasters that awaited her. Her head was foggy and she felt agitation taking over her thoughts. The nap hadn't been long enough.

She checked her phone. Easton had left her a text. *Checked on the old man. Call me when you can.*

Kat frowned. Sitting up, she glanced at Molly's empty bed and the closed bathroom door. She tapped the screen.

"Hey," his voice, low and soothing, crooned in her ear, washing over her like a warm wave. Just the sound of it gave her goosebumps.

"Hey," she echoed. "So he's all right? How about the house?"

Easton didn't answer right away. "I'm not sure. I mean, he seems all right, but he was short of breath and he was rubbing his left arm. I made a comment and he joked about taking his baby aspirin."

"Are you still there?"

"Yeah. When I got here he'd already cleared all the tree debris and swept your porch. I offered to put all the outdoor furniture back and for once he didn't balk at an offer for help. That's really why I'm concerned."

Kat stiffened. "I was going to go help deliver supplies to The Roosevelt. Do you think I should come home first?"

"I don't know. I just wanted to tell you he seemed a bit off. Might just be he overexerted himself. He says he's fine."

Kat reached for a strand of hair. She wrapped it around her finger as she considered what to do. "Okay. Please tell him I'll be home around in a couple of hours, then. See if you can convince him to move over to the big house for tonight."

"Will do."

Kat ended the call. She'd felt it coming. The tears spilled down her cheeks. She just sat there and let them come.

"Kat?" Molly's voice was soft. "What's wrong?"

Only everything. Kat swiped her eyes. "Just overemotional, as usual." She forced a smile. "You ready to go?"

"You bet."

Kat wondered how Molly could be so chipper after she'd lost the contents of her kitchen, most of her furniture, half her décor, and who knew what else. "Hey . . ."

Molly looked up.

"Why don't you stay with me? You don't need to cram in here or crash at your brothers' cabin. You could have any of the empty rooms."

Molly's eyes brightened and her mouth spread into a wide grin at her friend's generous offer. "Now that's an idea!" She smiled. "I'd love to, thank you! I'll crash here tonight and move in tomorrow!"

Kat laughed. "Great!" She'd be glad to have company in the expansive house. She opened the door to the hallway. "I'll drive."

Downstairs, Carol, Meemaw, and Frieda were busy prepping dinner for the resort guests who had stayed on to brave the storm. By the kitchen's back door, cases of water bottles were stacked next to boxes filled with nonperishables, paper towels, cleaning supplies, and more.

Carol spoke in a low tone to Meemaw, who nodded and strode over to the girls. "If you can fit it all, take it. We can spare more, but it's likely the power will be restored in a day or two. We can send a second and third load when and if we need to." She spoke directly to Molly. "Try to convince Grandma Vivi to come stay here for a few nights. We miss her, plus your dad and I won't worry about her so much if she's here."

"And I'd love to meet her!" Meemaw interrupted from the other side of the kitchen.

Kat flashed Meemaw a grin. "I don't know, she's quite a force!"

"Even more reason to meet her!" Meemaw retorted. They all laughed.

Kat had only seen Ms. Vivi once since she'd been back in town. The loss of Auntie Katie last summer had deepened her bond with Easton's grandmother that had already been strong after years of seeing her everyday at the stables. When she'd been on the road the last year, she called her often at the beginning, but once she broke off her engagement with Easton, her calls tapered to only about once every couple of weeks. She knew everyone had been disappointed, but they had understood. Still, she felt awkward about it.

She loved him. She knew he cared about her deeply, but lately she wondered if that love came out of friendship and duty, or a passion that burned when he wasn't taking care of her? She couldn't marry him if it didn't go deeper than that. When he refused to go on the road with her, she accused him of not loving her enough. Then he proposed. She was stunned, but she couldn't refuse him publicly, and certainly not in front of his family and the crowd at the resort's potluck dinner. She'd been blindsided and had so many questions. Why then? Why marriage? Where would they live? At Christmas, it had all come to a head.

Kat and Uncle Charley had been invited to Christmas Dinner at the main lodge. After the meal, they sat by the fireplace in the lobby, singing along to carols JC tapped out on the piano.

Kat was in heaven. This had been the big family Christmas she'd always envisioned. When they stopped singing for coffee and dessert, Carol remarked on it.

"Kat, it's been so wonderful having you and Charley here with us," she said as she handed Kat a slice of apple pie.

"It's been wonderful celebrating with you. My heart is so full."

Ms. Vivi put down her plate and asked point-blank, "So have you set a wedding date yet?"

Kat froze and set her plate on the coffee table. Dread and panic consumed her gut. She looked at Easton for help. She hadn't had a chance to ask him all those questions she had.

"Not yet. But soon, I'm sure." Easton grinned at her.

She smiled back at him, trying to stay cool. "Let's go for a walk before it gets dark. We can talk about it."

He gave her a funny look but went to get their coats. They excused themselves and walked over to the stables to watch the horses frolic in the dusty covering of snow.

"Easton, we can't set a date. I want to keep traveling. If I marry you now, how can I do that?"

His face, hopeful and happy, crumpled in confusion. "I don't understand."

She sighed and turned toward the horses. "It's my job. I don't have a college degree or any other prospects. I like to ride. I love to ride. Why don't you come on tour with me?"

"No, Kat. I do have a job, and it's here. You could work here, too. You don't need a college degree to give lessons. You love doing that."

She shook her head. "It's not enough."

He swung her around. "It's not enough, or I'm not enough?"

She froze. Desperately, she reached into her injured brain for something to say, anything. But nothing came.

Easton's eyes flashed with pain. "I see." His gloved hands rubbed at his eyes. "So you're going back and you can't tell me when you want to get married. It sounds like you don't."

She stared at him, gut clenched, frozen. "I'm sorry, I can't find the words I'm looking for. I—"

"Forget it." He began to walk toward the barn.

"Easton, wait!"

He called over his shoulder, "It's me or the tour, Kat. You either love me and want to spend forever with me, or you don't. If you love me, stay. Or else just go. And don't come back."

Kat's tears spilled over. Consumed by anger, she yanked off her mitten and pulled off her engagement ring. She ran through the snow to catch up with him. "Turn around!"

"What?" For the briefest second, she saw a glimmer of hope, but she couldn't stop herself. Impulsively, she hurled the ring at him. Her bottom lip quivered and her body shook with a fury she couldn't stop. She'd never forget the look on his face for as long as she lived.

Kat squeezed her eyes shut and pressed her hands to her head. She didn't understand why she had felt angry enough to end their engagement. Newly single, she had returned to the tour and was immediately pounced upon by the single males in the organization—and some not-so-single ones. She couldn't believe the way these guys behaved. They'd razzed her about her car, yes, but she'd thought it was in good fun so she'd smiled and brushed it off. Cowboys in general were usually polite and chivalrous. They'd been mostly respectful to her when she'd had her ring on, but as soon as it came off, the appreciative smiles and polite conversation accelerated into creepy full-length appraisals, catcalls, and suggestive pickup lines. They got bolder over time, trying to get her attention after Easton was out of the picture. She shuddered and tried to push away the memories that should stay buried. She'd been drinking the whiskey to help her cope.

Kat and Molly loaded up the back of her SUV and headed out to pick up the rest of the load, including Shelby, who was already at the church. Kat and Shelby had grown up together, good friends at school though they had different interests. While Kat was at home in the barn, Shelby preferred to be inside, holed up writing. In high school she had set up a makeshift office in her closet to write and pray in after her mother died. Kat and Shelby became even closer as they bonded over being motherless.

Shelby's father was the pastor of a small congregation, just over the Crane's Cove town border in Winter Harbor. A widower, he had raised Shelby and her older sister, Jane, after their mother passed away suddenly when they were teenagers. He hadn't remarried, and they'd become a tight family unit. When Jane had lost her husband to brain cancer two years ago, she moved back home with her son.

Shelby hadn't stayed in town for college. She'd

been back and forth over the last six years, getting her degrees and interning, assured by her sister that the church community was taking good care of her family. Kat was glad she was home for the summer while she figured out what to do next.

Kat navigated around downed trees, road signs, and other debris that the hurricane had dumped on the road. She pulled into the church and parked at the front door. Some shingles were missing from the roof, and one on the glass doors was cracked.

Kat and Molly entered the church. In the lobby, Tracy Walker, Outreach Coordinator and Sunday School teacher extraordinaire, stood behind a table bent over a clipboard with Mellie.

"Kat!" Mellie smiled broadly. "Hi, Molly!"

Molly laughed. "Hey there, sweet girl! Looks like your mom's got you busy. Ms. Tracy, how are you today?"

In her late thirties, Tracy was stunning. Her short blonde hair was coiffed into a side-swept bob, with a playful streak of platinum contrasting her golden locks. Her sassy but kind personality more than made up for her shortness of stature. She wielded an authority a drill sergeant would admire. She was well-liked and well-respected, and always ready to gift a smile or a squishy hug. She also never read a person wrong.

Tracy walked around the table and pulled both Kat and Molly into a fierce hug. "I heard you girls have had quite a day so far!" She looked at Kat. "Is Mocha going to be okay?"

"What happened to Mocha?" Mellie screeched, then bit her lip.

Kat explained. "We're hoping it's just a sprain. She's on three legs."

Mellie nodded, her mouth open in disbelief. Tracy returned to her place behind the table and assured her daughter. "You know that horse is just as stubborn as your father when you ask him for something he's already decided you can't have. I'm sure she'll be back on all fours in no time."

Kat was comforted by Ms. Tracy's encouragement. She nailed Mocha right on the head.

"All right," Tracy got right to business. "Mellie, go tell Shelby, her ride's here, and grab your brothers to load all that"—she gestured to the grocery sacks of hygiene supplies lined up by the door—"into Kat's car."

"Yes, ma'am."

When Mellie was out of sight, Tracy lowered her voice. "I'm concerned about the old folks that live there. That building is ancient. One of the generators didn't even turn on, likely worn out by its use last winter." She snorted. "Anyway, same drill as any other time we lose power, except no danger of icy roads, woohoo! Any questions, call me. Back up to their delivery door and ring the bell. Someone will meet you and unload. If they invite you to dinner, go. Text a full report on the status and constitutions of the residents by six forty-five. We need to know who to pray extra for at the staff meeting tonight."

"Yes, ma'am!" Kat and Molly chorused.

"Excellent. Knew I could count on you."

Kat, Molly, and Shelby helped Mellie and her brothers load the car. Molly filled Shelby in on the happenings at the resort while Kat drove to The Roosevelt.

"So you're moving in with Kat, then?" Shelby shifted in the backseat. The boxes and grocery sacks took up most of the space, leaving her pressed against the door.

"Till my cabin gets rebuilt."

Shelby was quiet for a moment. "Kat, do you have another open room? I can pay you a bit of rent. When Jane and Noah moved in with Dad, I gave the little guy my room. The attic gable room is fine since I'm home just for a few months, but—"

"Say no more! I'd love to have you. There's an old nursery suite on the third floor, with an adjacent small bedroom for a nanny or governess. The little room would be perfect for an office of your own, too. Better than your old closet or your dining-room table. And don't either of you think about paying rent." She spoke sternly, then smiled. "You'd be doing me a favor. I hate being alone in that big old house. We'll split the bills, but no rent. That's my final offer."

"Well, if you say so!" Molly acquiesced. Always the one to see the silver lining, she turned in her seat to face her friends on the driver's side of the car. "Let's decide right now to have the best summer ever!"

Kat exchanged a smile with Shelby in the rearview mirror. Though several years older than them, Molly had a playful spirit that often got away from her. Her positivity was contagious. Despite all she had been through, marriage, divorce, and now a destroyed cabin, she was the most upbeat of the trio.

Kat thought about Mocha. *She will heal.* She knew how strong the power of spoken affirmations was. "Yes, let's try to have some fun."

Easton had kept busy around the resort, and arrived back at the barn to find a container filled with Brunswick stew on his desk. Did they never run out of this stuff? He ignored it and went to check on Mocha.

She was dozing in her stall. He opened the gate and approached her cautiously.

"Listen." Mocha blinked and whinnied. "Kat needs you. And I need Kat. Work with me here." Easton stroked her face and sighed. "I miss when she used to need me. I would do anything for her. Which is why I am going to make sure *you* get that leg healed."

Mocha narrowed her eyes at him as if she could understand. She blew a breath and wiggled her lips.

"I'm glad we understand each other." He reached into his pocket and presented her with a handful of baby carrots. She snorted and moved her head toward them. "Ah, ah, ah . . ." He held them slightly out of reach. "You've got to get them from me." He took a step back.

Mocha stretched her neck. Just out of reach. She shook her head and whinnied. Adjusting her form, she stepped forward with her right front leg. Easton held a breath. Mocha lifted her injured leg and leaned on her forelegs for a moment, stretching her neck toward him. She sighed and eased herself back to her original position. *Almost.*

"Good effort, old girl." He fed her the carrots. "Next time, a full step on your own, okay?"

She snorted and scarfed them down. He patted her on the nose and retreated to his office.

He sat down to feast on the mystery-meat stew, which had been sitting on his desk for who-knew-how-many hours, but his phone rang. He pulled it from his pocket and grinned.

"Hey, bro, you too busy surfin' to check in on your fam?"

JC chuckled. "Nah, man, actually I've talked to Mom twice today, and Dad once. Oh, and Molly, too."

"So I should take your day-long silence personally?"

"Yup. Freezin' you out. It's so easy to do when you're a grump all the time."

Easton huffed. "I'm not a grump *all* the time."

"True. Just every time you have feelings for Kat, don't tell her, and she dates someone else or leaves or ignores you."

He cringed and sighed. "You got me."

"Dude, I don't know why this is so difficult for you. She's back, she missed you, she's sorry. *Bam.* Take her back. Happy Easton returns and we all live happily ever after."

"Can't do it. I took over the horses when Grandma retired instead of going to vet school because I thought Kat and I were going to build the stables back up to their old glory. She bailed on me. I hired on extra help in the barn and took on the lighthouse project. It's almost done and I've got other improvements to the resort lined up after that. I'm not going to drop anything just because her last thing didn't work out and good ol' Easton is always there to pick back up."

"Is that all?" JC asked.

"Isn't that enough?"

JC was quiet for a minute. "I think you're overlooking the fact that you two are meant to be together. You've been through a lot together, spent more time with her than anyone else over your lifetime, and I think that, despite what happened at Christmas, you know in your heart what you need to do. And you're paralyzed with fear."

"Maybe I am," he admitted. "She drives me crazy but I'm crazy for her."

"Isn't that when you know it's love, big bro?"

Easton jumped from the chair as the back door to the barn opened. He could feel her presence before he saw her. "I thought so," Easton spoke lowly into the phone as he leaned against the door frame. A few yards down, Kat spoke softly to Mocha in her stall. She walked right past him without so much as a hello.

"Then cast away your pride and get on it. Give her another chance, or at least an opportunity to explain. You know being irrational and impulsive are common with her brain injury. Whatever she said, maybe she didn't mean it. Simple as that."

"I can't really talk about it right now. She's here."

"Ah. Think about what I said then. Meantime, the reason I called is to tell you I'm coming home for a few weeks to help. I'm flying to Atlanta tonight and I'll crash there. Early flight tomorrow to Boston, then to Bar Harbor. Should be in around dinnertime. Steal some snacks from the kitchen for me?"

Easton's eyebrows lifted in surprise. "That's cool, man. Surprised you can leave for that long."

"My role is pretty fluid right now. They have plenty of volunteers coming in and my absence will give someone else a chance to step up. This is a big season for missionary trips so they won't miss me too much. Lots of help to go around." JC had been in Haiti since he'd graduated from college a year earlier. He'd only come home for a few days over Christmas. "Besides, I miss Frieda's cooking."

"Yeah, I miss it, too," Easton mumbled.

"What does that mean?" JC asked, slight panic in his voice. "Are the Sadlers not working there anymore?"

"Calm down, bro. They're here. Frieda's still overseeing the kitchen, but we have a sweet elderly guest from Savannah who is apparently an award-winning cook. Her grandson is getting married here on the Fourth, so she's teaching Mom and Frieda to make his favorite foods. And *we* get to eat them."

"Sweet! I love some good southern cookin'. Grits, greens, fried chicken, biscuits and gravy, and—"

"Ugh." Easton made a face. "Yesterday she made a huge pot of something called Brunswick stew. I was picking out the parts that were edible when you called. What's wrong with fish and chips or lobster for a wedding? It's New England."

JC cracked up. "Dude, you would never survive in Haiti. Save some of that for me. It sounds awesome."

Easton glanced at the bowl on his desk, the cover upside down and splattered with lima beans, mystery meat, and other lumpy things that reminded him of dog food. "You'll have to call Mom and ask." He walked to the doorway and watched Kat pull Mocha's gate closed and flip the latch. "Listen, safe travels, man. Kat's on her way out and I need to catch her before she goes."

She heard him and raised her head. He nodded at her and she headed toward him.

"Of course. Thanks. I'll see you tomorrow. Later, bro."

"Later." Easton ended the call and stared at Kat. She wore a mask of concern and exhaustion. Still, she was stunning. Hair escaped from a dark braid hung over one shoulder, the tail of it resting near the exposed cleavage above her tank top. As if she felt him staring, she tucked the stray hairs behind her ear and flipped the braid to her back.

"Hey," she said. "What's up?"

He didn't answer right away.

"Your grandma has been delivered to the main lodge and Molly is getting her settled."

"Okay." He ran his fingers through his hair and told her about Mocha attempting a step for the baby carrots. Her expression transformed into one of hope. "Do you have more carrots?" she asked excitedly.

Easton pulled the bag from his pocket. "Just a handful."

She grabbed them and ran to Mocha's stall. He followed her with interest. "She might be tired from her first attempt still," he said, warning her not to get her hopes up.

Kat wasn't listening. She baited Mocha with the remaining carrots. "C'mon, sweet girl . . . you know you want these. Maybe even some sugar cubes if you walk for me," she coaxed in a singsong voice.

Now, why hadn't he thought of that? Mocha was a sugar fiend. He left and returned with a handful of cubes, which he gave to Kat. She took them and held them just out of reach.

Mocha whinnied and shifted.

"Atta girl." Kat backed up a step.

Mocha leaned forward and lifted her front right hoof. He watched her in awe. Kat took another step back, and Mocha stepped forward. Kat stepped back again. "C'mon, sweet girl. You've got this. Just take it slow."

The horse was definitely trying. Mocha moved

forward, carefully and slowly. Tears welled in Kat's eyes. She fed her the sugar cubes, laughing and crying.

"Good horse," he whispered. "Good horse." A weight lifted from him, and he let out a breath he didn't know he'd been holding. Mocha got her footing, favoring the injured leg but steady enough.

Kat stepped back, out of the stall. She turned and wiped her hands on her pants. "She is." She turned to him. "I'm sorry."

"For what?" Easton asked.

Kat stepped closer and put her hand on his shoulder. Electric sparks shot through him, just like every time they'd ever made contact. Did she react to him like this? He covered her hand with his and gave a gentle squeeze, his eyes never leaving hers.

"For blaming you." The tears spilled over. He reached out with his other hand to pull her to him. It was a reflex, an instinct of sorts. Their bodies knew what to do because their hearts directed.

Easton bent his head down as she tilted hers up. His gentle kiss turned fervent, the passion they hadn't acted on since Christmas fueling them. Kat pressed herself against him. Her heart beat rapidly, pounding out a furious rhythm against his chest.

Kat pushed him against the wall between Mocha's and Buttons' stalls. She held his face, kissing him as if her survival depended on it.

"It's okay," he soothed when his lungs demanded air. "I know how upset you were." He tucked her head into his chest and held her, their hearts beating in sync.

Chapter 8

Kat stepped back, lips tingling and swollen, gasping for breath. This is what she wanted, what she missed. It felt so right to be in Easton's arms again.

He looked at her with a yearning that revealed the truth in his heart. She would have to move slow and prove to him he could trust her again. "I should go," she whispered.

"You don't have to—" He was still clutching her hand. She gently slipped it out of his grasp and trailed it down his arm.

"I do. I need to check on Uncle Charley and prep rooms for Molly and Shelby. They're moving in with me for a bit." She tiptoed up to give him a quick goodbye kiss.

He nodded. "Okay."

She smiled, amused at his lack of curiosity and words. "Did you already hear about it?"

"Molly texted me earlier. I don't think she was keen on sharing my space." He shrugged. "It's cool. Kinda glad she won't be there to force me to eat any of that weird healthy food she likes."

Kat raised an eyebrow. "You mean grown-up food?"

"Hey now." He lifted their held hands up and rested them on his chest. Kat felt his lean muscles through his shirt. His heartbeat was steady underneath. Goosebumps formed on her arms. "I don't make her eat burgers and fries. She shouldn't push her lettuce wraps and juicies on me."

"Juicies?"

"Yeah, that's what she calls those concoctions she makes in her juicer. I wonder if the tree took that thing out?" he asked hopefully.

Kat snorted. "If it did, she's likely already ordered another one."

Easton's smile lit her up. "Likely. Have fun with that." He pulled her toward him and planted a chaste kiss on her forehead. "Go take care of Uncle Charley. See you tomorrow?"

She wanted to pull his head down to hers and kiss him senseless, but she held back the urge. "See you tomorrow," she said, letting go. She turned and left, feeling his eyes burn into her back the whole way to her SUV.

The drive home was slow. Even in the dark, crews were still out in full force, clearing the main roads and fixing electrical lines. In a few more days, most areas would be back to normal, minus a few trees. As she turned onto Piney Point Road, she couldn't help but think they had been lucky. Crane's Cove had survived another storm.

She pulled into the empty space at Uncle Charley's cottage. His truck was in its spot. He probably wasn't convinced enough to move up to the main house. He answered after the second knock.

"Hey there, beautiful," he said.

"Hey there, handsome," she returned. She knew the old man wouldn't come willingly. She had to play this just right. "I wanted to let you know I invited Molly and Shelby to come live with me in the big house for a while."

"Shame about Molly's cabin." He stroked his barely there chin whiskers. "Nice that you'll have friends around. How's your horse?"

"She's hanging in there. We're praying she'll make a complete recovery in time." She pulled out a strand of hair from behind her ear and twirled it.

"Well, that's the best news I've heard all day. You're twirling your hair. That means you're thinking about something. Just spill it."

He knew her so well. "Um . . . well, with my friends moving in, and me at the barn so much while Mocha recovers, I was hoping you might stay up there for a little while, help them get settled in?"

"Kat Daniels, I do believe you are worried about me and you are using this situation to trick me into bending to your will." He put on his stone face, cultivated from decades of service and training sailors.

Kat gaped at him and swallowed. "Did it work?"

His stone face lit up with mischievous merriment. "It did! On one condition . . ."

"What's that?"

"I don't have to drink those foul juice things Molly makes."

"How did you—"

"Nevermind how I know. Deal?"

"Deal." She caught his eye and they burst into laughter. Suddenly, his laughs turned into coughs, then harsher coughs, until he was gasping for air. Kat wrapped one arm around his shoulder and took his hand. She guided him inside to the couch that faced the pool table.

A few minutes later, the coughing fit stopped. He met her eyes. "Gettin' old, that's all."

Kat didn't know what to say. "That didn't sound good, Uncle Charley."

In the time she'd been there, his face had gone from pale to ashen and he clutched his left arm. "I'm fine. Nothing new."

"But you're older," she persisted.

"Yes, I am." His hands shook as he took out a small bottle of baby aspirin from his pocket. He struggled with the lid. "And I'll manage till I can't." His response was kind but firm. "Go on up. I'll pack my duffel and be up soon."

"Okay." Kat felt helpless. She hugged him. "You better. Be careful going up the stairs. I'll check on you before I go to sleep."

He saluted her. "Yes, ma'am."

"Good soldier." Her phone rang from her pocket.

"Now go and answer that call and get settled."

She blew him a kiss as she closed the door behind her and swiped to answer the call.

"Hey, Carol."

"Kat, I wanted to tell you we're all praying for Mocha."

"Thank you." Kat felt another wash of relief as she got into her SUV to drive up to the main house. "Thanks for calling."

"Yes, well, I'm afraid that's not the only reason for my call. I need your help. The wedding planner the resort uses has resigned, effective immediately." Carol sighed. "Tragic, really. The house she and her husband just finished building was destroyed by that tornado that went behind the resort. She's up from us quite a ways, but the path was erratic. They lost everything. They'll be moving in with her in-laws in Bangor until they can figure it all out. So we need a wedding planner."

"Umm . . ." Was this one of Carol's famous reverse-psychology plots?

"Or two." Carol's tone inclined hopefully. "We don't do a lot of weddings at the resort, and we only have one on the books for July so far, the Owens-Saunders wedding. All the legwork has been done. I need you and Molly to take it over. Conroy Construction will be rebuilding the gazebo. We've got the kitchen set with Meemaw's recipes, and additional staff has been hired for the day of the event. Meantime,

I'll be looking for a new consultant, but we can't get one in time for this wedding. I hope Trisha's other venues have a backup plan. She feels terrible about it, so I reassured her we'll get it together. Her baby is due in September, so please add her to your prayers. She'll be available for consult by phone whenever you need her. What do you say? Can you meet with her and Molly at nine a.m. tomorrow before she heads out to Bangor?"

Kat's head began to throb as she tried to follow along. Her brain needed sleep. She tried to wrap it around the information overload. Since she acted normal most of the time, people tended to forget her brain couldn't handle what theirs could. She shook her head, grasping for some clarity. Plan a wedding? Never mind, she'd ask Molly tomorrow. "Nine a.m., sure I can be there. I'd love to help."

Except the last thing she wanted to take on was the wedding of the most picture-perfect, almost sickeningly sweet couple she'd ever met. Matt and Lanie had fallen in love over a few weeks, decided they couldn't live without each other, and planned a wedding just two months after they first met. Who did that?

"Oh, wonderful! I knew I could count on you. See you in the morning."

Kat held her phone out and stared at it, trying to retain the information before she forgot it. Too late. *Molly.* Right. If she played it right, Molly would fill in the gaps.

Hey, your mom just called. Looks like we are

planning a wedding!

Molly texted back immediately. *Yes! This is going to be fun! Wait, I shouldn't say that. I feel so bad for the wedding planner, Trisha. She and her husband are staying at the resort tonight. I told Mom that was a great idea to offer discounted rooms to townies who still don't have power by tomorrow. Mom said she'd talk to Dad about free rooms. Even better! I just love helping people!*

Kat couldn't help but smile. Molly's texts were usually all like this, about a mile long and slightly off-topic. *Me, too. So 9:00?*

You got it. Luckily, Trisha had everything planned out. I got all of her files. I might ask her if the other venues need help. I think wedding planning could be my thing. If I can't have a happily ever after, I can help others plan theirs.

Kat frowned. *Molly, you will get your happily ever after. The right guy is out there. Just wait on God's timing. You know He's got great plans for you.*

I know it. I'm just impatient. I'll be thirty in December. That's so depressing. I was supposed to have a brood of babies by now. Instead, I'm divorced and homeless. Jane and I had it all planned out, having babies together, raising them together. But her husband died and mine left.

Oh, Molly, please stop. Chin up before your crown slips! Remember who you are. You are the daughter of the Most High King. You are not homeless. And it's good you're divorced. Your ex-husband was a jerk. Anyone who is crazy enough to leave you is not the right person for you.

Kat's heart ached for her friend. Molly had been cast aside when she was at her most vulnerable. She couldn't imagine the pain she'd endured and couldn't understand how Molly wasn't still overcome with grief. She'd decided just recently to open up again, and when she'd connected with an undercover FBI agent, he'd left, too.

Deep down, I understand that. But it still hurts, you know?

I know.

We all realize it's complicated between you and my brother. But everyone knows how much he loves you and how long he's loved you. I want a love like that.

Kat's eyes stung. She wanted that love back, if indeed that was what it had been. How could she be sure? Could she ever know if Easton truly loved her the way she loved him? It was still love, though, and she'd taken it for granted. It was true that you didn't know what you had until you didn't have it anymore. Why had she ever put barrel racing before him? What did she get from it that she hadn't been getting at home?

Home. Being on the tour created a false sense of family. This was the real deal. And she'd left it.

Kat reached her room and laid her suitcase on the bed. She sank down next to it, thinking about Easton, their history, and how to respond to Molly. Her head throbbed. She massaged her temples with the thumb and middle finger of her other hand.

It'll happen, she reassured her friend. *Let's have a powwow here tomorrow night. See if you can get Jane to come, too.*

Great idea. Yeah, Jane could really use a girls' night out. I've known her all my life and I've never seen her so tense. Even when her husband was going through treatment. She's having a tough time lately. We should see if we can help.

Her son has been sick a lot, right? Shelby mentioned he's been getting a lot of headaches.

Yeah. Maybe he just needs glasses. She's got him an appointment in August with the pediatric ophthalmologist. They schedule wicked far out so they are just trying to manage it right now. I don't think either of them is getting much sleep.

Yikes. Kat knew what that was like. Kat heard the downstairs door open and close. *I've got to go. Uncle Charley just came up, way past his bedtime. He's moving in for a while, too.*

Awesome. Love that ol' guy! All right, I'll let you go. See you in the a.m.!

Kat plugged her phone into her nightstand charging port and left to meet Uncle Charley at the top of the stairs.

Sleeping in the barn meant that Easton was up with the horses. At first light, the animals began to stir and go about their business. He'd lain awake most of the night, unable to sleep. After checking on Mocha and the other horses several times, he'd finally gone into the office to rest. Time passed as he scrolled his phone, researching fetlock injuries and therapeutic ways to heal them. The barn came alive just when he was starting to drift off. He rolled over on the air mattress and pulled his pillow over his head.

"Easton?" Jordan's teenage tenor spoke hesitantly. "Are you awake?"

He stifled a groan and rolled over. Jordan's head poked through the opening in the slightly opened door. "I'm awake," he said, sitting up and grabbing his phone: *8:30 a.m. Already?* "C'mon in."

Jordan pushed the door completely open, revealing Mellie behind him. They glanced at each other, then at him. Mellie pulled in her lips and scrunched up her face.

"What is it?" Easton asked, standing.

Mellie nodded at Jordan, who looked up at Easton, worry painted in his expression. "We were going to clean Mocha's stall first, but she was asleep. Standing, but asleep. So we decided to save her for last. But now she's laying down, and she won't get up."

Easton sucked in a breath and pushed past his young barn hands without a word. He unlatched Mocha's door and flung it open. Mellie and Jordan followed. They observed him as he examined the horse. "Lungs clear, pulse normal." He stroked her muzzle. "Mocha." The horse's eyelids twitched. "You tricky horse."

The kids stared at him while he reached into his pocket and placed his hand, full of sugar cubes, under Mocha's nose. Her nostrils twitched, then her lips curled. She opened one eye and he challenged her with his gaze. What had made her lay down? Easton strained to keep his expression neutral, void of the panic and concern that threatened to scream from his body.

"It's all right," he said to Jordan and Mellie. "She's just being a drama queen." *Please, God, she needs to get up.* Mocha moved her mouth toward the sugar cubes. "Ah, ah, ah," Easton warned, holding them just out of her reach. "You want these, you have to stand for them."

Mocha heaved a deep breath and blew air out her mouth. She snorted in disgust, as if standing were beneath her station. Easton held firm, and a minute later she was standing and licking her lips, every morsel of sugar gone.

"Wow," Mellie said. "How did you know to do that?"

"I've known her all her life. This girl can be as stubborn as her owner." Easton flashed her a grin. "You two only have this stall left, right?"

"Yes, sir," Jordan confirmed.

Easton nodded. "Got any plans for the rest of the day? The horses need some exercise."

"Nope," Jordan said. "I'm just on call if my parents need me for anything." Being the son of resort staffers had plenty of perks, including a good hourly rate for miscellaneous jobs that came up. At sixteen and a half, Jordan had just gotten his intermediate driver's license and was saving for his own car.

"My mom is supposed to pick me up on her way to the church, but I'm not sure when." Mellie frowned. "I'm sure she could come get me at some point."

Easton tossed Jordan a key fob. "Jordan can bring you home or to the church whenever you need to go."

Mellie's eyes widened. Jordan rewarded him with a wide grin.

"I've got some business I have to tend to."

"Yes, sir!" Jordan turned to Mellie and smiled. Her cheeks reddened in a blush. Easton nodded at them and walked out of the barn. He was hungry.

He entered the kitchen through the back door. At the height of the breakfast rush, the kitchen was always a bustle of activity. His mother and Frieda were at the stove, short-order cooking. Two servers were in and out, delivering meals and refilling drinks.

"Mornin', Mom, mornin', Frieda," he called over the din, plucking a cheese blintz from a warming pan. His teeth sank into the soft dough, the cream cheese bursting out the end. Sweet and plain, just how he liked it. In two bites, it was gone, and he wiped his mouth with the back of his hand.

"Good morning!" His mom called over. "Can I make you some eggs?"

"Sure, thanks." He poured himself a glass of milk and chugged it in one gulp. He was starving. At the coffee station, he bypassed the standard coffee mugs and opened the cabinet above for the current selection of snarky mugs. A door slammed and Molly rushed in. He decided to mess with her and chose the mug that bore the message "No Talkie Before Coffee."

"Good morning, lil' big bro! Have you seen Kat?"

Easton almost spilled the coffee he was pouring at the mention of her name. He took a deep breath and added sugar and vanilla creamer to his mug before he turned around. He pointed to the drink with his free hand and grinned at his sister.

Molly snorted. "Fine. I'll find her myself." She glared at him playfully. "We've got a meeting in two minutes. Oh, and thanks for helping me move today. I think we can get it all between your truck and my car." She smiled slyly. "Unless you have other plans?"

He gaped at her.

"Great, then, see you at noon!"

She ran out before he could wrap his mind around what had just transpired. She beat him at his own game. He sat down at the small table the employees ate their meals at and texted Jordan to have his truck at the front door of the main lodge by noon.

"Here you go, sweetie," his mom said, setting down a plate of scrambled eggs, bacon, and buttered white toast in front of him. She pulled out the chair opposite him and folded her arms on the table. Her eyes twinkled. "Your sister got you pretty good there."

Easton sniffed as he gnawed on a slice of bacon. "I would have helped her anyway."

"I know you would. Listen, I want to update you on a few things going on. Your father and I have decided to open the last batch of rooms early this year for locals who still don't have power. It'll be another week or so before we hit full capacity. Also, JC is coming home for a few weeks to help get the resort ready for the busy season."

Her face brightened as she mentioned the arrival of his younger brother. JC was missed by everyone. He had the ability to light up a room like Molly, but in a manner of quiet presence like Easton. Where Molly was loud and excitable, he was calm and focused. Where Easton was introverted and shy, bordering on antisocial, JC was a people reader and focused on anyone he could help feel more comfortable.

"I'm looking forward to it." Easton polished off the rest of his meal in a few bites and pushed his chair out from the table.

"Easton." His mom stopped him before he could stand up, placing her hand over his and meeting his eyes. "I hope it's okay with you that I hired Kat back. We never really discussed it, you and I. It was Molly's idea and thoughtless of me not to have discussed it with you. I had hoped you would see her and you'd get back together," she admitted, looking away.

A muscle in his jaw twitched. "It's fine. She's like family."

"She is," his mom said, a wistful shimmer floating over her blue eyes. She patted his hand. "It's not my business, but as your mother, all I want is for you to be happy. As much as we all love her, if it gets to be too much for you, will you let me know?"

Easton's eyes narrowed. What was she up to? Was she trying some kind of reverse psychology on him? There was no way he'd ever have her fire Kat and she knew it. He didn't want to hurt her and that might just push her over the edge. He could face Kat. He wondered if his mother knew about all those years he'd pined for her. He could handle working with her.

"It's fine, Mom. I would have told you if it wasn't."

"Okay, then." She stood up. "But I do hope you two figure things out soon. The rest of us hate to see you both hurting so much." She walked around the table to hug him.

He hugged her back and squeezed tight.

Chapter 9

Kat and Molly sat across the table from Trisha, who rested one hand on her swollen belly and massaged her lower back with the other. Her flawless brown skin shone with a healthy glow. No makeup was needed to add to her beauty. Her black corkscrew curls, similar to Molly's blonde ones, were still damp from her morning shower and bounced as she spoke excitedly about the plans for the July Fourth wedding. Kat wondered how she managed to exude joy with bags under her eyes, her new house destroyed, her job loss, plus the obvious discomfort and lack of sleep that came with being seven months pregnant.

Almost immediately after Trisha started talking, Kat was inspired. Trisha had given Molly the file yesterday, which wasn't a file at all. Kat had gaped at the binder set out in front of them, organized into over a dozen tabs for venue, décor, wedding party, guests, food, photography, music, beauty, printed materials, checklists, etc.

"So, if you just flip back to the front section, there's

a set of checklists. Whatever is not checked off or crossed off is what still needs to be done. One month before, three weeks before, two weeks before, week of, night before, the day of, etc. The crossed-off items are things that either I've done, the bride has decided to do herself, or aren't applicable." Trisha's eyes danced from Molly to Kat and back to Molly. "And I was able to get Jenni Blythe to do hair and makeup for the wedding."

Molly looked up, a beaming smile matching Trisha's. "She is fantastic! I'm so impressed. She usually books out months in advance."

"She had a cancellation and called me first. You'll have to send me pictures."

"I—*we've* totally got this. I am so impressed, Trisha. No wonder Mom was panicked. I can't believe so much goes into a wedding these days." Molly frowned. "My ex-husband didn't want anything elaborate and I was just so eager to get married I didn't care. If I were to do it again—" She shook her head. "Anyway, you can count on us."

Trisha grinned. "I know I can. The Lord obviously has other plans for me right now, so I'm just going with it. I'm going to relax and spoil this baby till she or he is ready to come out. And then more spoiling."

Kat thought back to Molly's wedding. It seemed so long ago. It'd been a lovely summer evening down at the beach. She and Easton had danced in the moonlight under the stars. She thought Molly and her ex-husband, Kyle, had seemed perfect for each other. They were both young and wanted to start a family right away. She'd never seen two people so smitten with each other. But their love didn't last.

"Kat? Are you alright? I know it looks like a lot but we can totally—" Molly's concerned voice jolted her out of her memory.

"Sorry," she apologized. "Got lost in my own head. Still happens from time to time." She smiled at Trisha. "Of course we've got this. You've done just about everything for us. How can it go wrong?"

Trisha exchanged a glance with Molly and shifted in her chair. "What I've learned is if something *can* go wrong, it *will* go wrong, and it usually happens within the few days right before the event, or on the day of. Just stay on top of things and try to keep the bride happy. No one else matters, no matter what anyone tells you. Unless the bride turns into Bridezilla—but I've worked with a lot of brides, and I am ninety-nine percent sure Lanie Owens doesn't have a zilla bone in her."

Kat smiled. "I don't think so, either."

Molly agreed and stood up. "All right then. Lanie and Matt are in great hands. We'll call you if we need you." She walked around the table to help Trisha up. "You take care of yourself. We'll be praying for you, your family, and your house. Do you plan to rebuild?"

"Thanks. We'll see. I'm wondering if this wasn't a nudge to be closer to our families. I grew up with lots of aunts, uncles, and cousins. I'm thinking my baby might want that experience, too, but I'm not in any rush to decide yet."

Kat wanted that, too. If she married Easton and started a family, she wanted to stay here where her children would be surrounded by their extended family. She swallowed the lump that formed in her throat, and excused herself. She needed water.

At a quarter to five, Easton leaned against a column at the front entrance to the main lodge, waiting for JC's Uber. He looked up as an SUV approached. *Kat.*

Kat pulled up just past the doors, hugging the pavement so as to leave room for a car to go around her. His eyes followed her as she slipped down from her seat.

Molly hopped out of the passenger door and opened the trunk. "Hey, bro! Thanks for your help earlier! We've got one more load left upstairs. Help us again?"

Easton fumbled the button in his pocket and looked past her to Kat. "Sure. JC should be here any minute. Let's go."

He waited until Kat was beside him and reached for her hand. "Hey," he greeted her.

"Hey." She tilted her chin up and squeezed his hand. He grinned and bent down to kiss her.

"Not now," she giggled.

He shrugged. Inwardly, his mind screamed. He needed to kiss her, to feel her lips on his again. He blocked the warnings that told him not to, that getting close to her again would shatter his heart into even more pieces the next time she left.

They fell into step a few paces behind Molly and entered the lobby. When Molly started up the staircase, he gently tugged Kat toward him.

"How 'bout now?" His palms framed her face. In her eyes, he saw the spark he was looking for. She nodded, and he lowered his lips to hers.

Kat wrapped her arms around his waist and pressed her body against his. Their hearts beat in sync, and he was compelled to intensify the kiss. She returned his advances with a fervor that had his lungs begging for release.

Reluctantly, he stepped back from her. "We should—"

"Go help Molly," she finished, breathless. He laughed and impulsively drew her into a fierce hug.

Ten minutes later, they'd loaded the last of Molly's things into the Cherokee's trunk when a dark sedan pulled up behind Kat's SUV.

JC opened the passenger door and stepped out, sunlight glinting off his aviator glasses. His longish hair was tousled under a faded Cliff Walk Resort visor.

Kat was closest to the car. "Hey, handsome." She grinned as he gave her an affectionate hug.

"Hey, beautiful." He planted a loud kiss on her forehead. "Happy summer. Glad you're back. It gets boring around here with just these two," he teased. He hugged Molly, then looked behind him as the back door on the driver's side opened and a man stepped out. "I made a friend."

"Of course you did." Molly peered over his shoulder. A man with movie-star features and smooth light brown skin walked over and held out his hand to Easton. "Damon Saunders. Good to meet you." He greeted Kat and Molly. "You must be Molly and Kat?"

"We are. I'm Molly."

"My pleasure."

Molly giggled. "Saunders, huh? And a southern accent . . . you must be related to Matt?"

Damon grinned. "Cousins. Hope Meemaw isn't stirring up much trouble. I've heard she's already forced her Brunswick stew on you. They sent me up to bring her home since I've got some time off work, although she's never once let anyone make a decision for her."

"She's amazing," Kat said. "One of a kind." The automatic doors opened. "Speaking of . . ."

Meemaw strolled through the doors and straight up to Damon. She placed her hands on his cheeks and held his face in her hands. "My beautiful grandson," she said, her voice wavering slightly. He pulled her in for a hug and she backed away smiling. Her eyes narrowed. "I can't believe I have to come to Maine for you to visit me. It's a shorter trip to Savannah from Atlanta, you know."

Damon sighed and took his duffle from the Uber driver. "I know. I finally got that vacation you've been begging me to take. Thought I'd come up here and see if Matt's description rang true."

Meemaw slid her arm under his and walked him toward the door. "Did you call ahead? They may be at capacity, you know. We just had this hurricane and the locals are coming . . ." Meemaw's voice trailed off as they walked inside. Damon glanced back, a delighted and helpless grin on his face.

Amusement lit up JC's eyes. "She is everything he told me she was, isn't she?"

"And more." Easton took the handle of one of JC's rolling suitcases. He nodded toward the door. "How did you hook up with him?"

"The funniest thing, man. I was just standing at the curb, searching for an Uber, and he comes up to me and says he's going to the place on my visor. Turns out his grandmother is staying here. I realized she must be the Brunswick-stew chef, so I offered to share the ride. Cool dude. Cop from Atlanta, on vacation."

Molly frowned. "Hot guy like that coming to Maine to vacation with his grandmother? Is he for real?"

JC shrugged. "Maybe there's more to it, but I don't think so. He adores her." JC adjusted his backpack on his shoulder. "Speaking of grandmothers, how's Grandma Vivi?"

"She's great. Kat and Molly kidnapped her from The Roosevelt yesterday. You'll see her at dinner." Easton looked at Molly. "Will you be back for dinner?"

Molly nodded. "Just going to take the last load over and then I'll be back." She turned to Kat. "Want to join us?"

Kat shook her head. "Thanks, but I think I should hang out with Uncle Charley tonight. Especially since I'm here all day Friday and Saturday. I heard Country Night is still on? Maybe I'll swing by after he goes to bed."

Molly tucked errant curl behind her ear. "Yeah, Mom was going to cancel, but she's already had half a dozen regulars call to see if it was still on. Apparently, a hurricane isn't enough to keep people home. Sadie from the diner even told her she'd be here whether it was on or not."

JC laughed. "Good ol' Sadie! Well, I'm looking forward to it." He gave Kat a side hug and stage-whispered in her ear, eyes on his brother, "You got a date yet, Kat? I learned some new moves in Haiti."

Kat elbowed him playfully. "I'm working on it, silly." She rewarded him with a grin. "But if I wasn't, I would totally be your date. You're the funnest guy around."

"Ouch," JC said, grinning at Easton. "I do believe you've just been burned, big brother!"

Easton sighed. He was too tired to play along. "If that's all, let's get your things to the cabin so Molly can get back here."

JC turned back to Kat and mouthed, "Still bossy!"

She laughed. "I'm glad you're back, JC. See you tomorrow."

Molly hugged JC one more time. "See you at

dinner."

Kat's phone rang with Shelby's ringtone. "One sec. Hey, Shel—" Easton watched the color drain from her face. She stumbled and leaned up against the car for support. He couldn't hear what Shelby was saying, but it wasn't good. Kat sank to the ground.

He reacted instantly, taking the phone from her hand. Kat stared up at him helplessly. "Shelby, what's going on?"

"I just called 911. Those guys missed a board. Old Man Wetherby thought he could take it down himself. When I pulled into the driveway, he turned around to wave, lost his balance, and fell off the ladder. I don't know how bad he's hurt." She paused to take a breath. Easton could hear the sirens in the distance. "He grabbed his chest before he fell—"

Easton cursed under breath. "We'll be right there." He handed the phone back to Kat. "Keys?" She handed them to him. He looked apologetically at JC. "Kat's uncle fell off a ladder. Not sure I'll make it to dinner."

"No worries, man. We'll pray for the old guy." JC walked Molly to the SUV. "See ya later, sis."

Molly gave him a side squeeze. "I'll let you know if I won't be back." She climbed into the backseat and waved to JC.

Easton was in the car seconds later. Kat sat shaking in the passenger seat, fighting to keep her cool. As they pulled out, Easton laid his hand on her thigh and she gave in to the tears and sobs.

Chapter 10

They'd made it back to her house before the ambulance pulled away. Kat had ridden with Uncle Charley to the hospital. She now sat in a chair next to his bed holding the frail fingers of his right hand in hers. Across from her, Easton dozed, his hands clasped over his stomach. His thin green T-shirt stretched over his shoulders, biceps, and torso. It was tucked into loose-fitting jeans. At the stables, he usually wore a western hat, but when he wasn't working, he donned a decade-old beat-up Red Sox hat his grandfather had bought him on their first trip to Fenway Park.

Kat hadn't had a show that weekend, so Easton and JC's grandfather surprised the boys and their dad with tickets to Fenway Park. When Kat got in the camper with them the following Friday evening, her nose had wrinkled at the traces of cigar smoke, beer, and hamburger grease. The guys had talked about that trip for months. When his grandfather passed away, Easton told her that he felt his grandpa with him every time he wore the hat.

The hat had once been white, but like all things, time had made its mark on it. No longer new, the logo was faded, the material dingy. The brim, which he proudly molded all those years ago by dampening it and setting it in a water glass, still held its shape but was now tattered at the edge. She wondered if he still stuck it in a glass overnight every now and then.

What was he still doing here? It was after two in the morning. Molly, JC, and Shelby had all been by, and had left his truck in the parking lot for whenever they were ready to leave. He should be home, checking on Mocha and the other horses. Sleeping.

The next two days would be long ones for him. He had a full day at the stables, and there was still debris cleanup around the resort. Saturday was just as full, and culminated with Country Night, which she knew he was expected to help set up and break down.

Easton typically hung out at the barn during the event, but she planned to coax him to stay. Just like she'd always done. Easton had never felt comfortable at parties. He'd been working on his agoraphobia his whole life, and had gotten to a point where he could make it through an event without visible anxiety, but for the most part, if he wasn't required to attend, he didn't.

Kat used to love parties. Her traumatic brain injury had taken that from her. She became easily overstimulated and now had her limits. When she tried to push them, Easton was there to take her home. They were a perfect match now, she thought resentfully. She wanted to go to parties, dance, have fun, socialize, but her brain injury limited her. It wasn't fair.

Uncle Charley rested peacefully. He had a concussion, bruises, and a bit of angina. Kat and Easton prayed over him several times. The doctors had diagnosed him with coronary artery disease. Thankfully no heart attack, no broken bones. The doctor changed up his meds and assured her it should keep his heart under control. His chronic obstructive pulmonary disease complicated the condition. He'd have to rest and be monitored for a few weeks, which he wouldn't do if he was home. She'd called Ms. Vivi earlier to see if she could put a word in at the rehab wing at The Roosevelt. Ms. Vivi had moved to the exclusive fifty-five-and-over complex a few years ago. The facility also boasted a state-of-the-art rehabilitation wing. She knew Uncle Charley would receive the best care and attention if he was there.

"I see you staring at me."

Kat jumped at Easton's observation. So he was awake. "I'm not staring."

"You were." Easton pulled himself to a sitting position and rubbed at his eyes. He took his hat off and ran his fingers through his hair, then replaced the hat. "How's he doing?"

"About the same." She glanced at the beeping monitor, which told her his pressure was normal and stable. "You should go. I'll be fine here tonight."

He leaned over and studied the old man's face. "He's lucky to have you."

"I'm lucky to have him." He was all she had left.

Easton stood up. "Can I get you anything before I leave?"

"No. Molly and Shelby brought me a whole bag of snacks and my meds."

He nodded. "I'll be back later in the morning, then."

Kat hugged him goodbye. He pressed his lips to hers and quickly pulled away. She watched him go and wondered what he was thinking. He was acting like he used to, like they were a unit. She imagined, when other couples broke up, they didn't still accompany their exes to hospitals and drive their vehicles. He was continuously and constantly there for her. But she still didn't know where she stood with him.

It was times like this she wished she had a mother she could call. Auntie Katie and Ms. Vivi had been the closest things, but it wasn't the same. It was one of the things that bonded her and Shelby. Shelby's father had never remarried. He'd poured himself into the church when his wife died. Shelby and Jane had been looked after by a dozen or so of the church's most involved women. Ms. Tracy, especially, had taken it upon herself to make sure all Shelby's needs were taken care of while her father worked and Jane was away at college. But none of the girls had the kind of connection that Molly had with Carol, or that their other friends had with their mothers. No late night heart-to-hearts at the kitchen table or mother-daughter outings. As much as Auntie Katie and Ms. Tracy tried to fill the voids, they all knew it just wasn't the same.

Kat sighed and stood to stretch. Behind her, a pillow, sheet, and blanket had been left on the couch that set against the large window. She pulled the handle at the base and it popped out to a full-size bed. She had spent many nights on a bed like this the previous summer. Auntie Katie had been admitted for a broken arm, caught pneumonia, and died a few weeks later. Easton was her rock then as well. Her aunt had been so proud of her for being chosen to tour and thrilled for their engagement. When she'd died unexpectedly, Kat ran, throwing herself into her riding to forget all she had lost at home.

She needed to sleep. Kat spread out the sheet and curled up on it, pulling the blanket tightly around her. She adjusted the pillow under her head and closed her eyes.

Sleep eluded her. Her mind raced with thoughts, ideas, memories. She reached down to her purse on the floor, her hand searching for the nip of whiskey in the zippered pocket. Her meds were rarely enough to slow her thoughts, but a shot or two of whiskey worked every time. She swigged the amber liquid and tossed the bottle back in her bag. As she felt the effects take over her mind and body, she drifted off into a dreamless sleep.

Friday morning had dawned early, and by the time Easton finished administering the IV to Mocha and applying her liniment, Meggie, Maddie, and Mellie had arrived. They'd be resuming trail rides and lessons for the resort guests, and the whole day was booked solid with reschedules from the storm.

He gave the girls instructions, not that they needed them, and headed into his office to make a plan for the day. He told Kat he'd pick her up around lunchtime. He would also cover her morning shift at the barn. Easton was happy to give the children's riding lessons over to her, not because he didn't like teaching kids to ride, but because he loved watching her do it. She was meant for this, created for the sole purpose to teach kids to ride and love horses as much as she did. The joy on her face, in her posture, and in her voice filled him with a spirit that made him long to be a part of it, to connect with her. He hadn't realized how much he looked forward to watching her morning lessons until today. Her absence was deafening.

He opened the door to his office and his eyes widened in surprise. "Mom?"

His mother sat at his desk, looking over his schedule and making notes on a Post-it. "Good morning! I'm here to give you the morning off—"

"But we're already down one."

"Don't you 'but' me. I told your grandma what happened last night and she is more than happy to fill in. If you ask me, I think she misses it. I'll manage things here, and she'll do the kids' lessons."

"Umm, thanks?"

She patted him on the shoulder. "Go spend time

with your brother. He wants to see the lighthouse. You can take a load of stuff over and check on it since you haven't been there since before the storm."

"Sweet. But I told Kat I'd keep her company at the hospital later—"

She waved at him to stop talking. "I'll go sit with them. What time?"

"I told her I'd be there when I stopped for lunch."

"Perfect."

He was disappointed but didn't argue. "All right, then. Thanks, Ma."

"You're welcome, sweetie. Happy to. I've been cooped up in the main lodge for days. God bless Frieda." She smiled. "I like to think I'm useful and serve a purpose, but I know she's just humoring me. She could run the place in her sleep."

Easton headed back to his cabin, where JC and Damon gathered debris. "I hope he's paying you for that."

Damon looked up as he tossed a heavy branch effortlessly against the side of the cabin. "I prefer this to the fitness equipment."

"Meemaw kicked us out of the kitchen after breakfast and told him to make himself useful," JC clarified. "She's quite a delegator."

"Well, it's too bad you're busy. I was going to see if you wanted to come with me to check on the lighthouse."

JC pulled his yardwork gloves off. "I think we're

done here."

Easton laughed. "Then let's go."

The afternoon passed by in a blur. Easton relished the time with his brother and their new friend. The lighthouse had fared well, and he made plans the following week to return to it and finish the work. He'd come out with Matt a day before the wedding to customize the experience.

They decided to go to the pub for dinner and drinks before heading back to the resort. Settled at a high-top table in the back corner, they could still observe the crowd. Easton had just ordered a round from Paddy when his phone buzzed with a message from Kat.

Hey. I miss you. What are you doing tonight?

Hi, he texted back. *I always miss you. At the pub with JC and Damon. What's up? How's Uncle Charley?*

The drinks arrived. "Hey, bro." JC handed him a beer. "Check that later."

Easton took the beer but continued to stare at his phone.

"A girl?" Damon asked.

"Yeah," he sighed.

JC piped in. "Kat's the love of his life, but they're both too stubborn to do anything about it."

Easton glowered at his brother as another message came in. It was a picture of Kat holding up a sparkly pink flask. Her face drooped with sadness, her eyes heavy with the emotion he felt deep in his heart. *Cheers.*

Easton sat up straight in his stool and cursed, seething with anger and concern. She knew just how to get his attention, every time. He texted back furiously. *Why are you drinking? Do you need me to come get you?*

"Uh-oh. Lover's tiff, look out!" JC teased.

"Shut up. She's mixing whiskey with her meds again."

JC's eyes widened. "What do you mean, *again*?"

"She's been doing it since we broke up. She gets drunk and texts me. And I take the bait every time because she's a ticking time bomb. The doctors warned her long ago not to mix her meds with alcohol. She knows it's dangerous. She's smarter than that. So why is she being stupid?"

Damon had been silent, but now spoke up. "She's not stupid. Bad decision, yes, but she knows the consequences. Texting you about it is a cry for attention. Something had to happen to trigger it. You said she was away, right? Maybe something happened to her and she thinks she needs the alcohol to self-soothe."

"The only thing that happened to her was that she dumped me."

"It sounds like it was more than that. Could be she regrets it, but it could be more." Damon shrugged. "I've learned a lot about addicts while I've been on the force. There's always a trigger."

"She's not an addict."

JC put his beer down. "Did you ask her why she started?"

Easton's face flamed. He hadn't. "No." He held up his phone as a new text came in.

Whiskey helps clear my head. Uncle Charley is doing well. I'm home now. Maybe I'll come join you at the pub.

He punched back. *You're not driving, are you? Do I need to come get you?*

No.

Easton stared at the screen. Well, that was clear. He put down the phone and picked up his beer. "She says she might come here."

JC sipped his beer and leaned forward in his stool. "You want me to talk to her?"

"I want her to talk to me."

"Well, big bro, you aren't always so easy to talk to."

Easton upended his beer bottle and chugged the rest of the liquid. "Sure I am. Charming as can be."

Damon and JC stifled laughs. He knew he could be gruff, but she knew he cared. It irritated him to think something might have happened to her while she was gone. Wouldn't she have told him?

They ordered another round and were halfway through their beers when Kat, Molly, and Shelby arrived. Molly headed straight for them, her face lit up with her bright Molly-smile. He couldn't help but grin back at his sister. Life had put her through the wringer and she still found joy every day. He should be more like her.

"Hey! The three handsomest guys here! Got room for us?" Without waiting for an answer, Molly pulled over two chairs from the empty table next to them. Damon leapt up to get a third. Once they were settled, Molly looked around. "Oh! How rude of us Cranes. Damon, this is Shelby."

"Pleasure to meet you," Damon said, reaching out his hand across the table.

Shelby took his hand and blushed when he kissed her knuckles instead of shaking it. She pulled it back and tucked her hands in her lap. "Where did you find this guy?" she asked Molly.

They all laughed. Damon drawled, "Originally from Savannah, currently living in Atlanta."

"Well, Mr. Savannah-Atlanta, it's nice to meet you." A muscle in her jaw twitched as if she was keeping herself from smiling. Easton smirked at her flustered expression. He'd never seen it before. Shelby was always cool and commanding.

Molly had noticed, too. "Shelby, he's really sweet. Meemaw said so." She giggled. "I'll be right back."

Shelby raised a brow and looked at Damon. "All grandmothers are biased. But from what I've seen so far, yours seems to have good judgment. Mostly."

Damon laughed. "I trust it." Easton's eyes never left Kat as she went up to the bar and ordered a drink. While she waited, she took her phone out of her pocket and checked the screen. A second later, she violently shoved it back into her pocket. She carried her drink back to her seat next to his. He tuned out the group's conversation and leaned over to whisper in her ear. "Why are you drinking, Kat? You know you shouldn't." He went for it. "Did something happen to you on the tour?"

She stiffened, the color disappearing from her face. She gripped her glass so tightly her knuckles turned white. "Why would you ask that?" she whispered. She pressed her lips together and avoided his eyes.

Easton's stomach sank and a lump formed deep in his throat. Damon was right. How could he have noticed, and Easton hadn't? All this time, he could have been helping her. He stared at her, unable to form words in his grief.

"Who was that on the phone?" he pushed.

Kat slid off the bar stool, drink in hand, and headed for the door. He followed close behind, racking his brain for words, any words. No, he needed the *right* words.

He followed her outside and around to the side of the building. She slumped against the painted green shingles and met his eyes. "I don't want to talk about it. It's dumb. It doesn't matter." She chugged the contents of her glass and sank to the ground. "I just need to clear my head and breathe out my anger."

Easton's heart shattered. In all his years of knowing her, she'd never looked so hopeless, so sad. "Tell me. Please." He slid down next to her and pulled her head to his chest.

Her empty glass fell to the ground. "I . . ."

"It's okay," Easton soothed. "You can trust me."

He loosened his arms as she inhaled a deep breath. Her shoulders relaxed. "I just couldn't take it anymore. I had to leave."

"What couldn't you take?"

She lifted her head. Anger sparked in her eyes. "At first, they just said stuff, guy stuff, sometimes joking, but sometimes horrible things. Then, they noticed my ring was gone and that I was alone at the shows. After we broke up and you stopped coming to the events, they—"

Easton clenched his fists at her back. "They *what?* Who is *they?*" he asked through gritted teeth.

"I heard them. They made a bet. I told Troy about it, but . . ."

"Your manager? Did he stop it?"

"No," she muttered bitterly.

In an instant, her anger transformed into sobs. Her weeping sent chills through him.

"What, Kat?"

"He told me the only way he could make them stop was if I—if I—I—"

She didn't finish, but he could fill in the blank. He should have been there, protecting her from the scum, insisting she leave that tour. Another thought crept into his mind. If there hadn't been an issue, would Kat have come back? Or would she still be away from him, running? And how could he know for sure?

Chapter 11

Kat pressed her face into Easton's T-shirt. She wished the ground would open up and swallow her. She had decided weeks ago to forget about the reasons she left the tour.

"If you what?" Easton pried gently. He cupped his hand over her shoulder and stroked the length of her arm. "Did he hurt you?" he asked through his teeth.

Kat shook her head and inhaled deeply. Once she realized her manager had been serious about what she needed to do for him to put a stop to the harassment, she couldn't leave fast enough. He had been such a nice guy, supportive boss, and friend. She trusted him. But he had a dark side, and his anger at her rejection told her he wasn't accustomed to being told no. It took her over a week to drive Mocha home, and she hadn't planned to tell anyone why, ever.

A former bull-riding champion, Troy "Stetson" Boone had transitioned into the manager role after too many concussions had sidelined him from the sport. Last summer, he recruited Kat after a local rodeo. He even visited the Cliff Walk Resort to watch her train. He charmed everyone except for Easton, who had gone so far as to propose to her to keep her from going. She accepted his proposal and he flew out to most of her events as she traveled with Boone's company around the country. She knew the traveling had taken a toll on him, and his absence limited the equine activities for resort guests. Before the tour, Kat had only traveled outside of the state a few times by herself, and he'd gone with her. She hadn't thought about the resort's loss of revenue when he was gone, or the price of his traveling. She'd never had to think about money.

"Kat, talk to me," Easton pleaded. "Tell me how I can help."

She spoke into his chest, her voice a muffled sob. "I can't. Please, let it go."

"I'm going to take you home, okay?" He helped her up and pulled her close. She wrapped her hands around his waist and held him tightly. Why had she ever left him? What was she thinking? In her grief, all she thought about was herself. She couldn't imagine living in the big house without Auntie Katie, but why hadn't she ever pictured Easton there with her? Her life had been turned upside down last summer. The tour invitation, the proposal, and Auntie Katie's death, all in a matter of weeks. It was too much, and she ran.

"Hey," he whispered. "Whatever it was, it's over now. No one will hurt you." Easton's hand held her head against his chest. This man had always been there for her, and she took him for granted. If only she could know if his love was the kind she sought. Not a protector, but a partner.

Easton led her to his truck and she buckled herself in. Like she had the previous Sunday, she curled up against the door and pressed her face to the glass. Had it only been a week ago?

He settled into the driver's seat. "Hey, Molly." Kat turned her head and watched Easton talk into his phone. "I'm going to take Kat home. Can you bring JC and Damon back to the resort? Dinner's on me. I'll pay you back tomorrow." Easton started up his truck and turned the radio off. "Yeah, she's all right. Give us some time, though?" She strained her ears to hear Molly on the other end, to no avail. "Okay. Thanks."

Kat felt terrible. "I've ruined your night again. I'm so sorry, Easton."

He reached for her hand and squeezed it. "You could never ruin anything for me. I'm here because I want to be. I always want to be here for you, Kat. Why don't you understand that? I can't seem to prove that to you, even after all this time, after all we've been through together. Why can't you believe that?"

"Because I don't deserve you." There, she'd finally said the words. "Why would anyone give up his dream and spend years helping someone recover? What's in it for you? Nothing I can see, except a sense of duty fulfilled. I don't want to be your duty. I want to be your—"

The truck swerved off the road and he put it in park.

"My what, Kat? Look at me." She sighed and turned her head. "What do I need to do to convince you my love for you is unconditional? My proposal last year was not a scheme to trap you here. It was an honest request for you to spend the rest of your life with me. I've been miserable without you. We're connected by our hearts, whether you want to acknowledge it or not."

Kat swallowed hard, but try as she might, she couldn't hold her tears back. She wanted to say something, desperately wanting the look in his eyes to go away, but she couldn't speak. He needed to know how she felt about him. She leaned forward and cupped his chin in her hands. His cheeks were red, hot in her hands, heated with passion and frustration. She pressed her lips to his.

Easton's arms engulfed her and she leaned into him. Their kiss intensified. Sparks that felt new shot through her. She'd never felt so nostalgic for home. *Home.* The little town on the Maine coast. Sailing, seafood, salt, and snow. Safe.

Kat wrapped her arms around his neck and he pulled her into his lap. She was lost in the love she felt from his familiar kiss. She closed her eyes. Her heartbeat raced as his lips trailed from hers to the spot at the base of her neck that pulsed in tandem with her desire to be consumed by him.

Easton had been a part of her life since she was ten. He'd had no desire to see the world or sow wild oats. He loved his home, and he loved her. That was enough for him. Why hadn't it been enough for her?

He pulled his head back and sought her lips again. She returned his kiss as if his breath was the only air she could survive on. When she opened her eyes, she was stunned to see his face was streaked with tears, too.

Kat didn't think her heartbeat would ever slow. She slid off his lap but didn't break his gaze. The pure love and longing in his expression said everything she needed know. She'd been a fool to think he didn't love her for her. "Wow," she whispered.

He grinned. "Yeah. It's always like that for me."

She smiled shyly. "Like what, exactly?"

"I don't know. There's nothing even close to compare it to."

Saturday afternoon, Easton and JC laid out the dance floor for the Cliff Walk Resort's monthly Country Night. Across the room, Kat set the tables that had been rearranged along the perimeter of the expansive room. Every few minutes, one would catch the other looking.

JC had razzed him earlier that morning, but Easton wouldn't give him any details from the night before. Kat's secret was safe with him, even if he didn't yet know all the details that had brought her home. He was confident she'd tell him when she was ready. And then he would track down Troy Boone and make him wish he'd never met Kat. Easton wasn't going to let him get away with hurting her or anyone else.

He'd watched Kat teach the morning lessons and then he'd driven her to the hospital to visit her uncle. Old Man Wetherby was doing well and had enjoyed their visit, and encouraged her not to miss work that night. When the doctor assured her that her uncle was only being kept for observation, she agreed. Easton preferred she go home and rest, but he didn't dare suggest it. She wanted to spend time with Mocha.

They arrived back at the resort early enough for him to help with the event setup. He thought he might just decide to stay this time. He never grew tired of watching her.

She'd come so far. Over the years, she'd increased her stamina for loud and crowded events. He'd envied her in a way, as he'd never felt comfortable in a room filled with people and expectations.

When Kat was cleared to watch television after the accident, they'd watched the *Star Wars* movies more times than he could count. She'd never seen them and they became a tool to help recover her short-term memory, relearn math, and tell time. They also kept her from the despair and addictions that are common among those who suffer from traumatic brain injuries.

Six years after her accident, Kat was different, but the core of her hadn't changed. He was so proud of her. She worked hard to get her life back, and although it hadn't turned out the way she'd envisioned, he was confident she would find her way. He hoped it would be with him.

"Looks good, bro," JC observed after they snapped together the last square of the floor.

"Yep, let's get the side edging on and grab some food." It took about five minutes to secure the border of the floor, and the brothers slipped into the kitchen, where Meemaw was delegating from atop one of the wooden chairs at the old farmer's table.

"Gentlemen! Just in time!" Meemaw squatted down on the chair. Easton rushed over and extended his hand. She smiled and stepped down with a grace that belied her age. "Many thanks, Easton." She craned her neck up at him and JC. "Have a seat. Y'all and Damon are my guinea pigs tonight. I have orchestrated a complete Boardinghouse Dinner. Your job is to tell me what you like best. I have no idea what you picky New Englanders do for wedding food. I am tasked with planning the menu for my Matthew's big day and have got to somehow find a happy medium and infuse his and Lanie's favorites. And I don't want their guests to starve, so you eat, or don't, and tell me what to keep and what to cut. Understand?"

"Yes, ma'am!" JC grinned. "I actually love to eat, so I'm not sure how helpful I'll be in the cutting part."

"Damon!" Meemaw called. "Bring over the sample dishes." Across the kitchen, Damon picked up three bowls, one of which balanced precariously in the crook of his left elbow, and carried them to the table.

Easton stared with disdain at the bowl of soggy, steaming green leaves Damon set down in front of him. "Definitely cut that." He surveyed the other bowls.

"The fried chicken and sweet potato casserole can stay."

Damon laughed. "No can do. This is a Saunders staple. Turnip greens." He left and returned with cornbread, biscuits, gravy, and fried okra.

Easton plucked a piece of cornbread from the basket. Damon and JC watched him as he chewed and fought to swallow. "It's not sweet. How do you wreck cornbread?"

"True southern cornbread doesn't have sugar." Damon sat and grabbed a plate from the stack in the center of the table. He narrowed his eyes. "I dare you to try the fried okra."

"I don't even know what that is," Easton said.

"Then try it. You might like it."

"Okay, Mom."

JC plopped down into a chair and began spooning large quantities from each dish onto his plate. "No, worries, dude. More for me. I double dare you to try the okra."

"What are we, five? I'm a grown-up. I decide what I eat."

Meemaw, who had been observing the exchange, snorted. "Well, you don't sound like a grown-up."

Easton scrunched his face. "Fine." He held up one of the deep-fried spheres. "I will try it." They all watched him chew and swallow. "There. Done. What is it, anyway?"

Meemaw's mouth turned up at the corners. "It's a

seedpod fried in cornmeal."

Easton's fought his gagging reflex as his stomach heaved. *Hold it down, or you will never live this down.*

"You okay, bro?" JC teased.

Easton gulped. "I'll live." He filled his plate with fried chicken and sweet potato casserole. "I just prefer to stick to the normal food."

JC and Damon exchanged a glance, but Meemaw didn't try to hide her laughter. She let out a chuckle so deep tears formed in her eyes. She patted Easton on his shoulder. "Bless your heart, dear."

"Dude, she told you." JC smirked after Meemaw left.

Easton kept his eyes on her as she sliced cake. He shrugged. "If I ever get married, I'm planning my own menu."

Meemaw returned with three plates of cake. "Whiskey pecan cake. Might be more to your liking."

Whiskey. His appetite left him as his mind flooded with images of Kat and her new coping mechanism.

JC turned to Damon. "Guaranteed he and Kat will have the blandest wedding meal in the history of wedding meals. I can see it now, beer-battered fish and chips, coleslaw, clam chowder, and mac-n-cheese. No veggies, no greens, no spices. White cake with vanilla frosting." He and Damon chuckled.

Easton sighed. "Well, you don't have to worry about that anytime soon. Maybe someday."

"You and Kat getting married, or a bland menu?" Damon asked.

Easton let out a long breath through his nose. He'd lost his appetite. "Both." He stood up, holding his plate. "I'll take the rest to go."

He left the cake and strode to the side counter where the to-go containers were stacked. Behind him, he heard JC tell Damon he'd fill him in later. *Whatever.* He'd been in a great mood until his brother reminded him of the worst day of his life.

Chapter 12

In the employee-lounge bathroom, Kat donned dark fitted jeans and a sparkly ivory, teal, and navy plaid western shirt. She left the top two snaps open, folded back the cuffs to reveal the calico contrast fabric, and tucked it in. She slipped into her favorite boots and clipped a turquoise pendant around her neck. Ms. Vivi had given her the pendant after she won her first jumping competition. The oval stone was set in sterling silver, with a silver rose and leaves at the top. *Head to toe, accessories, hair.* She exited the stall and plugged in her curling iron next to the sink. She stared at herself in the mirror.

Kat was twenty-four, in the prime of her life. But she felt like she'd already lost her best years. She sectioned her hair and secured it with clips. Her eyes may betray her youth within their gloomy depths, her skin might have more freckles from the sun than ever before, but her hair was the one thing she had absolute control over. Styling it had not only helped her regain her fine motor skills, but it made her feel better, physically and emotionally. As she wrapped the sections around the styling wand, she spoke her affirmations.

"I feel refreshed and full of energy, ready to take on each and every day because I go to bed sleepy at ten p.m. I am so blessed to live in a historic beautiful home with my uncle, filled with beautiful treasures, surrounded by the sea and only a short drive from my beloved horse and a community of God-loving friends. I am full of energy, even more than I had as a teenager. My muscles are all toned up, and my brain is sharp. I am secure in my identity as a princess of the Most High King and I shine my light everywhere I go. I am an example of God's love and I lead people to accept Jesus in their hearts. I am blessed each and every day because I am abiding in God the Father with a continuous awareness of His presence, in conversation with Him throughout the day, everyday." Kat sighed. She'd been slipping lately. She needed to say these more often. She was forgetting who she was.

The door opened as she held the last section of hair around the iron. Molly slipped in and laid her hand on Kat's shoulder. "That was beautiful. I was listening outside the door and didn't want to interrupt you. Maybe you could help me write some new affirmations sometime? I don't even know what I want anymore, but I need to put some positive energy out there."

"Of course." Kat laid the curling iron down and unplugged it from the wall. *Makeup, purse, and outerwear.* She reached down to her tote bag on the floor and pulled out her makeup case. "Shelby helped me write them. She reminded me they should reflect my identity, who God made me to be within. Not just who or what I am now, but who I know I can be with God. You've got to believe them when you say them. That's where I'm struggling."

"I hear that." Molly sighed. "You trust God, but you have to do your part, too. He needs something to work with."

"Yeah." Kat opened the case and laid out each of the items. She arranged them in order of application. *Primer, foundation, concealer. Bronzer blush, brows. Shadow, eyeliner, mascara. Lip stain, lip liner, lipstick. Powder it in place.*

"You've got such a great system. I just pull stuff out of the bag and slather it on."

"I used to be able to do that before the accident. Afterward, I'd forget stuff, and the result would be scary. After one particular incident where Auntie Katie asked if I was going to a clown party, she helped me memorize this order. Now it's just a habit." She closed an eye and blended gold and rose shades of eyeshadow on her lid. "I've got it down to about five minutes." She blinked as she wiggled the mascara wand, taking care to coat each lash.

"You amaze me every day, sweet friend."

Molly's words touched Kat. She finished her makeup and put all her stuff back in her tote bag. *Makeup, purse, outerwear.* "Dang, I left my hat in the barn."

"I'll text Easton to bring it. Want me to drop your tote bag in the office? I'm heading there next."

"Sure, thanks. One sec." Kat rummaged in the bag and pulled out her flask. She poured the contents into her mouth, relishing the burn of the liquid as it ran down her throat and settled in her stomach. "Okay."

Molly tilted her head and furrowed her brows disapprovingly. "Did you just chug four ounces of whiskey? Before work?"

"I did. It helps calm me in that crowd." Kat avoided Molly's widened eyes. "It won't be a problem."

"I hope not." Molly slung Kat's tote over her shoulder. "I'll see you in the dining room."

Kat sighed after the door closed behind her friend. She turned back to the mirror. "I feel refreshed and ready to take on each and every day . . ."

Easton had taken great care in dressing for Country Night. He wore a new shirt, old jeans, and the black hat Kat had once told him gave him Tim McGraw sex appeal. That didn't mean anything to him, but if it turned her head, he'd wear it. The lightweight red-and-black plaid flannel shirt his mom had given him for Christmas was a perfect fit, and he rolled the sleeves up over his biceps. It was a cool seventy degrees, but he was warm with the anticipation and anxiety that preluded social events.

He retrieved Kat's ivory cowgirl hat from the tack room and caressed the felt. He smiled, remembering the day she'd decided to add a hat band for the turquoise and silver cross Shelby had given her for it. She'd just been cleared by her doctors to ride and the gift was a reminder that God was with her when she got back on her horse. He twirled the hat on his finger and caught it with his other hand. Whistling, he left the barn and made his way to the kitchen door at the back of the resort.

The employees working the event were gathered around the table, listening to instructions from his parents. Kat stood next to Molly, her back to him. Her chestnut waves cascaded down her back, a shiny brown waterfall over the plaid of her shirt. He wanted to touch it, wrap his hands in it. Hold her in his arms.

He bowed his head as his dad said a prayer to bless the event. His father was a man of great faith and a model example of how to spiritually lead a family. After his military service, he'd fallen in love with Easton's mother as they'd both mourned the loss of her first husband, Molly's biological father. God showed up for both of them, blessing them with each other, healthy children, and most recently, a career as resort owners when his parents retired.

The prayer ended. Easton walked up behind Kat and placed her hat on her head. She turned around and rewarded him with a smile that lit up her whole face. The ivory hat contrasted with her dark hair and made him want to touch it even more. Instead, he did the next best thing and reached for her hands.

"Hey," she greeted him.

"Hey." Her eyes pulled him in like magic. There was a mischievous glint in them tonight. Almost as if . . .

He leaned down and breathed her in. His heart sank as the scent of whiskey wafted up. He squeezed her hand. "Why?"

"Why what?" she asked cheerfully, squeezing his hand back. She stood on her toes and planted a kiss on his lips. "I have to get to work. You look so handsome with that hat on. Are you staying, then?"

"I was planning on it. But now I'm not so sure."

Kat's smile fell and she let go of his hand. Confusion clouded her eyes. "Why?"

Easton's eye narrowed to slits. "You shouldn't be drinking at work. How much have you had?"

"I'm not drinking at work. I had a drink before I started. It calms my nerves."

"It's not right, Kat. I'm beginning to think you've got a problem."

"I do have a problem," she seethed through her teeth. The pain behind her anger sliced right through him. She glanced left and right and lowered her voice. "But it's not what you think. I have to make adjustments every day just to get through the day like everyone else. You know this. You spent thousands of hours with me while I tried to figure out how to get my life back. I've had to relearn *myself.* I spent almost eighteen years doing everything I could to be the *me* I wanted to be, and then that girl was gone in a second. She'll never truly be back because she can't come back exactly the way she was. If you're waiting for that girl to appear one day, she won't. She's gone, and I'm here. And I found what works, what helps get me through times and events I once breezed through. As long as it's not a danger to me or anyone else, it's not a problem."

Easton stepped back. *Had* he been waiting for the old Kat to appear? Had he busied himself all these years helping her because he mourned the old her? No, he loved the old her *and* the new her. He just didn't like this whiskey-drinking selfish version she'd been presenting since she'd come back.

"I know a part of her never left you." He tapped his heart. "This part is there, and it's still hurting. I want to take that pain from you, Kat. The whiskey can't do that. Let me."

She exhaled loudly and shook her head. "It's not your problem anymore. You can't fix everything." Her lower jaw trembled, and her eyes pooled. "You can't fix me, or the overstimulation I get at events like this, especially when I'm working and need to think. You tried." Her chest heaved.

"I think you need some—"

"Yes, I do need some water," she spat. "Please tell Molly I'll be out to help her as soon as I can." She pushed past him and out the door he'd entered only a few minutes before. He stared at it and wondered if he should follow her.

"Hey." Easton jumped as JC appeared beside him. "Let me go talk to her?"

"I don't see what good it would do." Easton sighed.

JC shrugged and folded his arms. "She might tell me something she couldn't tell you."

"She can tell me anything."

JC raised a brow. "Can she?"

Easton inhaled and puffed up his cheeks. He let his breath out slowly. "Fine."

His brother nodded and disappeared out the door.

Easton joined Molly in the dining room and helped her seat the guests. The first hour of the event was the buffet dinner, followed by dancing and karaoke. Several of the regulars had already arrived and claimed their favorite tables.

From the buffet, a couple he'd known most of his life waved at him. Sadie and Steve Donovan were friends of his parents and owned the local diner.

"Easton!" Sadie called to him. "Great to see you here! Are you staying?"

"Good to see you both, too. I'll be in and out I think. Has Will left for Quantico?"

"Yes and no. He's on vacation with his girlfriend, then he'll head down there." Sadie scooped mac-n-cheese onto her plate and Steve's.

Steve radiated pride for his son as he held his plate out. "He's going to make a great agent, just like his mother." He beamed at his wife.

"Oh, stop it," Sadie hushed him. "He's working

hard and we're proud of him."

"Great to hear. How's the diner?"

"Just perfect. I convinced Shelby to work for us over the summer while she gets started with her freelance business." Sadie's eyes darted around the room. "Is Kat working tonight?"

"She is."

"Wonderful." Sadie took a plate from the stack at the end of the buffet and nodded at the silver chafing dishes. "I see you've changed up the menu a bit. No barbecue tonight?"

"We have a guest chef from Savannah. She's serving up what she calls her Boardinghouse Dinner tonight." Easton winced. "Complete with hot wilted leaves and cornmeal fried seedpods."

Sadie's face transformed from confusion to glee as she let out a loud snort. "Dear, dear boy. Do you mean greens and okra?"

"So they say." Easton spotted JC and Kat enter the dining room, carrying trays of water glasses, which they began setting down on the occupied tables. "Enjoy the mystery food. I'm going to help."

He said goodbye and trotted up to JC just as he was about to disappear back into the kitchen. "So?"

JC glanced around and gestured for Easton to follow him into the walk-in refrigerator. "I followed her to the barn. She's been hiding whiskey in the tack room. I convinced her not to drink any more than what she'd already had this time, but I'm really concerned. She's had enough already to loosen her tongue, but she seems to be in control physically. High-functioning." He rested his hands on his hips. "She told me she's afraid you love the idea of her, and not actually her. That you see yourself as her protector, but not as a partner. She loves you, but she's got some serious concerns, bro."

Easton reached up to grab the bottom of the top shelf. He buried his face in the crook of his elbow. "I don't know how to help her anymore."

JC placed a hand on his back. "Why not?"

Easton recalled the weeks and months after her accident. "I don't have instructions. There are no doctor's orders to follow, no checklists to complete, no games to play to help retrain her brain." He turned to his brother. "Her impulsivity makes no sense to me. I don't know how to fix her recklessness, the wanderlust that drove her away, the anger and fear that makes her drink whiskey. I don't know if she would have even come back if there hadn't been problems on the tour, and I don't know how to convince her that I love her for her."

"Did you just hear yourself? *Talk* to her. All she needs from you is love. You need to figure out and solve problems as you go, *with* her not *for* her. Most problems don't have fix-it checklists. Real life doesn't come with instructions. You've got each other, and you've got a mighty God who wants you to live a life of joy. You're forgetting the most important thing."

"What's that?"

JC grinned. "That you're not in control here."

Chapter 13

"Kat?"

She ignored Shelby's question and held her breath in an attempt to relieve the violent pounding in her temples. She was lying face down and clutching the pillow over her head didn't help. Still, she gripped it as if it were a lifeline. She'd forgotten to take her meds again last night.

Shelby sat on the bed. "Kat. I'm taking you to church. Let me help you get ready."

Kat groaned. She was in no shape to go to church, and she certainly did not want to hear what Pastor Porter had to say today.

"Don't you already have to be there?" Kat grumbled.

"I'm not serving today. I'll even sit with you in the back if you want. But you need to go."

"No, I don't."

"Yes, you do. JC texted me last night and told me I needed to get you there."

Kat bolted upright. "What else did he tell you?" she

asked, grabbing her head. Her heart beat double time. She didn't want Shelby to know she was sneaking whiskey.

Shelby drew back in surprise. "Nothing else. But if he cares enough to text me to get you there, you need to go."

"Ugh," Kat groaned and turned over, again covering her head with the pillow. "I'll watch the Facebook Live." The small church had begun streaming the sermons for the residents of The Roosevelt, families traveling on summer vacation, and others who couldn't make it to the service.

"You're coming with me."

"Just go, please."

"No."

Kat's head throbbed even harder when Shelby stood up, the mattress springing back to its original position. Shelby yanked the comforter off her and took her pillow. Her words were firm, but kind. "Come on. You'll feel better after some meds and a shower."

Kat pulled herself up to a sitting position. "I forgot to take my anti-seizure pill last night."

"Well then, you're lucky you've just got a headache. Come on, Kat. It's been two years. You risk losing your license, or more, every time you forget. I thought you set your phone alarm for that?" Shelby positioned herself behind Kat and began to knead her shoulders.

Kat closed her eyes and tried to release the tension.

"You are the *best* friend ever." She paused. "I forgot what you just asked me."

Shelby repeated her question. "I thought you set your phone alarm to go off when you need to take your medication?"

"I do. But I forgot to pack them and when I got home I went straight to bed."

"Hmm. Do you have an old bottle hanging around so you can keep some on you in case you're out?"

"Probably. That's a good idea." Kat pressed her index fingers into her temples.

"Go take a shower. Molly's making breakfast. I'll bring something up so you can eat while you get ready."

"Thanks," Kat whispered.

An hour later, the three friends entered the sanctuary. Kat was feeling better after Molly's juice cocktail of greens, fruits, and other antioxidants. The little white church had been built in the late 1800s. Its beautifully preserved pews and stained-glass windows offered a cozy respite from the rest of the world. After greeting Pastor Porter at the door, they found seats in the empty row behind the Crane family just as the worship music began.

Kat closed her eyes and let the music take over her soul. She held onto the back of the pew in front of her to keep her balance and sang along.

The pastor stepped up to the podium. "Good morning friends, family." He smiled down at Jane and little Noah in the front row and waved to Shelby. She waved back, her face reddening slightly. Kat smiled. Her friend's dad was a sweet guy and had been a surrogate father of sorts for much of her teen years. After Shelby's mom died, Kat spent many of the weekends she hadn't traveled with the Cranes at the Porter house. "Take a moment to greet those around you and offer them peace."

Kat was directly behind Carol Crane, who turned around and reached over, pulling her in for a hug. "Precious girl," she whispered in Kat's ear. "Peace be with you."

"Ahem," Molly teased. "Am I invisible, Mom?"

Carol grinned. "She was closer." *And so begins Church Musical Pews.* Kat leaned back and switched places with Molly so Molly could hug her mother. She turned to her right to shake hands with Joe Crane and stretched to give Ms. Vivi a hug, then JC. He switched places with Easton, who didn't say a word but took both her hands and placed a kiss on her forehead.

Kat switched places again with Molly and turned to her left. Beside her, Shelby was in conversation with Meemaw and Damon. His right hand held hers in a shake, and he'd brought his left hand up to hold the backside of her hand. *Interesting.* When they turned to face forward, Kat bumped Shelby gently with her elbow and raised a brow. Shelby shrugged and her face grew red again.

"Living on the coast of this beautiful state," the pastor began, "we are all familiar with fishing. We need a hook, or a net, or a cage of some sort. We need a line to connect us to our catch. And we need bait.

"What kind of bait gets the attention of the preyed upon? The bait that is attractive to the victim will catch its attention. The prey sees the bait and goes for it. It doesn't realize that hiding underneath is the hook. The hook is harmless until the fish bites the bait, then it pierces and takes hold.

"Satan knows how to bait each and every one of us. His bait is flashy, it catches our attention. It gets in our faces. But beware—when you take a bite on his line, you connect to his will."

Kat felt he was speaking directly to her. She reached for a strand of hair to twirl as she considered how she'd developed a pattern for letting herself get baited.

"Fear connects us to the will of Satan. It paralyzes us, makes us selfish. It pushes away love. Only fear or faith can reside in your heart, they can't cohabitate. You are either plugging into Satan or into God. Every decision, every feeling, every word you speak, every action you take is either toward or away from God.

"First Peter chapter five, verse eight reminds us to be alert and of sober mind." Kat sucked in a breath. Her cheeks flamed.

Molly's hand grabbed hers and squeezed. Shelby's dad had an uncanny way of speaking straight to Kat every time she needed it most.

Pastor Porter continued, "Your enemy prowls around like a roaring lion looking for someone to devour." He lifted his head up from his bible. "He will find you at your weakest, most vulnerable moments and dangle temptation or cause destruction. He makes you believe there is no hope, and you believe your line to God thins and unravels.

"The enemy pulls every stunt to disconnect you from your purpose. He wants to keep you from it and destroy your belief in God's unconditional love. He wants to break your line to God.

"There is nothing more dangerous than a person who has no love in his heart. Love is the ultimate Godly quality. Jesus pulls us in with his love. Feel it. Accept the love of the Fisher of Men. He's there to pull you out of the dark waters and bring you back to the light."

Kat didn't hear the announcements that followed. She wanted to hold onto every word, to remember this message. She could feel its importance. God was speaking to her through Pastor Porter.

She whispered to Shelby when the music started, "Do you think you could get his sermon notes for me?"

"Of course."

Kat relaxed her shoulders as she sang about being an overcomer. She *was* an overcomer. She'd survived a horrific fall off a horse. She'd recovered remarkably from a brain injury. She was still hurting from things she didn't want to think about and she would overcome them, too.

The service ended. "Go on with the Cranes to brunch," Shelby said. "I'm going to close up with Dad and then we'll be over. It looks like Noah is feeling better. I'm hoping they'll come, too."

"Okay."

Kat's headache had given up its residence and the service had lifted some heavy weights from her shoulders. She needed to think about her whiskey intake and deal with her demons instead of allowing them to harm her.

Molly led her to Easton's truck. JC held the door open for her as she climbed into the passenger seat. She tried to keep up with Molly's conversation on the short ride to the resort, but her mind wandered. She was looking forward to brunch. She hadn't attended an after-church brunch at the resort since last December. Easton was probably thinking similar thoughts. He hadn't said a word all morning.

Easton parked his truck at his cabin and the foursome walked the rest of the way to the dining room. Frieda greeted them and led them to the center of the room, where several tables had been pushed together, as was their Sunday tradition.

Kat hung back while the Cranes chose their seats. Meemaw and Damon filled in the rest of the far side, leaving her no choice but to sit next to Easton. The end of the table was saved for Shelby and her family, who arrived just as Freida returned to take their orders. She was glad to see Noah cheerful and Jane without bags under her eyes. She felt for them.

Kat ordered a mimosa and the Breakfast Sampler, a platter that consisted of one of each of her favorite things. A pancake, an egg, a slice of bacon, a link of sausage, home fries, a French crepe oozing with berries and cream cheese, and a slice of toast. She'd missed this and hoped she could finish it all off. She'd lost weight over the last five months and hadn't eaten this much in a single sitting since, well, last December.

All right, Kat, she coached herself. *Get a grip, ignore the baiting thoughts, and be pleasant. Enjoy yourself.*

Easton leaned toward her. His shoulder pressed against hers and the breath from his whisper caused goosebumps to form from her ear to her shoulder. "Guard your bacon."

A thrilling wave of joy ran through Kat. He noticed. "Guard your sausage." She giggled and he smiled back. It was a game they'd played for as long as she could remember. He'd steal her bacon, and she'd steal his sausage. She liked bacon, but not as much as he did. She'd been surprised the first time he playfully stole bacon off her plate. They were at a roadside breakfast buffet with Ms. Vivi. Kat had taken the last two slices of bacon, and when she wasn't looking, he stole them off her plate. She retaliated by swiping his sausage. She realized many years later it had been an attempt to flirt with her.

When she looked back, she realized she'd missed so many signs when they were younger that he had wanted to be more than friends.

The food arrived, and her bacon disappeared from her plate before Pastor Porter could bless the meal. She shook her head at Easton. "Before the prayer? You've really upped your game."

He winked. "I've been training all these months, waiting to make my move."

She smirked and stabbed his sausage link. "Still lost your sausage."

Easton put his fork down and reached for her hand under the table. He leaned into her ear again. "I lost my heart, too. And I'm so glad she's back."

Kat squeezed his hand and melted into her chair.

Easton and JC had offered to drive Meemaw and Damon to the airport after brunch. While they loaded Meemaw's extensive luggage collection into the resort van, she gave instructions.

"Now, I'll be back week after next. Molly, Kat." Meemaw looked at each of them in turn. "The menu is set. I'd advise you all to serve the new items a few more times in the next couple weeks to give your cooks practice with getting it just right. You two are doing a fine job planning this wedding and I am confident that it's going to be perfect."

"Yes, ma'am," Molly assured her as she hugged her goodbye. "We've got this."

"Of course you do. I have full faith in both of you." She turned to Kat and nodded her head toward the van. "See if you can get that young man of yours to expand his palate. I don't know how the poor thing survives on such a limited diet, bless his heart." Everyone within earshot of Meemaw's assessment laughed.

"Yes, ma'am," Kat replied. Easton had to give Meemaw credit. She was persistent.

Behind the wheel, Easton listened to Meemaw's stories during the hour-long ride to the airport but didn't comment or participate in the conversation.

On the ride home, JC called him on it. "Well, I think you get the Mr. Personality award for today." The sarcastic tone of his voice riled Easton. "Would it have hurt to contribute to the conversation?"

Easton shrugged. "You were doing just fine for both of us."

"Bro, you need to lighten up. I know you don't like to talk to people, but you miss out on so much when you close yourself off."

Easton sighed. He just didn't feel up to the conversation when all he could think about was where he stood with Kat. They rode the rest of the way home in silence.

He parked his truck at their cabin and went straight to the barn to check on Mocha. Kat's horse had been healing well and Doc Hill was confident she'd make a full recovery after a few months of stall rest and rehab. For Mocha, that meant no riders or saddles until she was healed. Unless Kat found another horse to ride, she was done barrel racing until Mocha recovered. He thought that would cheer him, but it made him sad. She lived for riding and competing had motivated her to push her limits.

Easton's eyes narrowed to slits as he approached the barn. Kevin's truck was backed in next to Kat's SUV. Kevin leaned casually against his truck as he chatted with Kat. She was animated, and whatever they talked about held her interest.

She spotted him and waved. Easton waved back but didn't stop. He went straight inside and to the fridge. He took out the bag of baby carrots and walked to Mocha's stall.

"Hey there, girl." He unlatched the door and went inside. "Brought you a treat." He stroked her muzzle and then brandished a handful of carrots. She munched on them like it was her last meal, snorting and nickering happily.

The barn door opened. "Crane?"

"Here."

Kevin appeared at the entrance to the stall and crossed his arms. "I unloaded all the lumber for the repairs. We'll start early tomorrow. You might want to move the horses at the other end of the barn."

"We have a plan for that. They'll be out in the paddock before you get here. Anything else?"

Kevin opened his mouth and then slowly shook his head. "I guess that's it."

Easton nodded. He turned to walk away.

"Crane?"

"Yeah?" Easton swiveled his head around.

"Can we be civil? Kat's made it clear she loves you. I respect that. I'm not going to try to steal your girl."

Kevin walked off before Easton could reply. He blew out a breath. A week with this guy in his space.

The week passed in a blur. Old Man Wetherby had been transported from the hospital to the assisted living wing of The Roosevelt for rehabilitation. After he was settled, Easton took Kat for a walk along the rocky stretch below her home. The wind billowed her long hair around her slightly sunburned face. Her silky mauve halter top barely reached the waist of her jeans, its lattice trim exposing her skin just enough for the mental image to replay in Easton's mind even days later, distracting him while he worked. He'd held her hand as they climbed from boulder to boulder, following a path they made up as they went, speaking little with their voices and much with their hearts. Their souls connected, and after a few moments, they chose to sit on a particular one, a place where they'd spent many hours in their past, watching the waves and sharing kisses.

Mocha had made great improvements, and between his work at the barn, avoiding Kevin and his crew, rides out to the lighthouse, and keeping Kat from self-destructing, it was Saturday before he knew it. To his knowledge, Kat hadn't imbibed all week. If she had, she'd hidden it well, and he didn't want to think about it.

Easton had just said goodbye to Doc Hill when Kat

pulled up in her SUV. She was dressed for the morning's riding lessons. Dark blue breeches hugged her slim hips. Her fitted V-neck T-shirt led Easton's mind from the Doc's report to places it shouldn't go at eight a.m. on a Saturday. Her favorite old western boots kicked up the dirt as she skipped over to him. Her eyes sparkled in the sunlight and her mouth turned up at the corners when she saw his gaze taking her in.

He held his arm out to the side, a silent invitation to a hug. She hugged him tightly and took a step back.

"It's 80's Night!"

Easton pursed his lips and tilted his head. "Mmmhmm." He had a feeling he knew where this was going.

"Aw, c'mon, Easton. I checked the main schedule. We both have the night off." She reached up to brush a runaway strand of hay off his shoulder. "We've worked our tails off this week. Go with me?"

He read the hope in her face and sighed. He would go, but he was going to make her work for the yes. He crossed his arms and leaned against the barn, "I don't have anything to wear."

"Sure you do. Find something."

"Hmm . . ." He stroked his jaw and pretended to think. "I think I have just the thing."

"Great!"

Easton turned and smiled. Her footsteps kept up with his as he made his way into the barn and rummaged through the pile of blankets in the tack room. He turned and held up the fringed Mexican blanket. "I can cut a hole in this and voila!" He draped it over his shoulders.

Kat wrinkled her forehead and squinted eyes, just the result he was aiming for. "How is that an eighties costume?"

"I can be Clint Eastwood."

"Say what? In the eighties?"

"Don't you remember *Back to the Future?*"

"Vaguely."

"I can be Marty McFly pretending to be Clint Eastwood."

Kat rolled her eyes. "Ugh." She took the blanket, folded it, and returned it to the pile. "Try again."

"Ye of little humor. What are you wearing?"

"Weeeell, I had an idea."

"Of course you did." Easton placed his hands on his hips and braced himself for her revelation. She was practically bursting.

"Remember Halloween two years ago?"

He groaned. "No." *Yes. Every day. Every time I touch that gray button.* He slid his hand into his pocket and closed his fingers around the momento.

"No, you don't remember, or no, you don't like my idea?"

"Both."

"C'mon. Reprise your role as my favorite space cowboy."

"It's not really a costume party."

Kat crossed her arms and stepped into his personal

space. She arched an eyebrow.

"Really?" Easton sighed. "Fine. I'll dig out the vest. What time are you picking me up?"

Kat whooped and pulled his face to hers for a hasty kiss. "I'll be at your cabin at six forty-five."

Chapter 14

Kat was still riding a high as she twisted half her hair around the spongy mesh hair donut. The morning's riding lessons went well, she spent the entire afternoon with Uncle Charley at his new place, and now she was getting ready for her date with Easton. *A date.* She hadn't had one of those in years. Had they ever really even dated?

She frowned as she pinned the ends into the hairpiece. After weeks in the hospital, she'd been released to home rehab. Auntie Katie had paid top dollar for the best physical and occupational therapists to come to their house. Easton would pick her up in the afternoons and for a long time they'd just watch movies or sit outside and talk. At some point, she realized she was falling in love with him—that she *had* loved him for a long time.

When she was first cleared to get back on a horse, Easton had led Mocha from the barn to the meadow. She'd been like a little girl on her first pony ride. Kat closed her eyes as she remembered sliding off Mocha and into his arms. He stared into her eyes and held her for just a bit too long. They both teared up, and he helped her down gently onto the blanket he spread. He guided the horse to graze in the meadow before joining her on the blanket.

Easton swiped his hand across his eyes before turning to Kat. He smiled shyly, then swung his gaze to the trees across the field.

"Why are you crying?" Kat asked. "I'm supposed to be the emotional one."

He scooted closer until his shoulders touched hers. He mimicked her position, leaning back on his hands with his legs straight out in front of him. "When you fell off Callie, I was so scared that you might die. Then you pulled through, and I wondered if you'd ever ride again. You came alive when you rode, Kat. And now you've beaten the odds, and gotten back on your horse, as cliché as that sounds. I'm just so happy for you."

Kat leaned her head on his shoulder. "You're a big reason why I was able to do that. You kept me going every time I wanted to quit. You never lost faith in me."

Easton lifted his right arm and wrapped it around her. "I knew you would do it," he whispered and kissed the top of her head.

Kat lifted her chin, nudging his head away from hers so he'd have to look at her. She locked her eyes on his, but didn't say anything. Instead, she was overwhelmed with the desire to kiss the lips that had spoken the words that resonated in her heart. She stretched up and touched her lips to his.

An instant wave of energy consumed her and ignited a flame deep within. Her lips sizzled as if electrified.

Easton was equally affected, and being a man of action rather than words, he took her face in his hands and kissed her so deeply and thoroughly she wondered how heaven could be better. Kat didn't ever want to stop; it felt like their souls were connecting.

In the moment before her mind cleared itself of all thoughts, Kat wondered why it had taken him so long to reveal the passion he held for her.

In the days and weeks and months and years that followed, they had been inseparable, in love, and in a constant state of joy. She never doubted back then why he loved her. She just basked in the glow of it. When Auntie Katie died, Kat was overcome with a feeling of numbness she couldn't shake. She'd withdrawn from Easton and her friends. Fear gripped her, and she lost sight of who she was, where she was going, and who she wanted to be. She needed clarity, and racing Mocha was the only thing that made her feel alive.

Kat knew her brain injury caused her to be susceptible to depression, but she didn't want to claim it. She kept herself busy and distracted. If she didn't have time to think about the pain, it wasn't there.

She thought about her injured mare. She wouldn't be riding her for a long time, until Mocha's fetlock was completely healed. She wondered why she didn't feel angry about being sidelined. Instead, she was hopeful.

Kat finished up her hair and makeup and slipped the white gown over her head. She wrapped the gray belt around her waist and fastened the two remaining fabric buttons. She'd lost the third at the Cliff Walk's Halloween party two years ago and had forgotten to hunt for a replacement. She sucked in her stomach and twisted the belt so that the buttons were positioned at the base of her spine.

Her cell phone buzzed, knocking her out of her thoughts.

Aren't you ever going to text me back? Troy Boone didn't deserve a text back. *He has no power of me, God. I will not let him make me feel bad.* Feeling empowered by her sudden revelation, she blocked his number. Why hadn't she thought about doing that before? Kat set her shoulders back. That felt good.

"Knock, knock!" Molly called.

Kat grabbed her white go-go boots and exited her walk-in closet. "Almost ready. Awesome outfit!"

Molly had gone all out. Her naturally curly blonde hair was teased to its limits under a hot pink scarf she'd tied in a bow. Under a blazer of the same shade of electric pink, she wore a fitted silver dress over black leggings, hot pink leg warmers, and black flats. She finished the look with a wide black belt and fingerless fishnet gloves.

"Love your outfit! Madonna or Cyndi Lauper?" Kat teased.

"Ha! I was going for Rockstar Barbie!"

Shelby poked her head in the doorway. "Are we

ready?"

Kat nodded. "I'm so glad you're coming out tonight, Shel. Let me see what you're wearing."

"Yeah, yeah. The sooner we go, the sooner we can get home. I feel ridiculous." She stepped into the room, revealing a strapless zebra-print ruffled dress with neon green accents. Her almost-black hair was crimped and highlighted with bright green hair chalk. She rolled her eyes and adjusted a black lace glove. Kat and Molly laughed.

"C'mon, *you* feel ridiculous? Have you seen my blue eyeshadow?" Molly batted her lashes.

Shelby raised a brow as she studied Molly's makeup. "Point taken. At least this old prom dress reject is classy."

Kat snorted. "Shel, you spent six years in Boston. You could never *not* look classy." She picked up her phone. "Selfie time!"

After several more ridiculous selfies, they set off for the resort. Shelby dropped Kat off at Easton's cabin.

Kat hesitated for a second, then knocked on the door.

It swung open to reveal JC in a cheetah-print vest, khakis, and shiny white oxfords. He held a faux black-and-white color-block jacket in one hand. She groaned. "Ferris Bueller, again? Don't you have anything else?"

"Princess Leia and Han Solo again? Don't you have anything else?"

"Fair enough. At least Easton and I won't be the

only ones cosplaying."

"Nope. Lots of locals coming tonight. It'll be a blast to people watch. I told Mom we should have prizes for the outfits." He grinned. "I'll see you over there."

Kat stepped into the cabin and closed the door behind her. She sat on the microfiber couch and thought about all the hours she and Easton had spent on it watching *Star Wars* movies. That was a simpler time, a time when she'd only had one focus—to get better. There had been no stress, no drama, no emotional pain.

Easton bounded down the stairs and bowed. "Your Worshipfulness."

Kat giggled and rose from her seat. "You ready to go, Space Cowboy?"

"Not yet. Let me look at you."

Kat felt a thrill as they drank each other in. He was every inch her fantasy Han Solo in his dark jeans, black boots, and utility vest. Underneath he wore a long-sleeved ivory shirt unbuttoned to his breastbone.

They walked hand-in-hand to the main lodge. In the dining room, all ages of guests and locals mingled and danced to the songs of the era.

"Oh my goodness," Kat hissed. "Easton, look at your mom!"

Easton's head swung to the podium where his mom, Grandma Vivi, Frieda, and Sadie crowded around the microphone, dressed as the Golden Girls. His mom, the tallest of the four, had pinned her long gray hair up in barrel curls to resemble Dorothy Zbornak. When the music stopped, she welcomed the guests.

"We just want to thank you all for being our friends, get it?" Laughter sounded from the crowd. "From our resort guests to our business partners, patrons, and community members, you all bless us so much, and tonight"—she paused for dramatic effect—"we have a special announcement!"

Sadie, dressed as a flashy Blanche Devereaux, took the microphone. "We've got a raffle going on with some prizes you are going to want. From a chef's table here with Frieda"—she gestured to the resort manager, decked out to look like Rose Nylund, complete with a white wig and long green button-down satin dress tied with a sash—"to gift cards for your favorite diner, and . . ." She handed the microphone to Ms. Vivi, who adjusted her knit shawl and squinted behind thick, yellow-tinted glasses, playing up the roll of Sophia Petrillo to the hilt.

"And for our special announcement," she spoke quickly with a sarcastic tone, "we'll be giving away a night for two in the resort's newest guest suite, which my grandson has been working on for months"—she winked at Easton—"inside Crane's Light!"

Kat gasped and squeezed Easton's hand. "You didn't tell me you finished it! Wow!"

Easton opened his mouth to reply but stopped when his mother got back on the mic. "Good luck, friends! Have a wonderful time tonight!"

Easton led Kat to a table for two by the window that overlooked the cliff. It provided a distant view of the setting sun behind his lighthouse. "It's not quite finished. I need to bring out a pair of deck chairs, and it'll still need some housekeeping touches the day before Matt and Lanie stay there."

"Still, that's amazing." She stared at it through the window. "I can't wait to see it."

"Wanna go tonight?"

The words left Easton's mouth before he finished his thought. It was a brilliant idea, if not well thought out. He'd just walked into the party and was already overwhelmed by the stimuli of the blinding colors and synthesized music.

Kat's eyebrows lifted in surprise. "Tonight?"

He shrugged. "Why not?"

"Like, when tonight? After the party?"

"Whenever you want to go."

He watched her bite her lip as she thought it over. "Maybe. But I want to dance with you first."

"Are you giving me an order? 'Cause I only—"

"We know, we know," JC said, clapping him on the back, "you only take orders from yourself."

"Exactly."

Molly and Shelby were right behind him. Molly spoke to JC. "Is this where I ask what the odds of my little big bro dancing are?"

Shelby snorted. "You guys are so weird." She grabbed Kat's hand. "C'mon. You made me come to this thing. Get your royal bottom on the dance floor."

"Yes, ma'am!"

Easton joined her on the dance floor when the music slowed. He held her to him and closed his eyes, getting lost in the sounds of Chicago and the scent of roses from her perfume.

A drop of water trickled from his clavicle down his shirt. What the—

Kat shook in his arms.

"Are you okay?" he asked.

She wrapped her arms around his neck and whispered into his ear. "I'm so sorry, Easton. I don't know what I was thinking to break up with you. I—"

"Kat, it's okay," he soothed. "We don't have to talk about this now." He stroked the top of her head. "Do you need some water?"

"No, I need to say this. I'm so sorry. I can't stop these tears anymore than I can pretend I ever stopped loving you."

His hands slid down her back to her waist. He hugged her close. The song transitioned to another ballad. "Someone here must be a big Peter Cetera fan," Easton mumbled.

Kat made an attempt to giggle but he wasn't buying it. "I never saw this movie, but I love this song. It's how it's supposed to be."

"What movie?"

"*Chances Are.* Listen." She was quiet, then recapped the message of the song. "This song reminds me that love changes as we grow and that if it's real it will never truly disappear. Even when one person goes away for a while." She looked up and slid her hands to his cheeks, pulling his forehead to hers. "I don't ever want to go away again."

His heart swelled and a wave of emotion coursed through ever muscle in his body. "It was my fault too, Kat. I don't want you to ever go away again, either." He hugged her to his chest and whispered, "You ready to get out of here?"

"Yeah."

An hour later, the resort's twenty-foot Cobia glided through the moonlit water. Easton positioned it at the bottom of the lighthouse's ladder and tossed the rope up to the platform.

"Give me a second," he told Kat as he climbed out of the boat and up the ladder to the lower deck. He wrapped the rope around the cleat to secure it. "All set."

Kat stood up in the boat and gathered the lower end of her dress to one side. "Don't get excited. I'm wearing shorts," she joked. She tossed the gathered material over one shoulder, exposing white thigh-length biker shorts.

"Impressive."

"Thanks."

"After you." Easton gestured to the three iron rungs built into the next level. Kat climbed up and waited for him at the door. He punched in the code and opened it. "Allow me to show you around. I'll get the lights as we go up."

"This is incredible."

Kat stepped in as Easton narrated. "The first level has been transformed from a utility room to a simple kitchen. There's a tiny half bath through that accordion door." The simple kitchen boasted a small refrigerator, a microwave, a camp stove, a Keurig, a gas oven, and a cooktop stove. "The cabinet under the sink holds the dishes and cookware."

Kat nodded and peeked into the bathroom. "There's no shower?"

"Nope, just the basics. We're giving guests a two-night maximum, and they get a discount if they book a room at the lodge following their stay as guest keepers."

"I could totally not bathe for a couple days here," Kat said. "Next level?"

"The living area. I'll follow you."

Easton had spent some time gathering nautical items, photos, and books to display in the built-in shelves. Two Barcaloungers sat facing a window that offered a view of the cove. Above the beach, the lights of the town shone across the inlet.

"So cozy. You did a great job." Kat touched the gilded frame that displayed a portrait of a long-ago ship captain. "I could sit here all day curled up with a good book."

"That's the idea. Ready for the next level?"

He climbed the stairs behind her. A plush loveseat sat underneath a painting of an eighteenth-century whaling ship. A model of a schooner sat perched atop a side table. Across from the couch was a flat screen TV with a built-in DVD player. A collection of movies lined a shelf underneath.

"I love it. The absence of windows makes it the perfect spot to watch TV or a movie," Kat said.

"Right. There's no cable or Wi-Fi, but the signal can pick up the local stations."

"No Wi-Fi? How will your guests survive?" she teased.

"Hopefully, they'll find other ways to occupy themselves."

Kat blushed at his comment, confirming where her mind had gone.

"And speaking of"—he gestured to the stairs—"the next level is the bedroom."

Kat ascended the staircase and paused at the threshold to the room. "Wow—this is the perfect spot for a secluded honeymoon."

She was quiet. Easton stepped up close behind her and cupped his hands over her shoulders. He wondered if she was thinking what he was thinking. That they could have been the first to stay here, had she not broken off their engagement.

"That's the idea." A bed and a nightstand were all that fit in this space. The room was windowless with an open staircase to the top level.

"It should have been us," Kat whispered. She rubbed at her temples. "I am so very sorry, Easton."

"Hey." He turned her around. "It's all right."

"It's not all right. I wasted a year of our lives,

maybe longer. That stupid tour. I regret every minute of it. It took me from you. From home. What was I thinking?" Kat's voice was harsh and her eyes flashed with anger. She turned away from him and took a long breath. "After already wasting years recovering, years before that not picking up on your cues that you wanted to be more than friends. What you must think of me . . ." She squeezed by him and hurried up to the top level.

Easton followed her. The new state-of-the-art LED light lit up the night outside the 360-degree windows. Kat pressed her face to the glass.

"Are you all right?"

"I'm a little nauseous."

"The lighthouse doesn't really float, Kat. Its base is built into the bottom of the cove."

She pinched the skin between her eyebrows. "Then why is my head spinning?"

Now it was Easton's stomach that dropped. "Your meds."

"Oh no."

He caught her before she fell.

Chapter 15

Kat slumped in Easton's arms. She was so dizzy. Her head throbbed everywhere. He guided her down the stairs to the bedroom level. "Lay down till it passes, then I'll get you home."

She curled up on the bed and pressed her eyes shut. Easton returned a couple of minutes later with an ice pack, extra-strength Tylenol, and a bottle of water. "I can't drink that yet. Can you open the pills for me, please?"

"Okay. You want me to stay here or go below?"

"Here, please," she whispered. She swallowed the pills and closed her eyes.

Easton lowered himself carefully onto the bed. She fidgeted, trying to get comfortable. With a sponge donut on each side of her head, she had two options: on her back or face-first into the pillow and on top of the ice pack.

"Kat, is it a migraine or an ictal?"

It felt like a migraine. She prayed it wasn't an ictal headache, which was a precursor to a seizure. She'd often gotten the two confused in the early years after her injury.

"I don't know." She opted for face-first and pressed her forehead to the bottom of the pillow so that her nose was off it and she could breathe. She pulled another pillow on top of her head to stabilize it.

Kat didn't move as Easton reached under the top pillow. It took her a moment to realize he was freeing her hair from the pins. He unwound it from the donut and removed the hairband that secured it. He slid the mesh donut down the ponytail, then gently removed the hairband at the top. A moment later, he sat on the other side of the bed and dismantled her other bun.

She shifted, pulling her knees up to her chest and turning her head slightly to the left. She pushed the top pillow and ice pack away. Most of the pain was concentrated to her right temple, and she pressed her thumb into the pulsating muscle.

Easton began to massage her shoulders. As the tension released, the nausea subsided. She needed to hydrate. "Water, please."

He rolled off the bed and appeared at her other side a moment later with a bottle he'd placed on the nightstand. "Can you sit up?"

She wasn't sure. She raised her head and leaned on her left elbow. "Whoa," she breathed as the room began to spin again. "This is the best I can do right now."

He twisted the top off and handed her the bottle. She was able to get a few ounces down and then sank back down into the bed. She peered up at Easton. She didn't like the way he was staring at her. "What?"

He sighed. "I don't want to ask, but I need to know. Did you have any whiskey or anything else tonight that could have caused this?"

"No," she stated firmly. "I didn't drink anything. Not this whole week. I didn't need to . . . This is what happens when I'm overstimulated, or stressed, and when I forget my nighttime meds—whether I drink or not. You know this. It's worse when I haven't had enough water throughout the day." She opened her eyes. "Please don't look at me like that."

His face relaxed. "Okay." Easton went around the bed. He laid down on his side and wrapped his right arm around her. "I'm going to set my phone alarm for one hour. Try to sleep."

Blinded by pain, Kat allowed her brain to succumb into nothingness. She drifted into a dreamless sleep.

She felt the vibrations of his phone at her hip before she heard him speak. "Hey." His tone was low and gave her goosebumps. "Can you get up?"

Kat turned her head slowly and looked up at him. "Let's find out."

Easton helped her sit up. She placed her hands flat on the bed to brace herself as he moved into position in front of her. She took her time standing up, testing her balance. The nausea had disappeared and what was once angry throbbing was now a dull ache.

She stepped carefully toward the doorway. "You should go first."

Easton moved to the stairs. He descended backward, one step at a time, eyes on Kat. She leaned heavily against the railing, but made it all the way to the bottom.

"Are you ready to get into the boat? Can you handle the ladders?"

Kat nodded. Outside, the air was especially crisp for June. Stars lit up the sky and cast light on her target. There was no wind, no waves. She made it down the short ladder with ease, but froze at the side of the lower platform. She peered over the edge to the boat below.

"Let me go ahead of you." Easton turned and stepped down the ladder, stopping midway to the boat. "Come down when you're ready. I'll be right here."

Kat threw her dress over her shoulder and climbed down. She hesitated at the step from the last rung to the boat, where Easton was waiting. He hovered behind her and when both of her boots touched the ground he guided her to the seat.

He was always so good to her. Her eyes didn't leave him as he returned to the lighthouse's platform to untie the boat's rope before seating himself and starting up the motor.

"Let me know if it's too fast or too bumpy," he told her. He navigated the craft around the lighthouse to begin the journey back around Piney Point to the marina.

Kat closed her eyes and gripped the sides of her seat. She tilted her head back as the wind picked up her hair and whipped it.

She was slightly unsteady on her feet after as Easton helped her up onto the dock. Somehow she managed to climb out of the boat and into his truck.

Easton drove her home. He helped her out of his truck and walked her to her door. "You going to be okay?"

"Yeah." She leaned into him and wrapped her arms around his waist. "Thank you."

He stroked her back and kissed the top of her head. "See you tomorrow?"

"Yeah. I've got brunch plans at The Roosevelt with Uncle Charley. I should be at the barn by one o'clock."

She pulled away from him. He tucked her hair behind her ears. "I'll miss you."

Kat squinted her eyes to alleviate some of the pressure from what was left of her headache. "I love you." She rose on her toes and captured his lips in hers.

"I know." He grinned and didn't turn away until she had locked the door behind her. She watched him drive away before she went upstairs.

As she changed into her pajamas, she realized she'd left her hairpieces and bobby pins at the lighthouse. She couldn't stop smiling. Despite her headache, it had been a night to remember. She hoped he'd take her back there to get them. She climbed into bed and texted Molly and Shelby not to wake her up for church. She needed a solid eight hours for her brain to rest and she needed to start sleeping now if she was going to get those hours in and be on time to meet Uncle Charley for

lunch.

Kat arrived at The Roosevelt with fifteen minutes to spare before brunch. She signed in and affixed her guest name tag to the front of her sundress.

The brightly lit dining room was abuzz with chatter from the seniors and family members who occupied the space. Ms. Vivi saw her just as she entered. She waved her over to her table where a handful of octogenarians dressed in vivid colors sipped coffee.

"Good morning, Ms. Vivi! Or should I call you Sophia?" Kat teased. *Was the 80's party just last night?*

Ms. Vivi snorted. "I don't know how Carol convinced me to do that. Must have been a senior moment when I agreed." Her friends laughed. "Sit down. I told Charley's nurse to seat him here. If he can handle it."

"You all might be a bit formidable, but he's a tough old guy." Kat remarked.

Ms. Vivi leaned over and held up her coffee. "Check out the typo on my mug." She pressed her lips together. "My Love Language is GIFs. Does that mean something?"

Kat snorted. "We really need to get you on social media! A GIF is an animated video clip that showcases a phrase or quote from popular culture. Let me show you."

Ms. Vivi waved her hand as Kat began swiping her

phone. "You can show me later. Back to Charley." She leaned in. "You should have known him as a teenager. He was a heartbreaker, that one."

Kat had forgotten Ms. Vivi was only a few years younger than Uncle Charley. "Aw, are you saying you had a crush on him way back when?"

Ms. Vivi humphed. "I'm not saying that. He was a bit of a troublemaker, but he was always good to your Aunt Katie and her friends."

"Now, Viv, stop spinning tales," Uncle Charley warned as his nurse rolled him up to the table. The chair next to Kat was removed for his wheelchair to slide in. He leaned into Kat, "If you want to hear tales, I can tell you things she did to try to get my attention." He winked.

"Ms. Vivi!" Kat exclaimed as her former instructor's cheeks turned pink. "I can only imagine!"

"Now, Charles, we do not need to resurrect old memories that should remain where we left them, dead in the past."

"Do you know my sister and this lady here"—he closed his fist and pointed his thumb in Ms. Vivi's direction—"once snuck into the trunk of my car when I was out with my buddy Stanley?" Uncle Charley commanded the attention of all the women at the table. "We had no idea. We parked the car at the town landing to go smoke and watch the boats."

"Charles, there is no need to rehash this," Ms. Vivi warned.

He chuckled and continued. "When we got back to

the car, we heard them. It was late and they had to go to the bathroom. I let them out and they ran like heck, but the marina office was closed, of course."

"So what did you do?" Kat asked Ms. Vivi.

"The only thing we could do." She sighed. "We went to the other side of the car and guarded each other while they had a good laugh."

Uncle Charley grinned. "Still laughing about it! Good thing it wasn't summer. They would have suffocated. They blamed each other, of course. I know my sister had a thing for Stanley, but she wasn't the type to think of that kind of thing." He narrowed his eyes at Ms. Vivi, whose pink cheeks transformed to crimson. "You had to be the brains of that operation."

"You'll never know." Ms. Vivi changed the subject. "How's that heart of yours doing?"

Uncle Charley sighed. "It's slowing me down. The double whammy of COPD and congestive heart failure is rough."

Kat squeezed his hand. "Have they told you when you can come home?"

"Soon, I hope. A couple of weeks. Right now they have to monitor my fluid intake, blood pressure, and oxygen level. And those foul breathing treatments need to taper off. They're cramping my style."

Kat reached over to give him a side hug. "Patience, patience. I want you healed fully, so don't rush it."

He grumbled. "Fine, fine."

The cart rolled up with the lunch trays. As Uncle

Charley picked at his food, she worried that he might never return home. The time in the hospital had taken a toll. Despite his still-sharp wit, he was frail and weak.

Lunch passed pleasantly. Kat said goodbye to Uncle Charley and the ladies and promised to visit the next day. She was meeting with Molly in the morning to make calls for their wedding-planning gig and then had the rest of the day off.

Kat checked on Mocha first thing when she arrived at the barn for her Sunday afternoon lessons. She changed quickly, plaited her hair into two braids, and hunted down the sugar cubes. She had a few minutes before her first student would arrive so she hurried to Mocha's stall.

Easton leaned against the doorframe, studying Mocha. "How are you feeling?" he asked as she joined him.

"All better."

"Good." She leaned into him as he tugged at one of her braids, pulling her toward him.

She melted into his kiss and tried not to forget she came to see Mocha. "I gotta see my horse," she murmured into his mouth.

Easton groaned in protest. "She's right over there."

Her toes tingled as he kissed her again.

"All right, lover boy, that's all you get. I have to work."

He pouted and then flashed a grin. "Join me for dinner and a movie tomorrow night? I'll tell JC to get lost," he added suggestively.

She lowered her eyelids. "Why? Do you have something scandalous planned?"

"You'll have to show up to find out."

"Is that a promise or a threat?" She raised her brows.

"Just be there." He stole another kiss and left the stall. She wouldn't miss it.

Easton was up bright and early Monday morning. Doc Hill arrived at the barn just after daybreak.

"She's doing better than I expected," Doc Hill reported. "You've done a spectacular job nursing her back to health."

"What's next?" Easton asked.

"Well, you can begin to ease her off stall rest. You can walk her around the ring, let her graze. Let her go at her own pace. We'll ultrasound every thirty days and go from there."

"I'll let Kat know. Anything else?"

"How's Old Man Wetherby doing?"

"As expected, as far as I know. He's tough old guy."

"Yes, he is. Send them my best. I'll see you next week." Doc held out his hand. Easton shook it.

Easton stroked Mocha's muzzle. "Good girl."

There was a gap in the schedule after lunch, and he decide to go for a ride. He could clear his head and check on the trails. He left Mocha and went to the tack room, where he grabbed gear to saddle up Bolt. He was adjusting the saddle when JC entered the barn.

"Late night, Saturday night," his brother commented.

"Yep." Easton wasn't going to elaborate.

"So what's going on between you two?"

"We're getting along."

"Mind if I ride with you?"

"Go for it." Easton finished and led Bolt out the newly constructed main door. The Conroy Construction crew had done a fine job and had even repainted the entire outside of the barn. He'd be glad when they finished the inside work.

Easton mounted his horse and jogged around the ring while he waited for his brother. He realized Kat hadn't ridden in several weeks. It must be driving her crazy.

JC led his horse out of the barn and mounted up. Slade was a dapple gray with a black mane, and at twenty years, he was the oldest at the Cliff Walk Resort. JC peered at Easton from underneath his visor. "So where are we headed?"

"The overlook." Easton led Bolt to the fork off Pine Walk Trail that would lead to the overlook, a clearing that afforded a look from the resort below to the lighthouse at the entrance to the cove. The dirt path was framed with pine, spruce, and white birch trees, which snaked behind and slightly above the row of staff cabins. As they neared Molly's cabin, downed and uprooted trees still lay on the hillside between her damaged home and the overlook directly above.

"Wow," JC said as he looked down at the damage. "I haven't been up here. That must have been wild, man. Imagine, a tornado, here."

"It was definitely wild. I haven't followed the whole route, but it took out a couple houses in that new development."

"No kidding."

The brothers continued their survey, clearing branches and other natural debris from the trail for the better part of an hour. Easton didn't offer JC any further explanation, so JC filled the silence with tales from his year-long trip to the Caribbean.

They headed back to the barn around noontime, prompted by the grumblings in their stomachs. As he approached the trailhead, Easton noticed a man leaning against the fence. The man held his phone in front of his face, as if he might be recording Maddie as she rode her buckskin quarter horse gelding, Mack, around Kat's barrels. The man wore shiny black jeans and a rodeo-quality plaid shirt. A tall, wide-brimmed hat perched atop his head.

The hungry rumblings in Easton's gut were replaced by a fiery churning of anger. He gripped the reins tightly and took in a long controlled breath.

JC pulled up next to him. "Hey, is that—"

"Troy 'Stetson' Boone?" Easton growled. "Won't be much left of him when I'm done." He kicked Bolt into a lope and rode him toward the man who had harassed Kat.

Easton stopped his horse a few yards away and slid off. He handed the reins to JC, who was already dismounting Slade behind him. Hunched forward, fists clenched, he stalked over to the man.

"Howdy!" Troy Boone tipped his hat, an arrogant smile on his lips.

"You have some unbelievable nerve. Get out of my resort."

"Ah, I see. So your ex-fiancée filled you in." He shrugged. "I came to check in on her, since she won't answer my texts. I introduced myself to Maddie and she filled me in on Mocha. I was sorry to hear about that." He frowned, then nodded to the girl riding behind him. "Maddie here has some natural talent. Would love to have her join the tour."

"She's sixteen." JC stepped up beside Easton, who was too angry to respond.

"Ah, too bad." He turned back toward the paddock and leaned on his forearms. "She's a pretty one."

Easton couldn't speak, but there were other ways to communicate. In two strides, he was upon Troy and grabbed him by the shirtfront. "Get. Out."

Troy regained his balance and stood to his full height. He and Easton were eye to eye. "Not till I see Kat."

"She doesn't want to see you."

"C'mon, man, just go." JC put his hand firmly on Troy's shoulder. "I'll walk you to your truck."

Troy's eyes narrowed. "Why all this fuss? All I did

was kiss her. After she dumped you."

That was it. Easton's fist connected with Troy's jaw. He'd kissed her? She'd left that part out.

JC steadied Troy so he didn't fall. The odious man had the nerve to laugh. "Guess she didn't tell you that part."

"Get. Out."

JC pushed him toward the parking lot. "Let's go. Don't ever come back here."

Troy chuckled. "Tell Kat I'll call her."

Easton rubbed his hand. *He'd kissed her?*

"Easton?" Maddie rode over to him. "What was that about? He said I was doing great . . ."

Easton relaxed his shoulders. "You were. That was about Kat. He was inappropriate with her. He's not a nice guy, no matter how cool he presents himself."

Maddie's eyes widened. "Ohhh. Well, that's terrible. I'm glad you and JC kicked him out."

"Yeah." He rubbed the back of his neck. "If he ever comes back here again, call me right away. We'll get the police involved."

"Okay."

Easton collected Bolt and Slade and led them into their stalls. He'd unsaddle them and wipe them down after he'd had a minute to settle. He paused as he approached the office door. Was that sobbing?

He peered in. JC held Kat, who shook in his arms. "Kat?" What was she doing here? It was her day off.

JC transferred the shuddering bundle to him and

tilted his head toward the horses. Easton nodded and eased her into his chair.

"Hey, it's okay," he soothed. He squatted to be eye level with her. She breathed long and slow to get her breathing under control. He pulled her close and tucked her head under his chin.

Finally, she spoke. "It's not okay. I never thought he would come here. And I wasn't completely truthful with you."

"I understand."

"It was awful. I went to him for help and he just grabbed me. I was mortified and ashamed. And so disgusted. How could he even *think* I liked him like that? I hadn't led him on. Or had I? I didn't think so. I thought he was my friend. It wasn't right. It might not seem like a big deal to some people, but it was to me. I didn't like his lips touching mine." She winced and closed her eyes. Easton waited while she collected her thoughts. "The only lips I ever want on mine are yours, Easton. I couldn't breathe. I didn't know what to say. I pushed him away and ran. All the way home. Like a coward. I should have faced him."

"I'm glad you came home." He hugged her tighter.

She leapt to her feet and rubbed her fists in her eyes. She stomped her foot and gestured wildly as if that would help her find the right words. "I saw you out there with him when I got back from the lodge so I waited in the office for him to leave. He must have seen my car and thought I was here." She sank back onto the hay. "I just couldn't face him. Do I need to face him?

Will that make me feel better?"

Easton shrugged. He let out a long sigh, perplexed. How could he help her? "I don't know what the right answer is, Kat." He felt helpless. "Just come over tonight. Please."

Kat exhaled a long breath. "Okay."

Chapter 16

The late-night *Star Wars* marathon with Easton was exactly what Kat needed to get her mind off Troy Boone. JC was out with friends, so they'd had the cabin to themselves.

She'd slumped against him for the first six hours or so, like the limp, dead codfish they'd ordered in for dinner from the Lobster Trap. The seafood stand was one of the few restaurants in the area that was open on Monday nights, and they delivered. They'd taken short breaks when the glare from the screen became too much. Now, as *Return of the Jedi* wrapped up, she sat up straighter, anticipating the kiss between Leia and Han.

The day after their first kiss in the meadow, they'd watched this movie. Though they'd seen it together countless times, there was a chemistry in the air that hadn't been there before. When Han and Leia kissed, Easton turned to her and all thoughts of the movie disappeared.

As that scene began, she turned and wrapped her arms around his neck. She pressed her lips to his and pulled him down on top of her as she fell backward into the couch.

She wanted him. She needed him. She gasped for air as he kissed her lips, then her jaw, and finally to that sensitive spot behind her ear…

"Easton."

"Kat," he mumbled into her neck.

"I love you."

"I know."

The next week and a half flew by. With less than a week left until the wedding, Kat was working her tail off between her regular duties and wedding preparation. Every employee at the resort was pitching in, and Carol had volunteered JC as their personal slave—his word—for whatever came up.

Lanie Owens and her sister, Caroline, had arrived early Thursday afternoon, a full five days before the wedding, for some sister "bonding time" and to help out with the planning. Kat had just finished her shift in the barn when JC texted her from the lobby that the ladies wanted to go for a guided trail ride.

She groaned. She didn't mind the overtime, but she needed to run an errand to Bar Harbor to pick up more tulle for the gazebo. The new structure was larger than its predecessor and she needed a few more bolts to achieve the look Trisha had sketched out.

Kat called him back. "Hey. Did they want to go right now?"

"Hey, yourself. Yeah, I checked them in and they're going to change and head over to the barn. Are you cool with staying late?"

"I am, but I need to get to the fabric store today, too. Would you want to take them on the trail ride?"

"Nah, I'll be your errand boy. Lanie's nice but her sister could freeze you with her eyes. Whatever you do, *don't* start singing 'Sweet Caroline' to her."

"That's funny!" Kat laughed. "Sounds like you're afraid of her."

"Let's just say the girl exudes negativity."

Kat couldn't help smiling. She'd met Caroline briefly over Memorial Day and hadn't gotten that impression, only that she may have been a little shy. JC wasn't often or easily intimidated. "All right, then. They're holding the tulle for me. Just give them my name and use one of the resort credit cards. I'll call to let them know you'll be coming."

"Will do."

Kat texted Triple M to saddle up a trio of horses and scarfed down her lunch. By the time Lanie and Caroline arrived, Buttons, Dottie, and Bolt were ready to go. Besides Mocha, they were the only horses that hadn't worked already that day.

"It's great to see you again, Kat," Lanie greeted her, stroking Buttons's nose. "And you, too, Buttons."

"Welcome back to the Cliff Walk." Kat handed

Lanie the reins after she'd mounted the mare. "And you, too, Caroline."

Caroline smiled. "You can call me Cara. It's good to be back. I'm taking my first official vacation for the next week. It's all about the celebrating and recharging for me."

"Well, then, you're in the right place." Kat held Dottie steady as Caroline swung up onto her. She climbed up onto Bolt and led them to the trail map posted under glass on the side of the barn. "For the sixty-minute ride, we usually begin at Birch Walk Trail and follow that up behind the meadow and around to the overlook, then descend by way of Mountain Walk Trail to Pine Walk, trot around the meadow or take a break, and then head back."

"Fantastic. Ready when you are," Lanie said.

"Let's go."

It was a picture-perfect summer day for a jaunt through the Acadian woods. It felt so good to be riding again. Kat had her eyes closed for a portion of the ride, trusting Bolt's knowledge of the trails to lead. The light sea breeze carried the salty air up into the trees, where it mingled with the scent of pine. Scattered along the trail, the lilies-of-the-valley, bunchberry, starflower, and goldthread were in full bloom, adding a floral note to the air.

They dismounted in the meadow. Kat spread out a blanket and they watched the horses graze. As the sisters chatted, she went through the running list of items she still had to attend to on the wedding checklist.

"What do you think, Kat?"

"Hmm?" Lanie's question pulled her from her thoughts. "I'm sorry, I was lost in my head."

"No worries. I was just talking to Cara about a bachelorette party. I hadn't planned one, and now I'm wondering if I should. The guys are going camping Sunday night, so I thought that might be a good time. What's around here?"

"That's a question for Molly. There isn't much around here, especially on a Sunday night. I know there are places to go in Bar Harbor and Bangor, but I've never been."

Caroline pursed her lips. "So no clubs in Crane's Cove, then?"

Kat laughed. "The pub is the closest thing we've got. They do karaoke on Saturday nights, but that's about as crazy as it gets."

"Sounds good to me. Saturday night, then?" Lanie grinned at Caroline. "Sorry, sis."

"Yeah, yeah," she grumbled, the side of her mouth turned up playfully. "When I get married, I plan to celebrate from Back Bay to the Leather District," she teased.

"I don't know what that means, but it sounds exhausting," Kat replied.

They laughed. Lanie stood up. "I'm ready to get back. This was nice. I'm glad we got here ahead of everyone else, Cara."

"Me, too," her sister agreed. "I could definitely get

used to this place."

"There's no place on earth like it," Kat said.

Back at the barn, they handed the horses over to Maddie, Meggie, and Mellie. Lanie and Caroline followed her down the stalls to check on Mocha. Kat felt a faint throbbing in her temples and excused herself to get water and ibuprofen.

She was rummaging through her purse in the office and jumped when Lanie called to her from the doorway. "Have you tried essential oils for your headaches?"

Kat popped four ibuprofen tablets and shook her head. She took a long sip from the water bottle. "No. There's a lot of misinformation out there. My doctor doesn't trust them."

"There is." Lanie said. "You just need the right brand, though. The ones I use are safe for internal consumption. They have supplement labels. Would you like to try them? Worst case, they do nothing. They won't hurt you."

Kat considered. She was so over her headaches. "Sure. I'll try anything at this point."

"Great." Lanie's eyes lit up. "Come up to our room. I love mixing remedies!"

Caroline rolled her eyes. "Everywhere she goes . . . she just can't help herself."

Lanie snorted. "Just like you can't help yourself whenever you find a great new bag you think everyone should have."

"Ya got me there."

They entered the main lodge through the lobby. JC was at the desk and waved them over. "Hey, ladies, did you have a *sweet* ride?" His eyes danced with mischief.

Caroline rolled her eyes. "You need some new material."

JC shrugged. "Nah. Not while it still gets me eye rolls."

"Is he this obnoxious to all your guests?" Caroline asked Kat.

Kat tried to hide her amusement. "Nope, just you."

"Wonderful." She headed for the stairs.

JC leaned toward Kat. "I think she enjoys the attention. I'm determined to de-ice her."

Kat laughed. "Good luck."

"I left the tulle in the office. You should have seen the looks I got at the store. Guess those old ladies don't sell much tulle to young studs like me very often."

Kat smirked. "I'll bet. Thanks for picking it up."

Kat followed Lanie and Caroline up to the third floor, which had been converted into suites after the family had moved out several years prior. It still had a homey feel to it. The wallpapered hall fanned out in two directions at the top of the stairs. To the right, two three-bedroom suites with private balconies stood on either side of the hall. To the left, they'd enclosed the former loft space into a luxurious two-bedroom suite that overlooked the front entrance.

Lanie and her family had reserved Suite 303, on the right side of the hall. She swiped her card and Kat followed them in. Across from the entry was a small kitchen with a laundry closet. To the left were the living and dining areas, which opened up to a balcony that ran half the length of the back of the lodge. To the right, a narrow hallway led to three bedrooms, two on the right side of the hall and the master suite on the left. Kat couldn't help but reminisce about when Easton, Molly, and JC occupied this suite with their parents. It seemed so long ago. Easton's grandparents lived in the rooms across the hall and she and Ms. Vivi had spent many nights curled up on sofas in the loft, watching equestrians and movies about horses.

Kat followed Lanie and Caroline into the master suite bathroom. On the counter, Lanie opened a case, displaying dozens of small amber-colored bottles.

"Wow, you use all those?" Kat asked.

"Most of them. I travel with all of them. You never know what you might need. Tell me about your headaches so I can choose the best ones."

"I have different kinds, but the worst tend to come on suddenly, usually a migraine on the right side, or a cluster." She pressed a finger into her temple. "They started six years ago with my brain injury."

Lanie nodded. "Okay. I'm going to start you with lavender, peppermint, and frankincense." She went to work filling three tiny bottles with liquid from larger ones. "Put the lavender wherever it hurts. It's anti-inflammatory and calming. Wait thirty seconds, then layer the peppermint on top of it. Then open your mouth and tap the peppermint bottle twice under your tongue to get a full drop out. These tiny drams only release half a drop at a time. Then, tap a drop of frankincense onto your thumb and press it to the roof of your mouth."

Kat sniffed the small vial of frankincense. "Smells . . . interesting."

"It's not so bad when you get used to it. We oilers like to say, 'If it was good enough for Baby Jesus, it's good enough for me.'" She grinned. "It's also anti-inflammatory, so you can also apply it where it hurts, even on top of the lavender and peppermint. Just wait thirty seconds between oils so they can each absorb into the bloodstream and do their thing."

"Can you please write that out for me?" Kat already had forgotten what to do with the lavender and peppermint.

"Sure. Let me know if it helps. We can tweak it and try other oils as well. Consider purchasing a diffuser to use with the oils. Diffusing Rosemary can help your memory."

"Thanks." Kat put the bottles in her pocket. If they worked, she'd suggest them to Shelby for Noah's headaches. "So when does the rest of your family arrive?"

Caroline chimed in from where she had plopped down on the king-sized bed. "Our grandparents arrive tomorrow. They're the ones who got us this fab suite. Almost feel guilty taking the master bedroom. They must be paying a fortune."

"Well, they have a small fortune," Lanie said as she

scribbled on a resort notepad at the desk. "Here ya go, Kat. Remember, only a couple drops at a time of each, and only ingest oils with supplement labels. Those knock-offs at the health-food stores are adulterated and mixed with who knows what, even though they claim to be pure."

"Thanks." She added the note to her pocket and joined Caroline on the bed. "Who else is staying here with you? I don't think Molly and I have a list of rooms yet."

"Our mom and my best friend, Sarah, are driving up Saturday. Dad and Aunt Liza and Uncle Leo are coming up Monday. They're in the suite at the end of the hall. Matt and his family are across the hall. They're all flying in tomorrow night." Lanie blushed when she said Matt's name.

Kat had to ask. "It's so wild. You've only known him a couple months. How can you be sure you want to spend the rest of your life with him?"

Lanie sank into the desk chair. "It's a feeling. I am so connected to him it feels supernatural. I just *know* deep down that I found my soulmate. So why wait? He decided to move up north so we can be together. It just makes sense to officially start our lives together."

Kat nodded. It did make sense. She and Easton hadn't been hit by cupid's arrow. They slowly fell in love after years and years of friendship. She'd never even so much as looked at another man, couldn't imagine herself with anyone else. But did that mean they were meant for each other?

Saturday afternoon, Easton and JC set up tables at the beach below the resort. This Saturday's theme was a Beachfront Potluck and a contracted serving staff would soon arrive with the main courses. They were sipping beers on the bench at the kayak shack when Matt and Damon Saunders bounded down the wooden steps set against the cliff face.

"Hey, look who's back!" JC stood up and pulled Damon into a bro hug.

"Your mom told us we could find you here. We had to escape Meemaw, so we volunteered to help set up. My sister wasn't so lucky," Damon chuckled.

Easton stretched his hand out to Matt. "Good to know we aren't the only ones afraid of her." He'd been avoiding the kitchen on purpose. "Great to see you again. Can I get you guys a beer?"

"Sure. It's great to be back," Matt said.

Easton went into the shack and reappeared with two bottles of his favorite local craft beer.

"Bar Harbor Blueberry," Damon said, reading the label. "Sounds interesting."

JC explained. "The Atlantic Brewing Company isn't far from here. Good stuff."

"Definitely different. I like it." Damon leaned against the shack. "So what do we need to do for the camping trip tomorrow?"

"Just head over to the barn after church. JC and I will load the gear and food into my truck and you can follow us. You have a rental?

"Yes, sir. My dad rented an extended cab." Matt looked at Damon. "When are your parents getting here again?"

"Not until Monday afternoon for the rehearsal. They want to make sure everything's set at the restaurant before they leave."

"That's right," Easton said. "Your parents took over the boardinghouse your Meemaw used to run, right?"

"They did. They converted the second-floor bedrooms into small dining rooms. They live on the third floor. Not too different from what you all did here, although it's much smaller."

"No wonder Grandma Vivi and Meemaw get along so well," Easton observed.

"Speak of the devil." Matt turned his eyes to the stairs, where his grandmother was bellowing instructions to the staff as she slowly made her way down.

"Let's hide!" Damon joked.

"Too late, she saw us." Matt tipped his beer and put it down on the bench. "Let's go save Rachel and the staff."

Damon's sister, Rachel, led the group down the stairs. She was overloaded, carrying a laundry basket of supplies and a tote on each shoulder. Matt reached her first and relieved her of the basket. She smiled gratefully at her cousin and handed the totes to her brother.

"Thanks. Whew! Those stairs are no joke." She lifted her hand to her head to shield her eyes from the sun. "You must be JC and Easton."

"You should pay more attention and flirt later, dear," Meemaw scolded.

"I promise you I'm not flirting." Rachel shook her head. "Meemaw's always forgetting I have a boyfriend back home."

"I don't forget anything," Meemaw defended herself. "I just don't like him."

They laughed. Rachel shrugged. "Doesn't bother me a bit. I'm just as stubborn as she is."

"All right, enough chitchat, let's get this beach set up." Meemaw led the way to the tables Easton and JC arranged. "If this strip of sand were more accessible, I could have brought the crockpots. These sterno-dish things, well, they just aren't the same."

Rachel pulled a tablecloth out of the tote she'd given to her brother and covered the table nearest to her. "Meemaw, they do this all the time, and they've hired an extra crew to take care of it today. It was nice of you to volunteer us to help set up"—she winked at the guys—"but I'm sure the catering staff knows what to do."

Meemaw sighed and straightened the cloth. "I suppose. But I *like* to be in charge."

Her grandchildren laughed.

"Don't we know it," Matt teased. "So what time

does this start?"

"Six. Want another beer?" Easton offered, watching Kat, Shelby, and Molly descend the stairs. Kat was wearing a mustard-colored cotton wrap dress that tied on the side. The deep V-neckline hugged the curves to her waist and then fanned out, the wind twirling it around her thighs.

"I'll take one," Rachel piped up, jolting him from his trance. Reluctantly, he dragged his eyes away from Kat. Matt followed him into the shack.

"So are things better between you and Kat?" Matt asked. "I've got a feeling I'm not the only guy here head over heels."

"She's everything, always has been." Easton cradled four bottles in the crook of his elbow and handed another to Matt.

Matt put his hand on Easton's shoulder as they exited the shack. "I know the feeling. I can't imagine my life without Lanie in it. The last couple weeks have been brutal being apart from her."

"Is she coming tonight? Molly mentioned a bachelorette party."

"She'll be here for a bit. Then they plan to party at the pub. I plan to crash it." Matt's eyes glinted mischievously. "Wanna come?"

"I'll think about it." They rejoined the group standing to the side as the catering staff set up the buffet. Easton handed the beers to JC, Damon, and Rachel and walked over to Kat, who was arranging plasticware into baskets.

"Hey." She turned around as he approached. "Almost done, wanna help?"

"I thought you weren't working tonight?"

"Your mom isn't feeling well. I told her I'd oversee the dinner so she could lie down. I sent Lanie to her. She has these oils . . . anyway, I am feeling great. Headache-free since I started using them yesterday."

"That's great. And the whiskey?"

"Not a sip."

"Good. It hurts me when you hurt."

Kat's expression softened. She touched his cheek. "I know."

He tilted his head and kissed her. "Cherry ChapStick?"

Kat nodded. "Blueberry ale?"

"Yes, ma'am." Her carefree laughter was music to his ears. Seemed like the old Kat was back. Finally.

Chapter 17

Kat was full. She'd filled up on Frieda's best seafood at the beach and gone for a walk along the water with Easton. Sipping on water, she waited at the high-top in the back of the pub for the guys to make their entrance. Lanie had invited her, Shelby, and Molly to her bachelorette party, and Easton had let it slip that Matt was planning to crash it.

Lanie was waiting to sing at the stage with Caroline when Matt, Easton, Damon, and JC entered the bar. "Perfect timing," Kat murmured to Lanie's best friend, Sarah, who was sitting beside her.

Sarah grinned and ran her fingers through her wavy red hair. "I've only recently met Matt, but I can tell you this is just the sort of thing he would do. In the sweetest way."

"No kidding," Molly said, waving them over. "Do you think she saw them?"

"She did." Rachel pointed to the DJ. "I think she's changing her song."

That was confirmed when Caroline headed back

toward the table. Eyes on her sister, she walked smack into JC. Her face glowed red and she steadied herself, then strode the rest of the way with extra purpose in her steps.

Shelby rolled her eyes at JC as Caroline reached the table, just ahead of the guys. "Smooth."

"I'm *so* embarrassed," Caroline hissed. "And do you know what he *said* to me?"

Before anyone could guess, JC answered, "What? I just asked her if she was falling for me." He winked at her.

Caroline rolled her eyes. "Not a chance, not ever."

"Aw, c'mon, Cara-"

"And don't call me Cara. Only my family and close friends call me that." Caroline turned away from him and smiled sweetly at Matt. "You might want to scooch up closer. She's singing next."

"Thanks for the tip." Matt excused himself and headed toward the makeshift stage on the side of the dance floor. Easton, JC, and Damon found seats as Lanie belted out the song.

"Oh, that's perfect." Molly sighed with a note of sadness as the beginning stanza of Katy Perry's "Firework" began to play. "They are certainly going to win the night on the Fourth of July. And her voice is perfect."

"Aw, Molly, are you getting sentimental?" JC gave his sister a side hug.

"Just a bit." She looked longingly at the stage. "You should have been here to watch them fall in love. It was so fast, yet so real. I'm happy for them." Her eyes glistened with tears.

"Hey, now, I'm supposed to be the emotional one. Do we need to cut you off?" Kat squeezed Easton's hand under the table.

Molly shook her head. "No. But I think I'm going to head out after her song. You should, too. Shelby will kill us if we miss church again tomorrow."

"Yes, I will. I'm ready when you are. I'm cutting myself off." Shelby pushed her drink toward the center of the table. "Anyone else need a ride back?"

Molly giggled. "I think you could have another Shirley Temple or two before you get totally out of control."

Shelby's jaw tightened. "I'll never get out of control."

Damon's face crinkled. "Why are y'all afraid of Shelby? She's as sweet as a warm biscuit on a Sunday morning." Shelby narrowed her eyes at him.

"Oh, puh-lease," Caroline smirked. "Do you guys really think your lines are going to get you anywhere?"

JC laughed. "Nah, but it sure is funny to see your reactions."

Kat was entertained by the cheesy pickup lines and banter. She leaned her head on Easton's shoulder.

Her phone buzzed in her back pocket. She leaned forward to pull it out. She swiped and sighed. Easton must have read the dismay on her face.

"He's still texting you?" he whispered.

She nodded. "From a different phone. I blocked him."

Easton let out a long, deep breath. He fisted his hands and kept his voice steady. "Kat, what do you want to do about this? Do you want to get a restraining order?"

Kat chewed on her bottom lip. She shook her head. "No. I just want him to go away."

"Okay. Do you want my help?"

"Yes." Her whispered response was weary but firm. "I know I should be strong and deal with this myself, but I need you, Easton."

Easton took the phone from her and punched the screen furiously with his index finger. *This is Easton Crane. If you ever contact Kat again or show your face in my town, we'll have the police and the press on you faster than you can rope a calf.* "That ought to do it." He hit the send tab and showed her the screen.

She gulped as she read the text. "I hope so. Thank you." Her eyes shimmered and he pulled her to him.

He spoke into her ear. "I'll always be there for you."

The song faded out. Matt walked up to the edge of the stage as Lanie finished her song and wrapped his arms around her waist to lift her down. He spun her around and she captured his face in her hands.

The hair on Kat's neck stood at attention when Easton moved behind her and whispered in her ear. "Wanna dance? I don't sing, but if I did, this is the song I'd serenade you with."

If Kat was the swooning type, she would have been

on the floor. "Wow." The man on the stage was singing Ed Sheeran's "Perfect."

Easton led her to the dance floor, where Matt and Lanie were locked in an embrace, hardly dancing. Her tiara was askew and her sash had fallen off her shoulder to her elbow. No one else existed. They truly were lost in each other's eyes.

Which was the next song. Easton held her tighter as the Debbie Gibson song played. Next to them, Damon had convinced Shelby to dance. Something was definitely in the air tonight. Kat couldn't remember the last time Shelby let loose. Despite her pursed lips and stiff frame, Shelby's cheeks were pink and she seemed not to be hating it. Kat tucked her head under Easton's chin. She never wanted their dance to stop.

Easton stood beside Kat in the pew. The scene from the night before kept playing over in his head. He tried to tune out Pastor Porter and attune himself to the dream standing next to him.

"Society tries to convince us that we are in charge of our lives. It's a lie from the enemy that the masses have come to believe. That we can be in control if we read enough, work hard enough, surround ourselves with the right people. These are all great things, yet people still suffer. The truth is, we can't control the people around us. We can't control the elements. The *only* things we can control are our reactions and our perspectives.

"Ever notice those people who seem to glow from the inside out? The ones who smile all the time, despite circumstances that have broken them? These are people who have given everything to God because they have realized they are not in control. They trust God and His timing, and they wait patiently. There is peace when you let go."

Easton thought of Molly. Despite her marriage struggles and divorce, his sister still smiled and exuded joy. She trusted God would provide for her, and bring her a better love than the one she had lost. She was one of those people Pastor Porter was describing.

He wrapped his arm around Kat's shoulders. She leaned into him. God had brought Kat to him when they were kids. He'd always felt connected to her, even then, and especially as teenager when he'd been too shy to act on his feelings. Somehow, deep down, he'd trusted God would help when His timing was right. He'd jumped ahead last summer out of desperation, letting fear get the better of him instead of waiting on God. The time felt right now, in a way that it didn't last year.

"Wake up early. Spend time in prayer. Listen. Look for God everywhere you go, in everything you do. There are no coincidences, no luck. Only God. When you make connections, it's God. When your seed produces fruit, it's God. When you are awarded a harvest, it's God. Have faith in His timing. Have patience in His love. Praise Him, and he will bless you beyond your wildest dreams."

Easton was still thinking about Pastor Porter's sermon later that day as he and JC led Matt, Damon, and Matt's father through the winding paths of Mount Desert National Park. He had forgotten to look for God and to appreciate His timing. Evidence of God's love was everywhere around him, and though he didn't care for God's timing when it conflicted with his plans, things always turned out better when he trusted.

At the tail end of the off-season, the campground's many empty sites afforded them a level of privacy they wouldn't get later in the summer. After checking in at the office, it was a short drive to their waterfront campsites along Somes Sound. They'd set up their tents, packed their gear for a day on the trails, and set off deep into the woods. The trees were alive with the songs of the native birds. The sea breeze caressed the pine branches, and the cool fresh air filled their lungs.

"Definitely a different experience from camping back home," Damon observed as they stopped for a water break at a collection of boulders in a clearing. "I almost miss the alligators and poisonous snakes."

"I like this kind of desert." Matt, a retired Army Ranger, had spent many years overseas in a different kind of desert climate. "What's the biggest danger here? Bears?"

"Actually, it's slipping on rocks," JC replied. "Rope rescues are a pretty common thing here."

"Seriously?" Damon asked. "I'll be careful to watch my step, then."

Matt's father, Clay Saunders, patted his nephew on his shoulder. "Don't worry. Wouldn't be the first time we caught you when you fell."

For a brief second, a shadow appeared over Damon's eyes, then he grinned. "I was a klutzy kid," he explained to Easton and JC.

"And then you turned into a big showoff," Matt added. "You were always trying to prove yourself."

"Trying? I believe I succeeded, cuz," Damon shot back. "Once I figured out I had a talent for basketball, things fell into place."

"And despite all that fancy footwork, you still manage to trip over your own feet when you're off the court."

"All right, all right," Matt's father interceded. "Ready to move on up the trail? I'm curious to see what's up ahead. That park ranger was pretty tight-lipped, but I could tell he was busting at the seams when you told him where we were headed."

"You won't be disappointed. We're not far," said Easton.

"Well, then let's go." Matt slid his water bottle in the side pocket of his backpack and pulled it over his shoulders. "After almost nine miles, I was starting to wonder if you'd lost your way."

"Not a chance, funny guy. Follow me," JC retorted as he set off on the path.

Up ahead, the tree line broke, revealing the ocean beyond. A salty breeze caressed their noses and blew through the tall grasses. Easton climbed onto a flat boulder and passed his binoculars to Matt. "Take a look."

Down below, dozens of speckled harbor seals lounged on the rocks. "If that ain't the bee's knees," Matt murmured. "Damon, feast your eyes on that." He held out the binoculars to his cousin.

"Can we get closer?" Damon asked. He passed the binoculars to his uncle.

"Sure. You can climb down this way." JC pointed to a series of rocks that led down to the sand.

Clay handed the binoculars to Easton and followed JC, Matt, and Damon down the path. Easton hung back to take in the seals. Through the binoculars, he scanned from left to right, his eyes coming to stop on a rock farther out, where a tiny gray pup lay by itself. Its eyes were closed, and it was shivering. He lowered the binoculars and headed down the trail to get a closer look.

His companions had reached the bottom. They sat on the rocks directly below where they'd been standing. Easton dropped his pack and discarded his shirt, socks, and shoes.

"Going for a swim with the seals?" JC asked.

"Nah. Gonna check on that baby out there."

Easton could feel their eyes burning into his back as he navigated the sharp rocks and waded out to the pup. Blood stained the far side of the rock. A jagged white shark tooth lay in the middle of the red stain. "Hey there, little fella." The pup opened one eye briefly and let out a silent cry. Easton talked to it in a soothing voice as his hands explored the folds of loose skin, indicating it was underweight and malnourished. "You've got a swollen flipper."

He couldn't find a source for the blood, but on the underside of the seal, he felt the pup's umbilical stump. Likely a shark had followed the trail of the afterbirth to its prey. This baby wasn't more than a few days old. "Where's your mother?" he asked.

The pup opened its mouth again, and again no sound escaped. With great care, Easton lifted the pup to his chest. "We've got to get you warm or you're not going to make it out here."

He turned to find JC waiting, perched on the rocks a few feet above him. "Dude, that's a federal offense."

"It won't survive if we wait for help."

"All right, then. Hand the little guy up."

"It's a girl. She's freezing. Likely her mother was snatched by a shark. I've got to get her to Doc Hill or she won't stand a chance."

"Hey, little girl." JC stroked the pup on the top of its head. He looked up at Easton. "Easton Crane, seal whisperer," he half joked. "Let me get something to wrap her in."

"No," Easton said. "The shivering is the way seals thermoregulate. You can actually cause more harm if you wrap her. She could overheat. I do need something I can use to splint her flipper, though. It's swollen."

"You sure you should be removing her from the beach?" JC asked.

"Not at all. Just going with my gut. It'll take hours for someone from the triage center in Bath to get out here and find us. I can get her to Doc Hill in half an hour. He can stabilize her while he waits for them to pick her up."

"Isn't there anything closer? Can a park ranger help?" Matt asked.

Easton shook his head. "Up until a few years ago, the University of New England had a rehab program. When it shut down, a lot of pups had to be euthanized. Last year, a nonprofit, Marine Mammals of Maine, opened a triage center a few hours south of here. They stabilize and then transport them somewhere else. Last I heard, though, the closest marine response team to here is in Wells. It's about a two-hundred-mile drive from here."

Damon let out a low whistle. "That's a shame."

Easton nodded. Matt climbed down with the first-aid kit. Easton transferred the pup to JC. His eyes scanned the sand until he found a stick the length of the injured flipper.

Matt handed him the tape from the kit. "This will only hurt for a second," Easton promised the animal as he secured the splint.

"Nice job. I've never splinted an animal before. Impressive," Matt said.

"He wanted to be vet once upon a time. Worked with Doc as a tech for a bit before he took over the barn," JC said.

"Long time ago." Easton silenced JC with his tone. "Let's get this girl up."

"It's a nine-mile hike back to the campsite." Matt's eyes darted up to where his dad and cousin stood, his gaze on the trees behind him. "Should we construct a stretcher?"

"No." Easton shifted the pup in his arm and pointed up. "There's a road just on the other side of those trees. I can call for a ride."

"Okay then. Let's get this pup up." JC scaled the rocks until he was about three-quarters of the way up. Matt followed, stopping halfway. Easton handed the pup to Matt, who boosted it up to JC, who passed it up into Damon's waiting arms.

The men began their ascent to the ground above. Easton went last. He'd been climbing these boulders his entire life, and no one was more surprised than him when his hand slipped on a moss-covered rock. It threw off his balance. He waved his arms as he lost his footing, scrambling to right himself as he fell backward. He twisted his body in an effort to keep his head up as he went down, but despite his maneuvers, it slammed into a rock. His last thought was of Kat as everything went black.

Chapter 18

Late Sunday afternoon, Kat and Molly gathered with Lanie, Caroline, their mother, Ellen, and Matt's mother, Grace, around a table in the resort's dining room. As they went over the details for the rehearsal dinner and wedding, Kat couldn't push away the envious thoughts that took up residence in her head. Breaking her engagement with Easton was by far the worst thing she had ever done. Not a moment went by where she didn't feel regret. For every moment she spent planning Lanie's wedding, she spent two moments wishing it was hers.

So how did she fix it? She'd wounded his pride and hurt him deeply. What could she do to rebuild what she'd knocked down? Every day, she conveyed to him that she loved him. She spent time with him and welcomed his affections. Was it enough? Would come around? And if he did, was she ready to be married?

"What do you think, Kat?" Molly's question brought her out of her thoughts.

Kat apologized. "I'm sorry, I totally tuned out."

"Is it another headache? Do you want to try some different oils?" Lanie asked.

"No," Kat smiled. "Actually I haven't had a headache since, which is incredible."

Lanie beamed. "I'm so glad." She turned to her mother. "Another success story!"

Ellen Owens smiled widely. "People still think I'm crazy, but they do work. I'm glad they are helping you, Kat." She glanced at Molly. "We were debating on doing the rehearsal dinner on the patio instead of in the dining room."

"I think that's a wonderful idea." Kat flipped a page in her notepad and began to sketch out tables. "It's a small party, and we can arrange the tables like this." She turned the notepad around for them to see.

Grace Saunders studied the design. "I think that would work. Just be sure to have enough seating for yourself and Molly and the rest of the Crane family, too. Meemaw would have my head if y'all didn't stay and eat, especially if she's cookin'."

"Yes, ma'am. That's very nice of you, and I can tell you none of us have any intention of ever getting on Meemaw's bad side." Her last comment was met with knowing laughter. Molly pointed to Kat's sketch. "If we moved the sweetheart table to this side of the door and the buffet table to the other side, we can fit an extra six-top table here. It will give the illusion of two long tables with breaks in the center to make an aisle from the stairs to the door. The dessert table can go in the corner here and we can put the drink dispensers on it."

Kat made the necessary adjustments, which were met with approval. "Next order of business, the menus." She found the tab in the wedding binder and unclipped a handwritten note from the first page. "Wedding dinner is seafood-southern combination, selected by Meemaw, and currently is as follows: fried fish, fried scallops, fried chicken, crab stew, steak fries, mashed potatoes, coleslaw, cornbread, turnip greens, butterbeans, fried okra, cranberry sauce, and biscuits with gravy. Is there anything you'd like to add or omit?"

Lanie nodded. "Can you add some mac-n-cheese for Bella? It's her favorite."

"I'm so glad Bella was able to come," Caroline said. "She's such a sweet girl. I enjoyed coaching her when you were away."

Lanie's flower girl, Bella, an eight-year-old swim student of Lanie's with Down Syndrome, was a talented swimmer and Special Olympics champion. Lanie had a deep bond with her and talked about her often.

"Meemaw makes a mean mac-n-cheese," Grace said, sipping her sweet tea.

"Sure. That's easy enough." Kat flipped another page. "Rehearsal dinner menu. I don't have a list for that meal, just a note from Trisha that says, 'Meemaw's Choice.'"

Grace answered. "My mother-in-law is running that show. We haven't the foggiest idea what she'll be serving."

Meemaw chose that moment to walk out of the kitchen. "My apologies for being late. I wanted to help with the box lunches before I came out." The resort was closed for lunch on weekdays, but guests could order boxed lunches to be picked up or delivered to their rooms.

Molly gestured to the empty chair to her right. "I bet Mom and Frieda were thrilled for the help. They might not let you leave."

Meemaw smiled and shared a glance with Grace. "I might stay the whole summer. I like it here. I find the lack of humidity refreshing." They all laughed. "So, what did I miss?"

"We were wondering what you were cooking up for the rehearsal dinner," Kat said.

"Ah!" Meemaw clasped her hands in front of her face, which lit up with excitement. "I just sent Frieda out. We're going to do fancy-simple. I just *loved* the Cliff Walk's signature lobster rolls, so I'm letting Frieda do her thing. I'll be mixin' up my pasta and potato salads, and we'll do some deviled eggs, potato chips, and I've been soaking my cucumbers all week. My Matthew insisted on peach cobbler and praline cookies for dessert. And, of course, a few giant jugs of my sweet tea."

Grace laughed at the blank stares from the native New Englanders at the mention of soaking cucumbers. "You'll love them, trust me. You slice up some cucumbers and an onion, and you soak them in water, vinegar, sugar, salt, and peppercorns for a few days.

Dee-lish-us!"

"We look forward to trying them, then," Ellen said. "Is there anything we can help with? I don't know how you all pulled this together in such a short time. Surely you could use some extra hands?"

Lanie shook her head. "I told you, Mom, Matt and I wanted to keep it simple. There really isn't a lot to do."

"Well, all right then. What about decorations?" Ellen asked Kat.

Molly slid the binder over and turned to the décor tab. "Just a few bolts of tulle. Wildflowers for the aisle-side chairs and gazebo. The wedding party's flowers will arrive from the florist tomorrow morning. We'll save some for the cake. Sadie will arrange them at the base of your intertwined swans cake topper and they'll cascade down one side. She's in the kitchen now working on it if you want to take a peek when we're done here."

"Sadie makes cakes?" Lanie asked.

"She does," Molly said. "She usually makes them at the diner during their slow time, but occasionally she'll do them here for events since our kitchen is closed a few hours each day."

"So interesting!" Lanie's face lit up with admiration for the former FBI agent turned diner owner. "I would love to hear how she came to learn that skill."

"My dad said she learned it while she was working undercover in a bakery." Molly flipped to the next tab in the binder. "Let's get back to the reception. Our guests have been informed the dining room will be closed Tuesday night. We usually do a potluck at the gazebo for the Fourth of July fireworks, anyway, so that will be set up following your ceremony. What you have to decide now is where you and Matt want to watch the fireworks from, if you do. If you leave the party early, you could watch them from the lighthouse. Sunset is around eight thirty, so you'd have to leave before eight."

"That would be *so* romantic," Caroline said. "I would totally leave my party an hour early for that."

Lanie's eyes sparkled. "I'll talk to Matt. I'm all for it. I don't mind missing the last hour."

Kat took a sip of her water. Maybe she could join Easton on the ride to the lighthouse. They could watch the fireworks in the resort boat on the way back.

Her reverie was interrupted by an insistent buzzing. It took her a minute to realize it was her phone vibrating on the table. "Sorry," she said as she swiped to decline the call.

A few seconds later, Molly's phone rang. "Oops! Forgot to turn my ringer off, too!" She silenced it and tossed it into the tote bag hanging on the back of her chair.

Lanie's phone was the next to ring, "Goodness!" She reached into her purse. "It's Matt. Excuse me. I'll ask about the fireworks." She swiped the call, pushed back in her chair, and stood up. "Hey, babe." Her face fell and she sat back down. "Yes, we're all here. Hold on."

She handed the phone to Kat. "Hello?" Her heart began to thump double time.

"Hey, Kat. Now don't get worried, but Easton slipped down some rocks when he was rescuin' a seal pup. I think he's got a concussion."

"He did what? *A seal pup?* Is he okay?" The thumping morphed into a pounding. Her free hand pressed into her chest.

"He hit his head and needs to get it checked out, but he's being stubborn. Says he doesn't want to ruin my camping trip. I'd feel better knowing he got an okay from a professional. Can you come get him? He refuses to let any of us here take him. JC is going to bring the seal pup to the vet." Kat could hear Easton in the background, insisting he was fine.

"Of course. You're in the park, right? Can you text my phone your coordinates?"

"Sure thing."

Kat handed the phone back to Lanie. "I have to go. Easton fell and hit his head."

Molly's face scrunched. "Is he okay?"

"Matt thinks so. I'll call you later." She rushed out before Molly could answer, then ran to her SUV.

As Matt filled Kat in on his fall, Easton tried to make sense of what had just happened.

He'd been climbing up and then he was on his back, opening his eyes and blinking into the blinding sun. He lay sprawled over the bottommost rocks, his head in the sand.

Matt was the first to reach him. "You okay? You fell pretty hard. What's your name? Do you know where you are? What day is it?"

He squinted up at Matt. Man, his head hurt. He reached to the back of his skull, where a lump was forming, and winced. His brain felt foggy. "Just bumped my head. Easton Crane, Mount Desert National Park. It's Sunday. Or maybe Monday? Monday is Kat's day off."

Matt flashed a grin. "I'll let her know you're thinking about her." He peered into Easton's eyes. "Did you black out? Do you feel nauseous?"

"Um . . . maybe? I don't remember." Easton lifted his head and rolled to one side, pulling his legs from the rocks. "My head is killing me."

"I'm thinking you've got yourself a grade-three concussion, seal whisperer." Matt turned to JC. "Help me get him up?"

On Matt's count, he and JC lifted Easton to his feet. The blood rushed to his head and he swayed. Matt tightened his grip.

"Whoa, bro. You gonna make it back up?" JC's eyes were full of concern.

"Sit." Matt guided him down onto a boulder in the shade of the cliff. "I'll stay here with him till he's steady. You get the seal to the doc. Have your Uber drop Dad and Damon back at the campsite on your way. They can drive the truck back to get us."

"Yes, sir."

Easton peered up at his brother. "Thanks, man."

JC shook his head. "Can't believe you slipped on the rocks. Rookie mistake."

"Shut up." Easton apologized to Matt. "Sorry to ruin your trip."

Matt reached up to catch the bundle of cloth JC tossed at him. "It's not ruined at all. Never thought I'd hold a baby seal." He glanced up at his cousin, who still held the pup. "Just sit still. Put your shirt on and rest your noggin' till we can get you checked out."

"I'll be fine." Easton pulled the shirt over his head.

He leaned his head back against the wall of moss-covered granite and closed his eyes. "So two days till you're a married man. How do you go from not knowing someone to knowing unquestionably that she is the one you were meant to spend your life with?"

"I thought I was the one asking the questions," Matt joked. "Easy. I just know. It's more than an attraction, more than butterflies. It's a deep connection that I have never felt before. And I don't want to waste any time overthinking it or second-guessing. God brought us together and the spiritual world is on our side. I don't care two wits what the earthly realm thinks. It's a divine connection, one only God could have orchestrated."

"Makes sense. I know that feeling."

"Seems you do. You gonna do something about it?"

Easton closed his eyes. "Eventually."

"Don't wait too long, man. She came back to you,

right? Like a butterfly."

"She came back because her boss was harassing her. I know she loves me, but I can't help but wonder if that hadn't happened, if she would have come back. When her aunt died last summer, it hit her hard. She became so reckless and the walls went up."

"You think too much. You know how your heart feels. What does your gut say?"

"My gut says you ask too many questions."

Matt laughed. "Sounds like the Easton I've come to know. Glad your head seems to be fine. You ready to head back up?"

"Yeah."

Chapter 19

Kat set a tray of sandwiches on the coffee table and sat next to Easton. "You should eat something. And hydrate." She twisted the cap off a water bottle and handed it to him.

"I'm fine." He placed the water bottle on the table and stretched his arm over the back of the couch. "C'mere."

She scooted closer and searched his face. "Are you really okay? A concussion is no joke."

"I know."

"Is JC coming back tonight? The doctor said you shouldn't be left alone for twenty-four to forty-eight hours."

"No, I told him to finish out the trip." He turned to look at her. "Seriously. I'm fine."

"I'm going to stay with you."

"Seriously, I'm—"

Kat placed a finger over his lips. "Shut up. You took care of me for *years,*" she reminded him. Her voice softened. "Let me do this. Let me take care of you." She shivered at the sudden jolt of warm electricity speeding through her. She sucked in a breath as he tilted his head and trailed his lips to the tip of her finger. She pulled it away before he could capture it with his mouth.

"Uh-uh," Kat scolded. "You will not distract me from my nursing duties, especially with amorous intentions."

"What else am I supposed to do?" he sulked. "Brain rest is overrated."

"Trust me, you'll thank me later." She snuggled into him. "And you get a few days off, so relax and enjoy your mini vacation."

"That just forces others to pull my weight."

"It's taken care of. Molly and I have been texting. JC will take Matt out to the lighthouse when they get back to make final preparations. You can rest all day tomorrow until the rehearsal dinner, which you are expected to be at. Your dad and Terrance can set up for the ceremony on Tuesday. If you're good, I *might* just let you unfold a chair or two. You can still drive the landau to and from the ceremony and take Matt and Lanie to the lighthouse after the reception, but I'll come with you to drive the boat."

"JC can drive the landau."

"Nice try." Kat smirked. "They requested you specifically since you drove them last time. They want to create new memories over the bad ones. And besides, you look incredibly handsome dressed as a nineteenth-century hackney driver."

"I look incredibly ridiculous."

Kat lifted her chin and pressed her nose to his. "You know, talking isn't good for brain rest. Shut up."

His lips crashed into hers. Everything inside Kat craved him as she returned the kiss. It was a good thing she was sitting down. The power he held over her clouded her mind and made her knees weak.

Kat closed her eyes and let him move his lips to her cheek, behind her ear, the side of her neck. She couldn't move, couldn't think. She let all her defenses down and basked in the loving tenderness of his touch.

At first, she ignored the knocking on the door. Then it got louder. Easton pulled away. She opened her eyes.

"Someone's at the door." His husky voice sent a thrill through her.

"So?"

"I don't think they're leaving. They know we're here."

She sighed. "Fine." Grudgingly, she shuffled to the door and peeked through the peephole. Surprised, she opened the door to reveal Doc Hill.

"Hey there, Kat. How's Easton doing? Can I come in for a minute?"

"Sure." She stepped back.

Doc entered and Easton started to stand. "No, no. Don't stand up." He lifted up a chair from the kitchenette and set it down across from Easton. "I just wanted to come by and check on you while I was here looking in on Mocha. And to tell you that you did a mighty fine job splinting that seal pup's flipper. It was risky moving it. But from what JC said, it was likely she was motherless."

"It seemed that way," Easton agreed. "I know that it's not unusual for a mother to leave her baby for an extended period of time while they forage in the water. Had to go with my gut." He closed his eyes and rubbed the back of his head. "Definitely worth this bump if she lives."

Doc Hill considered Easton's response. "It was the right call. She needs to fatten up and learn to swim, but she'll make it." He scratched his head. "Listen, I know you've got the barn to run, but if you were ever to consider vet school again, you know I think you'd make a fantastic vet. I've told you before. I'd love to have you come work for me."

Easton pursed his lips. "The closest DVM program is five hours away. It'd be asking a lot of my family to invest all that time."

Kat sank onto the couch next to him, weighed down by guilt. She spoke softly and laid her hand on his thigh. "It's because of me you stopped at a vet-tech certificate. I can run the barn, Easton. That's my dream. It's time for you to follow yours."

He shook his head. "I'm good here."

"All right then." Doc Hill stood up. "Just hate to see natural talent not cultivated. You've proven that your instincts are right on more times than I can count, most recently with Mocha and Pepper."

"Pepper?" Easton raised an eyebrow.

"JC named the pup. Think about it, when I'm not

around anymore, this area may have a tough time finding a replacement if you're not it. Just promise me you'll consider it more carefully when you're feeling better?"

"Sure."

Kat locked the door after the Doc left. She sat in the chair he'd vacated. "Easton . . ."

"I'm not leaving Crane's Cove to be a vet." He closed his eyes and crossed his arms.

"Why not?"

"Because I have other plans. I want to build a life here with you, not leave you for five years. We were talking about adding jumps and doing horse therapy. Now you want me to be a vet?" Easton's voice dripped with impatience.

"Like I said, those were *my* dreams. You have to chase yours and then we can work our dreams together."

"Do you ever get tired of telling me what to do?"

Kat gasped. "What?" She stood up, sudden anger pulsing through her veins. "Telling you what to do? I've never told you to do anything."

Easton narrowed his eyes. "Not with words. But you've dictated my life, one way or another, for the last six years. I'm done. Let it alone." He closed his eyes and leaned his head back into the couch.

Kat's body began to shake. She raised a hand to her mouth as unbidden tears streamed down her face. She gripped the back of the chair for support. "You're *done?"* she squeaked.

"Yep."

She couldn't breathe. Everything had been going so well. She thought they'd turned the corner back to where they used to be. So close. He'd even just told her he wanted to build a life with her. But evidently she'd misread that somehow. What he wanted then versus now. She kneaded her fists into her temples. She couldn't think. The lump in her throat prevented her from speaking. She had to get out of there. She bolted for the door and slammed it behind her.

Frantically she texted Molly. *Can you stay with Easton tonight? I need to go home. Headache.*

Sure. Molly's text came through right away. *How soon do you need me?*

Now, if you can make it. Kat replied as she started up her vehicle. *I'll wait for you outside the cabin.* She left it running and went to sit on the cabin's steps.

Okay. I'm just down the lane at Mom and Dad's. Be there in 5.

Kat felt horrible for tearing Molly away from visiting her parents, but she couldn't stay with Easton one moment longer. Overcome with what she could only describe as the worst feeling she'd ever experienced, she slumped as she waited for her friend.

Easton's eyes snapped open when he heard Kat's motor turn on. Where was she going? He listened as it pulled away. *Strange.*

His question was answered a moment later when Molly stormed in. "What do you mean you're *done?* What in the holy name did you say to her, Easton?" she said, anger dripping from her voice. She clenched her jaw.

"Huh?" He opened his eyes. "Say to who?"

"Kat," she spat. "I have never seen her so upset, not even when her aunt died. What. Did. You. Say. To. Her?"

Easton uncrossed his arms and scratched his head. It hurt. What *had* he said? "I don't know. I don't remember."

Molly crossed her arms and tapped her feet. "Let me press the refresh button for you since you're suffering from a head injury. So you didn't just insult her by accusing her of dictating your life and inform her you were done? 'Cause those were your words. What else did you say?"

Easton cursed. "That's not what I meant. Doc was here. He wants me to go to vet school, so I can take over for him someday. She told me to go. Things have just been getting back to what they were. I don't want to leave her now." *What did he say? Think, think.* His eyes widened as his brain played back what he'd said earlier. "Oh no."

"Oh no?"

"I meant I was done with her telling me what to do, not done with *her.* Ugh." He sat back down and pulled at his hair. He looked at his sister. "I love her, Molly. I never stopped loving her."

"Well, you certainly made a royal mess of things."

"How do I fix it?" He felt his world slipping away. "What do I do?"

"Right now you need brain rest. Sleep. Maybe she'll take pity on you and forgive you because you are literally messed up in the head."

He deserved that. He hadn't exactly been forgiving or welcoming when she'd returned last month. He groaned. "She must be a mess. I have to call her."

Molly unplugged his phone from the counter and tossed it at him. It went straight to voicemail. He called Shelby. Straight to voicemail. He cursed.

"Stop swearing. Grow up. Fix this." Her voice softened. "But sleep first. You'll be no good to anyone if your head doesn't heal. C'mon."

Molly led him up the stairs. "Take a shower, and go to sleep. I'll be right across the hall if you need anything."

Easton awoke the next morning clearheaded and with a plan. He spent the morning resting his brain and planning. The resort buzzed with activity in preparation for the rehearsal and dinner. He took advantage of the chaos to lay low until he made his move.

Tracy Walker pulled up the barn at 4:45. Mellie hopped out of the passenger seat and met Easton at the back of the van. The trunk opened and he and they each lifted a box of the supplies he'd requested.

Tracy's window slid down as he approached her

window to thank her. "You sure you don't want any help?" she asked.

"No. I got it. Thanks for bringing this to me. They won't let me drive yet."

"Not a problem. I prayed over that stuff. It's gonna work. I can feel it."

"Thanks, Tracy."

"You got it." She reached out and squeezed his shoulder. "Don't burn down the barn, lover boy."

Easton chuckled as he and Mellie carried the boxes into the barn. When she left, he began setting up the contents. Jordan entered a few moments later. "Bolt all set?" Easton asked.

"Yes, sir. He's all saddled up and ready to go just past our cabin."

"Perfect." Easton stood up wiped his hands on his jeans. "Wait for my text, then finish this up and get lost."

"Got it." The teenager grinned. "This is gonna be epic."

"Let's just pray it works."

Chapter 20

It had been a heck of a day. Kat went through the motions, ticking items off her checklist and trying not to think about Easton, or how she had sobbed herself to sleep the night before. As the wedding party and out-of-town guests walked from the gazebo to the main lodge, Kat reflected on how stupid she had been in coming back here. She thought she could just come home and life would return to how it was. She was so wrong.

"Hey, Kat." Molly fell into step beside her as they turned off Birchwood Lane toward the patio at the back of the lodge. "I told Meemaw I'd help in the kitchen. You got the patio if she holds me hostage?"

"I can take kitchen duty," Kat suggested hopefully. Anything to avoid Easton. If he showed up.

"No, no." Molly held up her hands. "I am afraid of what will happen to me if I don't show up." She laughed. "I shouldn't be too long. Meemaw is planning to enjoy the dinner with her family."

"Okay."

Molly went ahead and Kat followed the guests up

onto the patio. She had rearranged the place cards earlier so that she and Easton would be as far away from each other as possible.

He still hadn't arrived by the time she filled her plate. She sat down to eat and began to breathe easier. Until her phone buzzed with a text.

She had to read it. She couldn't not. She'd been praying Easton would text her all day. *I'm sorry. I have to talk to you now. Can you meet me outside the Sadlers' cabin?*

It didn't make sense. The Sadlers'cabin? She left her food and found Carol. "Excuse me, I'll be back."

Kat hurried down the steps. The quickest distance between two points was a straight line. Rather than take the paved lanes, she crossed over Carriage Lane and cut through the Cabin 6 site. She emerged from the trees on Crane's Lane opposite the Sadler cabin and sucked in a breath.

There, decked out in his hackney driver suit-and-tails kit, was Easton. Behind him, Bolt was hitched to the landau.

"We don't need that tonight. I know you have a concussion, but—"

"This is for you." He stepped toward her and took her hands. "I'm so sorry, Kat. I was literally out of my mind last night. I didn't mean I was done with you. Not at all." His eyes pleaded with her for understanding.

Kat sought clarity in her mind, and in his gaze. This didn't make any sense. "I don't understand."

"Come for a ride with me?"

"Okay." Only it came out more like a question. He assisted her up to the bench seat. He settled in beside her and steered Bolt down the lane toward the stables.

"I always say the wrong thing. I've never been good with words. When you fell off Callie, I saw my chance to show you how much I cared for you." He stopped Bolt and turned to face her. "I *chose* to end my education with a four-year degree in veterinary technology because I *wanted* to be with you. Not because I felt pressured or thought that was what you wanted me to do."

Kat's eyes misted. Easton's voice ached with the sincerity in his words.

"I wanted to make all your dreams come true. When you were ready to ride again, I was so happy. When I'm with you, the rest of the world fades away. I couldn't imagine leaving the barn. I woke up every day to see you, be with you, watch you ride. Life was perfect."

Kat hung her head. That was right about the time when she'd begun to feel restless. "I can't really explain . . . I just felt that I needed to leave, to *go* after Auntie Katie died. I had to get out and feel something. I was numb. She was gone so suddenly, Easton. I needed to figure out what was next, who I was, who I wanted to be. I was so broken and lost."

He nodded. "You got better and wanted to race again. We all thought it was a good idea. Taking you to competitions and rodeos, it almost felt like old times. When you got that offer and then your aunt died . . . my perfect life started to crumble."

Kat placed her hand over his. "Worst mistake I ever made."

"I was wrong, too. I let you go without a fight. I thought you would miss me so much you'd come back. Then I gave you that stupid ultimatum at Christmas. I should never have done that, and I regretted it as soon as it came out of my mouth."

"I regretted leaving you the second I began walking away," Kat whispered.

She leaned on him as he finished the loop. He parked the landau by the newly repaired main entrance to the barn. He climbed down and secured Bolt to the hitching post.

"Let me help you down."

Kat put her hand in his and stepped down. He led her to the barn door.

"I want to give you something," Easton said.

He opened the door. Inside, dozens of flickering electric candles inside mason jars lit up the interior space between the stalls. A large sheet hung suspended from the ceiling. She stepped inside, slowly walking around the candles until she could see the message on the sheet. In the soft glow, the words *For You* were painted onto the white background.

"I don't understand."

"Here." Easton pulled a folded-up piece of paper from his pocket. He picked up a mason jar so she could read by the glow of the candlelight.

Her hands shook as she unfolded the paper. She gasped as her eyes scanned the words.

In his messy, Easton handwriting, he'd scrawled, *I, Easton Crane, of sound body, mind, and spirit, do hereby give the future of the Cliff Walk Stables and all property of mine belonging to it, to Kat Daniels, for as long as she wishes to have it.* It was even notorized.

He put the lantern down and cupped her cheeks with his hands. Tears ran down her face, mirroring those that streaked his. "I'm giving you the barn and everything in it. No matter what I decide to do, your dream is here. If I'm wrong, if it's not, then take Bolt and go back to riding if that's what you want to do. I'll take care of Mocha and keep tabs on your Uncle Charley if you decide to leave. All I've always ever wanted was your love. If I can't have that, then I want to make you happy, even if it's without me."

"Please," Kat begged. "Shut up." She shoved the paper back into his pocket and wrapped her arms around his neck. "I've been a terrible person this last year." She pressed her thumb to his cheekbone to wipe away his tears. "But I never stopped loving you. I want to be with you, Easton. Here. Or if you want to go to vet school, I can go with you. Or I can stay here. You can go to Tufts and come home on the weekends. What matters is we never break apart again, ever." Kat pulled his face down to hers.

Her kiss ignited a fire that rivaled the flames from the candles around them. She surrendered her thoughts to oblivion and kissed him with all the passion she'd ever felt for him.

Tuesday afternoon, Easton helped Lanie down from the landau. She clasped her fingers around a colorful bouquet of Acadian wildflowers. The weather couldn't have been more perfect. It wasn't too humid or too cool. A soft breeze stirred the salt of the ocean with the scents of the pines and flowers. It was this kind of Downeast day that seduced the tourists each summer and reminded him of how blessed he was to call Crane's Cove home.

The bridal march played as Lanie's father took her arm. They strolled toward the newly constructed whitewashed gazebo where Pastor Porter waited with Matt and the wedding party. As much as he hated to admit it, Kevin and his crew had done a fine job and he was grateful for it. He'd even managed to send him a thank-you email for getting the work done so quickly.

Matt was sharp in his dress blues, and Lanie was every bit the vision Kat had described to him. Though stunning in a sculpted lace halter that fanned out into a gathered twist of bell-shaped satin, it wasn't Lanie that Easton was watching. His knuckles tightened on Bolt's reins as his gaze swept over Kat's pale shoulders, exposed by the slip of her pashmina. The wispy, delicate fabric of her turquoise dress hugged her in all the right places, places he wanted to memorize and lose himself in. The passion she'd reawakened deep inside him could never be extinguished. He wanted to be hers forever, take care of her, comfort her, love her—in good times and in bad. They'd gotten through plenty of bad and it was time to even the memories out.

Easton's left hand sought the button in his pocket. Next to it was a small velvet drawstring bag just waiting for the right time to be opened. This time, he would wait for God's whisper and obey His timing. Today, tomorrow, sometime in the future, he wasn't sure of anything except that the timing would be perfect and the reasons would be right. He would be ready.

Easton turned his attention back to the ceremony. Lanie and Matt faced each other, holding hands, looking at each other as if the rest of the world had fallen away.

Pastor Porter's soothing voice held the guests mesmerized. "Ecclesiastes chapter four, verse twelve tells us a person standing alone can be attacked and defeated, but two can stand back to back and conquer. Three are even better, for a triple-braided cord is not easily broken. And that triple braid is made up of Matthew, Allaina, and God. This is an unbroken, beautiful bond, and from this point on, your power in the spiritual realm is multiplied. God's Word tells us where one can chase a thousand, two can put ten thousand to flight. You can take authority. The opposition will come, but know this: love defeats everything. And you've got that. And it's based in the covenant that God has for you. Love conquers all."

Easton imagined himself and Kat at the gazebo,

joining as one, taking on the world and growing old together. He wanted this more than he wanted his next breath.

"Lanie," Matt said, his voice just audible despite the microphone clipped to his lapel. "The moment I met you, I felt our hearts connect. Neither of us was in a place where we could see the light, or the future. I thank God every day for bringing us together. No one else but Him, through you, could have healed my pain."

"Matt." Lanie reached up to caress his cheek. He leaned into her hand. "When I came here, I was terrified of my own shadow. I'd lost my faith in people, in everything. You pulled me out of the darkness. You helped me learn to live in a new normal. I couldn't imagine living a moment of this life without you. God is so good."

Lanie gave her bouquet to Caroline. Damon handed over the rings to Pastor Porter, who led them in the traditional "I do's." Kat turned around and caught Easton's eye. He winked back at her. She blushed and turned back to the ceremony.

"Matthew, do you take Allaina to be your wedded wife, to live together in God's ordinance in the holy state of matrimony? Do you promise to love her, comfort her, honor and keep her, in sickness and in health, and forsaking all others, remain faithful to her as long as you both shall live?"

"I do."

"Allaina, do you take Matthew to be your wedded

husband, to live together in God's ordinance in the holy state of matrimony? Do you promise to love him, comfort him, honor and keep him, in sickness and in health, and forsaking all others, remain faithful to him as long as you both shall live?"

"I do."

"Dear Heavenly Father, we ask Your blessing upon these two lives and the home they are establishing today. May the love they have for each other grow deeper and stronger because of their love for You. Today is the beginning of your new life together. God knew your needs when he brought you to each other. He knew exactly what each of you needed to make the other complete. He has chosen to complete you as one. By the power vested in me, I now pronounce you Mr. and Mrs. Matthew John Saunders. Matt, you may kiss your bride."

Matt's grin could have lit up a starless sky. He pulled Lanie into his arms and kissed her thoroughly, inciting whistles from his side of the aisle. There wasn't a dry eye among the guests. Even little Bella was overcome with emotion, dropping her empty flower-girl basket and running to Lanie. She wrapped her arms around her coach's waist and sobbed into Lanie's dress. The bride and groom hugged her.

Again, he watched Kat. She dabbed at her eyes. He wished he could read her thoughts. Caroline followed Lanie into the landau and arranged her dress around her. She stepped down and Matt took his spot beside his bride. After the photographer snapped a few pictures,

Easton took his place at the front and navigated Bolt down Lover's Lane toward the main lodge for the reception.

Later, as he slow danced with Kat at the reception, he reflected on all that had transpired over the last year. They'd cleared all the doubt and faced their fears together, and they would face the future together. It had been a struggle, but it had been worth it for all the wisdom he'd gained along the way.

Out of the corner of his eye, he spotted the intertwined swans at the top of the wedding cake. He guided Kat's head onto his shoulder. She sighed and a wave of comfort washed over him. They were going to be okay. Like a swan, her transformation was beautiful. She found her grace and they would glide into their future, their hearts and souls connected for all time.

The music faded out and Shelby's voice over the microphone cut through his thoughts. She stood on the stage, dressed in her waitress uniform from the diner. "Sadie, I hope you'll forgive me for closing up a little early tonight." Sadie was in attendance, as she had been part of the effort to capture Lanie's stalker back in May.

Sadie called out, "Shelby, I've never known you to do anything without a good reason. So get to it!" A titter of laughter hummed throughout the dining room.

"Well," Shelby paused for full effect. "There I was, menus in hand, ready to place them on a table when I realized who'd just sat down." Shelby's eyes found the newly married couple. "My old friend, back in town, having dinner with her mother. I believe some of you know her . . ."

Shelby gestured toward the door to the kitchen JC held open. A petite young woman in jeans and a red peek-a-boo shoulder ruffle top strode up to the stage and waved. Her cascade of light brown highlighted waves bounced as she leapt up next to Shelby.

Kat gasped. "Macy's back in town?"

Shelby continued. "Ladies and gentlemen, I'm not usually sentimental, but I did what any of you all would have done. Those of you who weren't here for Lanie and Matt's karaoke debut last May have no doubt heard about it over and over again from Sadie or others in this room. So I fed Macy and her mom, bribed them with free meals forever, and held them hostage until she consented to sing Lanie and Matt's song tonight."

"You did good, Shelby!" Sadie called out. More laughter.

Easton watched Lanie, who stared up at the stage. Wonder, and joy lit up her face.

Shelby bowed. "Thank you, thank you, I know, I know. I'm wicked awesome."

"Yes, you are!" Damon called out from the bar. Her face flushed and she glared at him. Easton chuckled at the southerner's most recent effort to get Shelby's attention.

"Without further ado, I present Miss Macy Wells, hometown girl, lead singer of the Harbor Lights, and writer of the song that brought these two lovebirds together." Shelby passed the microphone to Macy and stepped down. She disappeared through the kitchen door as covertly as she'd come.

"Congratulations to the bride and groom!" Macy gestured to them. "Can we get some spoons clinking on glasses?" Matt led Lanie to the center of the dance floor as the collective sound of metal on glass reached a crescendo. He twirled her in a circle, dipped her low, and held her in a kiss that would have impressed Rhett Butler.

Easton moved behind Kat and wrapped his arms around her waist. His lips dipped to her ear. "Showoff."

Kat giggled. "He's always been one to go all in."

"I've noticed."

Easton twirled Kat to face him and clung to her while Macy crooned "Just Be," the ballad that had gotten her and her two older brothers the attention of a label in Nashville.

Suddenly, Kat jerked her head up. "I'll be right back!" She weaved her way through the crowd. At the stage, Macy sang the last note and then bent over so Kat could whisper into her ear. Macy nodded and spoke briefly to the DJ as the guests shouted for an encore.

Easton's eyes never left Kat. "Just Be" faded out, and she arrived back in his arms as Macy began their most recent hit, "I've Got You."

Kat was no singer, but she sang along softly as they swayed. Her low alto projected the most beautiful words he'd ever heard.

My dreams had left me

I fell into despair
I didn't answer
When I heard you there

You came to me
When I needed you most
I pushed you away
And you became a ghost

I let you haunt me
But still, I stayed away
Never knowing
You could love me that way

Easton's arms tightened around her and bent his head to sing the chorus in her ear. Her voice wavered as they harmonized the familiar words.

You told me, "I've got you"
You took my hand
I tried to let go, to break free
You didn't deserve the wreck that was me

Still, you loved me
Still, you cared
You put me first
Even when I wasn't there

His lips met hers as the instrumental riff began. He didn't care who was watching, didn't care that people around him were whistling.

"Dude, get a room," JC elbowed him in the shoulder as he danced by with Caroline. Easton laughed.

Kat smiled slowly and opened her mouth to begin the next verse.

I was lost without you
You were my compass, my rock
I took you for granted
I locked up my heart

Now I see you never left me
I understand why you care
I left our path
You found me in a snare

Her eyes brimmed with tears. Easton sang the chorus with her again. The music rose to its crescendo. "Last verse," he whispered. By now, everyone was singing along.

"Together." Kat sang with him, at full volume and a bit off-key.

You restored me
You restored my faith
And now it's my turn
I've got you, every day

"Every day, Kat. Every day, always."

She looked up at him, tears spilling over. "I love you, and I've got you, every day, always. She kissed him again. Can we get out of here?"

Kat cut the engine just as the first fireworks lit up the sky. On the dock, Easton secured the boat. Instead of offering his hand to help her out, he leapt back into the boat. In two long strides, he was in front of her, his lips meeting hers.

Her brain, overloaded by the physical stimuli and sensation, drained any part of her will that might resist. She gripped his biceps to steady herself, dizzy with desire. The deck beneath her disappeared as Easton carried her to the cushioned bench at the back of the boat. She sat on his lap, disoriented, fighting between letting her barriers down and regaining her bearings.

"I love you, Kat Daniels. There's no living without you." She'd never felt as wanted and cherished as she'd felt in the past twenty-four hours. This flame, with him—she never wanted it to be extinguished.

She pulled back. She didn't even care this time that she couldn't control the tears that flowed down her face. "I love you, too, Easton Crane. Existing without you isn't living at all. Let's never be apart ever."

"Do you really mean that?" His eyes welled with sincerity. They burned into hers, intense and bursting with emotion.

"I do. I promise you, I do." Her lips fluttered against his nose and she smiled.

He shifted her on his lap and reached into his pocket. "Well, then. If you're sure . . ."

"Never been surer." She squinted in the flickering light at the small velvet bag he'd pulled from his pocket.

"I'd like to give this back to you."

Kat took the bag and opened it. She gasped and a

sob escaped her lips. "Oh, I am *so* sure." She tipped the bag upside down and shook its contents into her palm.

Easton took it from her hand. His heart picked up speed and he was filled with a peace and confidence that transcended his whole being "But only if you're *really* sure." He was teasing now. "If you're not, you can hang onto it for another time . . ."

"Oh, shut up. Please!" She laughed and held up her left hand.

Easton slipped the platinum solitaire diamond on her ring finger. Molly had told Kat he had it custom made. Tiny turquoise accent stones sat flush with the band, on which a swirling pattern had been hand-engraved. Milgrain beading ran down the edges of the band giving the design a vintage touch. She couldn't have imagined a more beautiful ring, but that was what he did. Easton knew what she wanted and what she needed before she knew it herself.

"Can I talk now?" he asked, the intensity morphing into a boyish grin.

"No." She wrapped her arms around his neck and laced her fingers in the hair at the nape of his neck. She needed to kiss him, needed to convey how much she loved him. She took her time, kissing his forehead, the tip of his nose, each cheekbone, and finally his lips. Only then, when she was satisfied he got her message, did she let him speak. "You may talk now."

He took a deep breath. "We don't have to plan anything now if you don't want to. I was thinking I might go to vet school, or—"

"I'm ready."

But wait, there's more!

Enjoy the soundtrack for *Love on the Rocks* on Spotify at *http://bit.ly/LoveontheRocksSoundtrack*

Did you miss the first book in the series, *Love on the Edge*? You can find Matt and Lanie's story here: www.amazon.com/Love-Edge-Cranes-Cove-1/dp/0999586114

Want Meemaw's recipes? Sign up for my newsletter at KerryEvelyn.com.

Please consider leaving a review online. If you loved it, I want to know!

I'd love for you to join my reader group! Lots of surprises, bonus material, contests, games, and giveaways await at www.facebook.com/groups/CranesCoveCrew

Want to return to Crane's Cove? Turn the page to check out an unedited sneak peek from Damon and Shelby's story, *Love on the Beach*, coming in 2019!

Keep in Touch!
- Facebook: www.Facebook.com/KerryEvelynAuthor
- Twitter: @theKerryEvelyn
- Instagram: @KerryEvelynAuthor

Love on the Beach

SUMMER 2019

Chapter 1

The eyes glowed from the middle of the road, two silver disks reflecting the light from the moon. Shelby's breath caught and fear trickled down her spine. She slammed the breaks of her father's Jetta. The tires screamed as the car came to a violent halt. The eyes continued to stare, mocking her. *Only a deer.* It scampered into the trees. God knew the number of her days, and her heart thundered as it hit her how close she'd been to a serious accident.

Shelby shuddered and steered the car onto the shoulder. Her fists gripped the wheel. She breathed in, then out, long and slow as she'd been taught years ago. After a few minutes, her heartbeat slowed and became regular.

Red and blue lights flashed in Shelby's rearview mirror. *Are you kidding me?* It was late, and she'd just delivered a trio of twenty-somethings to their homes after they'd imbibed too much at the pub. Her fingers closed around her mother's diamond-embedded silver cross at her neck. "Not this week, God," she muttered under her breath

She wiped her tears and debated reverting to her "pastor's daughter" mask of pleasant face and voice. The handful of cops stationed in the cliffside town of Crane's Cove, Maine knew her, and she knew them, and they knew why she was out late at night. She'd been a designated driver volunteer for Paddy's Pub and Grill as soon as she'd turned eighteen. Her father didn't like it, but he understood her need to do it.

The fear transformed into agitation as the police SUV pulled up behind her. She tapped her fingers on the wheel, mouth set, jaw tight, she glanced at the clock. She had to be at the diner in five hours. *Just perfect.* "Keep it together, Shelby. You know these guys."

Or did she? She rolled down her window and squinted at the side mirror. The bulky shape of the approaching officer was similar to Will Donovan, but he had left weeks ago for FBI training. As the figure approached, his easy swagger registered and sent off alarms in her head. None of the other officers in town were in that good of a shape. In fact, that particular shape almost reminded her of---

NO. WAY.

"You *moved* here?" Shelby spat before the officer could ask for her license and registration. "Why?"

Damon Saunders, dubbed Atlanta's Hottest Bachelor by the Peach Gazette, stood before her in all his muscle-hugging-uniformed glory. His eyes met hers and his stone-faced cop expression transformed into the most swoon-worthy, genuine grin she'd ever seen. He recognized her. *Don't stare, don't stare.* She fought the magnetic pull and struggled to look away from his flawless light-brown skin and dark eyes illuminated by his flashlight. Resolute, she crossed her arms, tilted up her chin, and stared straight out her front window.

"Yes, ma'am." His deep baritone drawl prompted a shiver. "Seemed like a nice place. You came back after being gone. Why?"

"Turned out city life wasn't for me." After six years back and forth to Boston, including a year of interning at what was supposed to be a humanitarian-focused publication, she'd toughened up and learned what she didn't want to do with her life. She'd come home to her small town on the Acadian coast and gotten a part-time job at the diner to supplement her freelance work while she figured out her future.

"Seems we have something in common, then."

"I'm sure we have nothing in common." She didn't want to have anything in common with him. She was back home for the summer only, to regroup and refocus, and so far everything was going according to plan.

She did not have time for dating, no matter how interesting or hot the man was.

"I'll bet we do. Music, for example. As I recall, you crashed a wedding with the lead singer of the Harbor Lights. How'd you manage that?"

"We went to high school together. She used to sing with me at my dad's church." She shrugged.

"See? Another thing in common. I used to sing at church, too."

Wonderful. She sighed, rolling her eyes.

Shelby had met Damon through friends when he'd been a guest at the town's Cliff Walk Resort for his cousin's wedding a month ago. He hadn't kept it hidden that he was interested in getting to know her better. The guys had crashed the bachelorette party, and in a moment of weakness, Shelby had agreed to let him pull her out onto the dance floor. He was sweet, smooth, and smokin' hot. She'd let her guard down, and let him kiss her as Whitney Houston belted out about wanting one moment in time. Freaked out by how it had consumed her, she'd bolted to the parking lot before he could ask for her number. As she sat in her car waiting for her friends, she went over all the reasons she couldn't get to know him better and vowed—unsuccessfully—to never think about him ever again.

So much so, she'd volunteered to work the night of the wedding to avoid him. In any other time, in any other place, she might be interested. And not because he was Mr. December on the Atlanta PD's charity calendar. Yeah, she'd googled him. But there was more in those eyes than just pretty specs of light. She couldn't fight the draw, and she'd been glad when he'd gone home to Atlanta.

But now he was here and she didn't know where she was going. The idyllic New England coastal town was fine for vacationers and townies who wanted to remove themselves from the ugliness of the world. Not for her. She wanted to make a difference. And she couldn't do it here. Here in this small town, she couldn't make her mark on the world. Here, there were memories of her mother everywhere she went. Here, it was too painful.

"Well, get it over with," she said through her teeth. Her jaw remained clenched and she held her posture so rigid her friend Kat's great-aunt would have been proud.

Damon rested his elbows on the open window ledge. She leaned away from him. "Get it over with? You got someplace you're supposed be?" Any closer, and he'd be invading her personal space.

"Home. In bed." Her cheeks heated after she spoke those last two words. She cringed. Oh, the things his easy southern drawl conjured in her mind! She swallowed. "I have to be at work early."

Damon shifted his weight to his left arm and peered at her. "Mmhmm. Well, you were speeding pretty fast when that deer came up on you. And your center backlight is out. I suppose I should write you a ticket or give you a warning, but I already feel like I'm on your bad side." He pressed his lips together. "But I'm new in town and I want to be your friend. What do you say?"

Shelby whipped her head toward him, incredulous. "Are you trying to bribe me? Aren't I the one who's supposed to try to get out of this?"

He grinned. "Did it work?"

Is he for real? Shelby let out a long breath. "Fine.

Thank you. I will try to be pleasant when I see you around town."

Damon's grin stretched wider, if that was even possible. *Look away, Shelby. He's everything you don't want.*

"Sweet! That's all I ask." He stood up and tapped his hand on the window ledge. "You have a good night, Shelby Porter. See ya around."

Shelby nodded and waved half-heartedly. Her tongue had turned to jelly. She couldn't have spoken if she tried. Thank God he hadn't noticed she'd been crying.

Damon pulled into the diner as the first light of sun painted the horizon. *She wasn't kidding. She did have to work early.* Shelby's car was parked along the side of the building. He wasn't stalking her, not really. He was just hungry after his first overnight shift at his new job. And the diner was the only place open. And yeah, he was hoping to see her again.

He'd looked for her at Matt and Lanie's wedding, and was disappointed when he learned she was working. But then she'd strode in with Macy Wells, lead singer of the Harbor Lights, whom she'd convinced to sing the bride and groom's song. Once Macy started singing, she was gone again.

And so was he.

Damon couldn't pinpoint what drew him to her. He

was easygoing and friendly. Shelby was wound tight, cynical, and didn't waste any words. But he knew that was just for show. He'd seen her interact with her nephew, and it was contrary to the act she presented to everyone else. He closed his eyes and imagined her regarding him with that degree of warmth she bestowed on little Noah. He wanted to know why she barricaded herself behind a series of protective walls, and how he could break through them.

His eyes roamed over the old chrome and maroon railroad car that had been converted into a diner and reflected on the difference in working overnight in Crane's Cove versus the graveyard shift in Atlanta. Here, he'd sat by the side of the road for most of the night. Every hour or so, he'd cruise around town, checking the neighborhoods and familiarizing himself with the streets and layout. In Atlanta, he often went an entire shift without a break. He stocked his car with protein bars and a cooler of bottled water, and he'd go straight home and collapse if he wasn't required to put in overtime.

Damon shuddered thinking about his last job. He'd been so proud when he'd made detective. Despite five years on the force and having seen the worst of humanity, he couldn't have imagined the degree of cruelty he came across digging into the crimes he'd been assigned to.

That last bust had been his breaking point. His boss granted him time to process, and he'd flown up to

Crane's Cove to visit his grandmother. Meemaw was enjoying her summer away from the heat of Savannah as well as helping to plan his cousin Matt's wedding. He'd gotten to know some of the locals and begun to think he could fit in here. Dread had consumed him each time he'd thought about going home to Atlanta and his job.

That was a month ago. Meemaw had sensed he wasn't in any rush to return, and when she learned that the police force in the little town was down a man, she suggested he apply. On a whim, he did, and was surprised when he got the call. He'd flown back up last week and was already at work. Now he just needed to find an apartment. The extended-stay hotel in Winter Harbor was nice, but he couldn't live there forever.

Damon jogged up the steps to the diner and opened the door. "Hey, Ms. Sadie," he called out to the matronly woman filling sugar containers behind the counter.

"Look at you!" she clucked. Sadie set the sugar down and lifted the countertop at the end so she could approach him. She reached out and straightened the flap on his collar. "Yes, sir, you will fill my Will's shoes just perfectly. I'm so glad you took the job. Here, have a seat anywhere you like." She gestured to empty restaurant. "How was your first night?"

"Mostly uneventful." He took a seat on a stool at the bar, trying not to be obvious as his eyes scanned for Shelby. Sadie went back around to her side of the counter. In less than a minute, he was staring down into a hot cup of coffee with a menu beside it. "Night and day from Atlanta."

"I'd imagine so." Sadie sighed. "Did your Meemaw tell you that I was with the FBI?"

Damon's eyes widened. "No. Makes sense though. You must be so proud of Will."

She beamed. "I am. He's working hard, but it's no picnic. I'm glad he was able to take his girlfriend on vacation between jobs. He won't get another one for a while." Sadie leaned in. "I'm retired, but I assisted when your cousin's wife was abducted." She shifted her gaze toward the windows in the swinging doors that led to the kitchen. "If you're waiting for the muffins, they should be out any minute, dear." She lowered her voice. "I worked some cases that rattled me to the core. The worst ones were the children." She shook her head. "You can't imagine how creative some people can be to induce suffering on babies."

"I can. I have nightmares about it." He raised his eyes to hers. "I don't mind the night shift. It's easier for me to sleep during the day."

The door to the kitchen opened. Shelby stopped dead in her tracks as she caught his gaze. The tray of muffins shifted in her hands as she steadied herself.

"Mornin', Shelby!" Damon sipped his coffee and winked.

Shelby avoided his eyes and set the tray on the counter. "Good morning, tough guy." She opened the clear glass cabinet and began loading the muffins into it.

Sadie glanced between the two of them. "Seems you two already know each other. Wonderful! Shelby, be a dear and grab his order for me? I'll finish up the baking."

Damon fixed his eyes on her as she slowly arranged the muffins on paper doilies in the cabinet. He moved his head around to try to catch her eyes, but she kept them down.

When she finished, she took a spiral pad out of her apron pocket and finally looked up. His heart thundered in his chest as Shelby flipped her long bangs to one side. Her almost-black hair was highlighted in lighter tones and pulled back from her face in a long slick ponytail, accentuating her high cheekbones and tanned skin.

Her words came out in one breath. "Today's special is a French crepe with pears, walnuts, spinach and brie, with or without eggs. Comes with the diner's famous fried potatoes and your choice of toast, cheese roll, or English muffin. Add a side of bacon, sausage, linguiça, or ham for two dollars more." She blinked at him three times and then held his gaze.

"Ahh---" Damon hadn't heard a word she'd said. "Sure, I'll try that." He handed her his menu.

She blinked again. "Toast, cheese roll, or English muffin?"

He pointed to the muffins in the case. "One of those, please."

"And did you want to add a side?"

"Of what?" He knew he was staring. He couldn't help it.

She sighed. "Bacon, sausage, linguiça, or ham?"

"Bacon, please."

"Egg or no egg?"

"Egg whites, please."

Shelby raised a brow, made a notation on her notepad, and disappeared into the kitchen. She returned with a small plate that held a muffin and a pat of butter. Her shoulders relaxed. "This one is fresh out of the oven. It's still warm. And it's on me. Thank you for not citing me last night."

Damon was touched. "Well now if that ain't sweeter than Meemaw's peach pudding!"

Shelby held up a hand. "Save your southernisms. Enjoy the muffin."

She disappeared again into the kitchen. Damon set about making his coffee drinkable. Four Splendas and four French vanilla creamers usually did the trick. He wondered if he could order tea here without being laughed at.

The bell above the door rang, signaling new customers. Damon turned his head and raised a hand in greeting to a trio of middle-aged men who took seats at the other end of the counter.

"Howdy," Damon greeted. "Nice mornin', right?" The men narrowed their eyes and nodded at him.

Sadie pushed through the kitchen doors and set out three mugs in front of the men. "Damon, meet some of the regulars. George, Al, and Simon are lobstermen. Guys, meet Damon Saunders."

George nodded at Damon. "Morning." He turned to Sadie. "They hire him to replace Will? Where's he from?"

"Yep. Damon was a detective in Atlanta."

Al gave him an appraising look. "How did they convince you to move here?" He turned to Simon on his other side. "He might rethink that move come winter."

Simon snorted. "Maybe. Nice to have some new blood in town, though."

Damon bristled. The men were talking about him instead of to him. "I heard 'bout the opening last month when I was here for my cousin's wedding. Sounded like a nice change of pace."

"I'm sure it is," George agreed. "Biggest excitement you might get is moose holding up traffic."

Sadie shot him a look of warning. "Not funny, George."

"Oh, right. Yeah." George looked chagrined.

Damon chuckled. "Sounds more exciting than a gator."

The men blinked at him. *Ba dum bum.* Sadie noticed the awkward moment and smiled, but he was sure it was just to be kind. *Different sense of humor here.*

"Let me get you guys some breakfast," she said. "Your usuals?"

The men nodded and Sadie shot him an apologetic smile. He stared at the kitchen door, willing Shelby to come out.

A moment later, she did. "Hey, guys," she greeted the men.. "I see you've met my friend, Damon." She glanced at him with a small smile. "Now don't go giving him any trouble."

Simon grinned. "Aw, Shelby. You're no fun."

"Ain't that the truth." She set three ramekins of butter on the counter, one in front of each man. "I'm serious. He's new in town, and you best make him feel welcome – or don't expect any extras you're accustomed to from me." She lifted her eyebrows to reinforce her words and disappeared back into the kitchen.

Damon grinned. He wondered how he could get her to treat *him* like an old friend, or more, without coming on too strong.

Sadie breezed out a few minutes later with Damon's breakfast and cheese rolls for the lobstermen. Damon waved her over. "Top you off?" she asked, glancing at his mug.

"No, thanks." He inhaled deeply and met her eyes. "So, how does one go about getting a singing gig at Pastor Porter's church?"

Acknowledgments

I will be forever grateful to God and all my family, friends, colleagues, and readers who continually help me to find the words to bring the people of Crane's Cove to life!

God, thank you for blessing me with a passionate, creative mind and an outlet to express it. You bless me daily with more ideas, vignettes, scenes, and storylines than I could possibly ever write down. You want these stories told and it is my great honor and privilege to tell them. From your spirit to my words to readers' hearts, I pray each and every story I write is told in such a way that blesses the reader, ignites hope for the suffering, and brings You praise.

To Anthony, Kailyn, and Nicholas, thank you for allowing me the time to write and grow, and for keeping the puppy dog eyes minimal when I have to miss a day at a theme park to meet a deadline. Huge thanks to the Laundry Fairy, the Dinner Fairy, and the Cleaning Fairies for their help when I get lost in my cave (or head!) and neglect the practical things!

To my mom, Judy, for her gifts of time and for sharing in the chauffeuring duties. I would not have been able to carve out the time to write this book without you. I'm so glad you finally escaped the Frigid North to come live near us in sunny Florida! To Dad, Amy, Brenda, Roger, Sally, Frank, and Doug – thank you for keeping the kiddos busy and entertained while I spent months revising and editing. Seven drafts! I am hoping never to break that record, haha!

To my family and friends who shared their TBI stories—thank you from the bottom of my heart for sharing your pain and the agonizing and challenging details of your everyday. You helped me illustrate Kat's day-to-day frustrations in a way that I hope will bring new awareness to readers who don't understand how a TBI sufferer can look well on the outside and struggle so much on the inside, even years after the injury occurs.

To Pam Boutte and her girls, Madelyn and Megan—I couldn't have written this book without you! Your horse knowledge, ideas, videos, and fantastic stable tour made Mocha and the Cliff Walk Stables come to life! Triple M and Mack will be back for adventures of their own – stay tuned!

To Erica Long, equine veterinarian and riding expert—thank you for reading my story and recommending changes to make the conflicts and solutions more realistic. Even after months of interviews, research, and YouTube, I had no idea what I didn't know. I'm so thankful to you! I'm so psyched that this story is "horsegirl approved!"

To Courtney and Travis Spain—thank you for letting me borrow the beautiful words from your wedding ceremony for Matt and Lanie. And to Hannah Keeley, author of those words, for sharing them. Hannah, I'm still so incredibly awed by you and how the Holy Spirit speaks through you. You bless me infinitely.

To the Master Moms who have been a part of this process from the beginning, thank you, sisters! Especially to my Mentor, Rebecca Kirchberg, who was and is instrumental in getting me to follow this calling, Becky Bullock who mails me encouragement every week, Pat Akey who blessed all of the women she coaches with copies of *Love on the Edge*, my Minties for giving me grace when I disappear for days or weeks, and all the Mamas who have purchased, read, and/or reviewed my work. God was so good to bring me to you all!

To my beta, gamma, and delta readers—thank you for reading one, two, and some of you even three, versions of this book and helping me tighten and strengthen it each time. I'm grateful for your time, patience, and love. Abbi Stebbins, Allison Fessler, Becky Bullock, Belinda Villafane, Beth Ledesma, Bonnie Dueck, Chelsea Fuchs, Gwen Haas, Hannah Kartagener, Jennifer Cepuder, Jennifer Markiewicz, Jennifer Schutz, Jill Kulbok, Judy Marshall, Katie Carley, Kayla Qualls, Kim Lukens, Kolie Dee, Nicole Harding, Pam Boutte, Stephanie Harrell, Tiffaney McCarthy, Tonya Spitler, and Wynell Tastinger—I am forever indebted to you!

To my homegirl, Tracy Walkons—thank you for being a wonderful friend and inspiration! I hope you get a kick out of Tracy Walker and her adventures—there are more coming! XOXO!

To Chelsea Fuchs, Tonya Spitler, and Stephanie Harrell—YOU ROCK! I could write out several pages listing all the reasons I am grateful for you including random Facebook messages and texts at all times of the day and night as ideas strike, but instead, I'll just send you gifts!

To Julie Faye, my "writing wife," who is talented beyond measure. My creativity and motivation always spark when we are together. You are an amazing friend and I'll always be grateful to you for encouraging me to take action and get the words "someday" out of my vocabulary. And thank you for the stunning painting of the swan. I look at it every day and think of you!

To Lorelei and the Lit Lair Ladies and Readers—your support is everything to me! Thank you for your friendship, time, support, reviews, and encouragement. No one would know who I am if not for you all!

To Anabelle Bryant and Nancy Herkness—Y'all make me want to move to New Jersey to stalk you! But, snow. You are safe. Ha, ha!

To the Members of the Orlando East Writers Group, Spacecoast Authors of Romance, and Central Florida Romance Writers—thank you for the love, knowledge, support, opportunities and help over the last year. I continue to absorb your expertise like a sponge and be in awe of you all. I'm incredibly blessed to be in your company!

To Rob Hare, photog extraordinaire and benefactor of dreams—No mere words can fully express my gratitude. I look at the leap of faith you took when you began your journey to do what you love and I'm inspired to keep going and do the same. You are a great friend, an incredible success, and an example for all of us who are just starting to follow their dreams. Your hard work, thoughtfulness, generosity, and giving heart will always make you stand out in the best way, and is appreciated beyond measure by the countless people you have blessed over the years. I can't thank you enough for the beautiful covers and all you have done for me. Sarah Masry and John Kelley – you capture the essence of Kat and Easton flawlessly. I couldn't have imagined a more perfect couple for my cover! Thank you infinitely!

To Nicole Ayers—I just love working with you! Thank you for the love, care, understanding, and attention to detail you put into my work. I'm so blessed to have found you and I'm so glad we have more projects coming up!

To Racquel Henry, Valerie Willis, Laura Perez, Paige Lavoie, and Arielle Haughee at The Writer's Atelier—I love the tribe you have created and your vision behind all you do. You have helped, inspired, taught, and blessed countless writers over the last five years and I'm thrilled to be one of them. You all are so stinkin' talented, loving, generous, accessible, encouraging, kind, and brave; you bless all whom you encounter, and when I'm with you, I'm convinced I can do anything.

And finally, to my readers and fans! Thank you for your continued support. I am so incredibly blessed you have fallen in love with Crane's Cove just as much as I have. You loved my secondary characters so much, you wanted a series and I am happy to oblige! I've got enough material in my head right now for seven books, so stay tuned. I can't wait to bring back the good friends you have grown to love and introduce you to new ones along the way. XOXO!

About the Author

Kerry Evelyn has always been fascinated by people and the backstories that drive them to do what they do. A native of the Massachusetts South Coast, she changed her latitude in 2002 and is now a crazy blessed wife and homeschooling mom in Orlando. When she's not teaching or writing, she's mentoring moms through Mom Mastery University, sharing essential oils, and planning super fun events for her kids and their friends (although her own kids have yet to be impressed, being that every event has some sort of learning involved, thanks to her earlier career as an elementary school teacher). She loves God, books of all kinds, traveling, taking selfies, sweet drinks, and escaping into her imagination, where every child is happy and healthy, every house has a library, and her hubby wears coattails and a top hat 24/7.

Made in the USA
Columbia, SC
21 November 2020